The STARS That TREMBLE

KATE McMURRAY

Dreamspinner Press

Published by
Dreamspinner Press
5032 Capital Circle SW
Ste 2, PMB# 279
Tallahassee, FL 32305-7886
USA
http://www.dreamspinnerpress.com/

The Stars That Tremble
© 2013 by Kate McMurray.

Cover Art
© 2013 Aaron Anderson.
aaronbydesign55@gmail.com
Cover content is for illustrative purposes only and any person depicted on the cover is a model.

ISBN: 978-1-62798-135-4
Digital ISBN: 978-1-62798-136-1

Printed in the United States of America
First Edition
September 2013

"Nessun dorma! Nessun dorma! Tu pure, o Principessa, nella tua fredda stanza, guardi le stelle che tremano d'amore, e di speranza!"

"No one shall sleep! No one shall sleep! Not even you, o Princess, in your cold bedroom, watch the stars that tremble with love and hope!"

—Giacomo Puccini, *Turandot*

ONE

THE girl had the voice of an angel.

Gio could say that with some authority, since there had been a time when many people had said the same about him.

But this girl. She was tiny, maybe four foot eleven, and very fine-boned, and her application indicated she was fourteen years old even though she barely looked a day over ten. Gio eyed the row of parents sitting in folding chairs or on the floor off to the side of the studio and tried to guess which of them this girl belonged to. Probably an overbearing helicopter mom. There were a dozen of those in the crowd of parents. Usually, you could spot the one who belonged to the auditioning kid because she sat forward in her seat and mouthed the words along with her child. But, no, in this case, all of the moms looked on either with disinterest or in naked shock that such a big sound had come out of such a tiny girl.

Gio was sympathetic to the latter feeling.

Although, there was one person in the crowd of parents who caught Gio's attention, a handsome man who seemed a little out of place. He was *very* handsome. He had messy brown hair and a square jaw, wide shoulders atop a strong body, and he wore gray trousers and a blue button-front shirt as if they were jeans and a T-shirt. Gio wished he hadn't noticed the man, because now he'd be distracted through the rest of the auditions.

But back to the matter at hand.

"Miss McPhee," he said. "That was really lovely. Would you indulge me by singing that last part again, starting with 'Tu che di gel sei cinta'? Okay?"

She nodded and launched back into the Puccini aria. Her Italian was pretty good. It wasn't perfect, which indicated to Gio that she'd learned the aria by listening to recordings and mimicking rather than really understanding and learning to correctly pronounce the words, but he could work on that. Because this girl was *it*. She would be his protégé, his muse, the next great star of the Metropolitan Opera!

And she was only fourteen.

Tiny Emma McPhee finished singing. The faculty panel, Gio included, applauded her enthusiastically. She bowed and moved back to the area where the other potential students of the great Giovanni Boca's opera workshop were waiting. She glanced toward the crowd of parents, probably looking for her mother, but then she took her seat and chatted with another girl.

"Have you ever?" said Dacia, who was sitting next to him. She leaned close and blocked the parents' view of them by holding up a piece of paper. Her eyes were wide.

"She's mine," Gio said.

"I thought you might say that." Her expression turned wry. "You want her to be *la tua stella*."

"*Sì*," he said. "*Ha la voce*." Gio knew without a doubt this girl had the voice to be a star.

Dacia nodded. She threw her long, dark-gray hair over her shoulder and softly crooned a few notes in her smoky mezzo voice. She put the paper down and said, "*Avanti*. Let us continue."

The next hour passed the way these auditions always passed: there was a mix of kids aged thirteen to seventeen, some of whom were terrible, some of whom had a bit of vocal talent, and some of whom had the raw material but needed refinement. Emma McPhee remained the only shoo-in for the workshop, although Gio had made a list of potentials and had pretty much decided on his twelve students by the time the auditions were winding down. The other faculty members on the audition committee always forced Gio into the song and dance with head shots, vague remembrances of the performances from people with bad recall, and usually Sam, the violin teacher, said lecherously of some talentless girl, "But she's just so beautiful," as if beauty had ever actually been linked to skill. Gio indulged them because he figured he shouldn't bite the hand that fed him, since the Olcott School continued to employ him every year, but the final decision was still his.

He tuned out a particularly bad audition by mentally listing who he wanted in his class. He'd scrawled notes on his pad about why he wanted each one in case Sam or Dacia or even Jules, the quiet pianist, somehow thought a teenager with middling talent belonged in the most prestigious workshop in the city for young singers. And then, mercifully, the last audition was over.

Dacia stood and announced that the faculty was going to meet for about an hour to discuss and then the accepted singers would be posted on the bulletin board outside of Gio's studio. She welcomed them to stick around or go grab a bite to eat and come back.

Gio stood, ready to shuffle into his office for an hour of nonsense, but he caught little Emma McPhee jogging across the room and then, much to Gio's surprise, throwing her arms around the handsome man who had been distracting Gio for the better part of the audition process.

Merda.

Gio considered walking right up to the man and informing him that his daughter was definitely getting a spot in the workshop, just to get a closer look, but Dacia hooked her hand around his elbow and pulled him away.

A miserable forty-five minutes ensued in which three kids were obviously in, six were mostly agreed on without controversy, and three were furiously debated. Gio wanted a sixteen-year-old tenor with a voice like honey, but Sam wanted a soprano from New Jersey because, of course, "She's just so pretty."

"So we're clear," Gio said, "this is Giovanni Boca's opera workshop, not Collective Olcott Music Faculty's workshop. In my opinion, yes, Julie is a very pretty girl, but Tyler has the real potential here. His voice is a little thin right now, but he has a good sense of pitch and rhythm, and I can work with that. Julie was a half step sharp through most of her audition." Luckily, Dacia and Jules sided with Gio, so he got his way in the end.

Needing some air outside of his stuffy office, Gio volunteered to go hang up the list. His assistant typed it up and printed it, and Gio took it and a pushpin to the bulletin board outside of his studio. About two-thirds of the prospective students and their parents were milling around in the hallway.

Gio spotted Emma McPhee with that man—her father, presumably, although there wasn't a great deal of resemblance—and he smiled at the guy, who just looked back, biting his lip. There was something endearing about that. Surely he knew how much talent his daughter—or whoever she was—had.

He cleared his throat and said, "If your name is on this list, my assistant Angela will be e-mailing you or your parents with a class schedule and syllabus within the next forty-eight hours. Everyone else, better luck next time."

He posted the list and barely got out of the way before the horde descended. He managed to catch Emma's attention and crooked his finger, inviting her to follow him down the hall. The man trailed after her.

"I wish I had spared you the wait," Gio said, which got him two horrified expressions in return. He laughed softly. He probably could have said that more nicely. "You were in from the moment you opened your mouth. I haven't heard a voice like that in quite some time. I look forward to working with you, Miss McPhee."

Her eyes were like quarters. "What? Really? I got in?"

"Yes. And classes start on the twenty-eighth. I expect you to be there."

She turned to the man. "Daddy, did you hear that? I got in! I got in!" The words came out in a squeal. She jumped up and down a few times.

By now, the assembled crowd had gotten to the board, and there were assorted whoops of joy and groans of disappointment. A couple of the parents gave "buck up" speeches, or said something like, "We'll try again next year," although Gio knew some of those kids would never be good enough. Perhaps that was a harsh way to think of it, but he'd been around music long enough to know that talent was not something that could be taught.

Pushing that aside, Gio extended his hand to the man. "It's a pleasure to meet you. Your daughter is an extraordinary talent."

The man blushed and took his hand in a firm handshake. "I'm Mike McPhee."

"Giovanni Boca, but I suppose you knew that."

"Emma is thrilled, obviously," Mike said. "We're really honored just to audition. It means a lot that you see so much in her." Gio detected a local accent—Brooklyn, maybe.

"It really was a splendid audition. Does this kind of musical talent run in the family? Do you sing?"

Mike shook his head. "No, not at all. Don't know where this voice came from. I don't know much about opera at all, either, but Emma loves it. Her voice teacher—do you know Tina Moretz from the Academy of Music?—well, Ms. Moretz thought Emma's voice would be good for opera, so that's what she's been studying for two years."

Mike's voice quivered a little, as if he were nervous. There was something about the man that softened Gio's heart. "I know Tina Moretz a little. She's a good teacher." Gio glanced at Mike's hand. No wedding ring. "Is there a singer in the family? A wife? A husband, even?"

Mike frowned and shook his head. He briefly looked very sad. There was a story there, for certain.

"Nah," Mike said, "just me and Emma." He put an arm around his daughter and hugged her close. He was not a small man—just above six feet, if Gio's guess was correct, and he was on the bulkier side, though up close it looked like the bulk was mostly muscle—so little Emma's head rested near his armpit.

The rhythmic clack of heels walking on the linoleum told Gio that Dacia was coming to fetch him. "I have a faculty meeting in twenty minutes, or I'd chat more," Gio said to the McPhees. "It was wonderful to meet you, though, and I will see you in class."

"Yes, definitely!" Emma said.

MIKE had been at this dad thing for fourteen years, and the one thing he'd figured out for sure was that parenting involved a lot of multitasking. Thus, the night after the audition, he was watching the Yankees game while also ironing Emma's school uniform while also keeping an ear on her giddy phone conversations, because she apparently had to call half the planet to tell them she got into Giovanni Boca's workshop.

Mike did some quick calculating. Four more days of school; then she got a long weekend off before starting the opera workshop. Maybe they could do something special that weekend.

He was still a little surprised that Emma had gotten into the opera workshop. Ms. Moretz had assured him that Emma had what it took, but Mike had tempered his expectations, not wanting to get Emma's hopes up too high and risk disappointment. Turned out his fretting had been for nothing, thank goodness.

And that Giovanni Boca was a trip, wasn't he? Really good-looking guy in a sleek Italian way, with silver-flecked black hair and a bit of a barrel chest. Mike reasoned he'd have to have a chest like that to produce the sounds he had. Emma had shown him a few online videos, and Boca had been even broader back when he sang, a good thirty pounds heavier than he looked now. The audio quality on those videos hadn't been great, but the sound was still incredible, a voice unlike any Mike had heard before.

Emma had said Boca had lost his voice a few years ago. He had some kind of throat problem and they'd done surgery. Now he couldn't sing anymore and his voice certainly had a raspy quality Mike hadn't expected (though he'd had the slight Italian accent Mike *had* expected). Mike supposed that was why he was teaching.

Emma burst out of her bedroom. "Daddy? Are you working Monday?"

"Yep. Finishing up that Upper West Side job."

"Can Isobel come over after school?"

"Sure, sweetie. You're not going to have any school work this late in the year, are you?"

"No." She rolled her eyes and lifted her phone to her ear. "Izzy? Dad says it's okay." She walked back into her room and started talking rapidly with her best friend.

Emma was a good kid. She hadn't turned out the way Mike had thought she would. At first, he'd tried teaching her about his interests. He took her to baseball games and gave her lots of puzzles and blocks to play with. He wanted to encourage her to be athletic, but she'd always been small for her age and the bigger kids pushed her around. But then one day she'd started singing. So he revised his plan and decided he wanted her to be herself above everything. When she'd wanted to quit sports and take voice lessons instead, he'd agreed. The singing took him out of his comfort zone, into a world he didn't know anything about, but he was willing to go there for Emma.

It had been tough to know what to do in those days. The single-dad thing was not what he'd signed on for. He'd been all of twenty-three years old when he'd let Evan talk him into adopting a baby. He'd always wanted a big family, so it hadn't taken much work on Evan's part, granted, plus they'd thought they'd have to wait years before an agency found them a child. Then this pregnant teenaged girl had picked Mike and Evan within weeks of their completing the paperwork.

But four years after that, Evan was dead and Mike was trying to figure out how to raise his sweet, beautiful, high-energy daughter on his own. His relationship with his own parents was dicey and none of his siblings had had kids at the time, so most of the time, he had to forego advice and just do what seemed right, what his instinct told him to do.

He was pretty sure he got it wrong a lot of the time, and yet Emma was becoming a smart, well-behaved teenager. He would have to beat the boys off with sticks once she started high school in the fall, but that was a mountain he'd climb when he got to it. In the meantime, she seemed happy to practice her singing and hang out with her girlfriends, and most of the time she did well in school. And now she'd been accepted to the best opera workshop for teenagers in the city. So he must have done something right.

She came back out of her bedroom, off the phone now, and threw herself on the sofa with a huff. "Who's winning?" she asked.

"Yanks are up two, bottom of the fifth."

She yawned and settled into the cushions. "What did you think of Giovanni Boca?"

"I think you've got your work cut out for you, kiddo. Ms. Moretz said he's a hard-ass of a teacher."

"He's the best, though. One of his students from a couple of years ago is in a Met production this season. She's one of the youngest actresses to get a starring role."

"Wow."

"I know. That could be me, Dad."

"It could be, yeah. Or you could finish school."

"Well, yeah, duh. I'm going to get into Juilliard."

He leaned over and kissed the top of her head. "You haven't even started high school. How can you be so sure?"

"I'm sure. Giovanni Boca's workshop is my ticket."

He chuckled, admiring her confidence. He'd wondered sometimes if he thought so much of her talent because he was her father, if having raised her had biased him. But now that others saw that magic in her too, he knew he hadn't been mistaken. She could very well go to Juilliard and sing at the Met and tour Europe and all of those things.

"Plus, he's kind of cute, don't you think?" she asked, her expression a little dreamy.

Mike burst into laughter. "Yeah, sweetheart, I guess he is."

TWO

GIO talked while he plugged his MP3 player into the speakers. "I had a voice coach when I was living in Milan who thought the best way to inspire his singers was to scare the living hell out of them. So now I will do that to you."

Twelve teenagers sat rapt on the studio floor, staring at Gio. He found "Der Hölle Rache" in the list of songs. "This is June Anderson singing from *Die Zauberflöte*." He hit play. "It is famously referred to as the Queen of the Night's aria, although she sings another earlier in the opera that is nearly as good. Here, she is singing, 'Hell's vengeance boils my heart.' She is not having such a good time, eh? And Mozart is about to put her through hell vocally too. Listen."

It was clear from their expressions that a few of the girls knew this aria. Emma McPhee certainly did. The girls who didn't blanched when the singer got to the run pattern between the verses.

"This," Gio said when the aria finished, "is coloratura. Literally, it means coloring, but in the context of an opera, it means to add these vocal flourishes. They are beautiful but extraordinarily difficult to sing." He smiled, trying not to freak the kids out too much. "That is, coloratura was often added to songs in the bel canto tradition. Can any of you think of other examples?"

About half the class was with it. Emma cited Rossini, the obvious example. Marie pulled out an obscure Mozart piece, which allowed Gio to freak the class out more by pointing out that this particular part was written for a castrato. Most of the boys winced at that. Greg knew "Every Valley Shall Be Exalted" from Handel's *Messiah* was a coloratura tenor aria.

"Good," Gio said. "Now I will blow your minds some more. This one is from *Nixon in China*."

After playing a few more arias, he had the class stand and he ran through some vocal exercises, mostly scales and weird syllables and matching pitch to the piano. It was a good crop of students, no doubt about that. Still, he said, "The expectation is not for you to sing like June Anderson when you finish my class, particularly since you are all teenagers and your voices are still developing. But I want you to think about what you might do in the future, what you're capable of. Maybe one of you will play the Queen of the Night at La Scala someday."

He gave them homework, asking them to find their favorite aria in their own voice range, something they could aspire to. Then he warned them, "This session was easy. After today, I will put you through your paces. I will challenge you to sing things you never thought you could sing, and I will teach you technique and style and grace. We will read music and we will learn languages. It will not be as easy as this. Fair warning." He put his hands on his hips and aimed a stern look at them. "All right. Class dismissed."

The kids gathered up their things. A few of the parents filtered into the studio, including Mike McPhee, who grinned when he saw his daughter. The fanatical stage parents often picked up their kids, but it seemed weird for someone like Mike—today in beat-up jeans and a paint-splattered T-shirt—to pick up his daughter when she could just as easily get home by herself on the subway, like most of the kids in this city. Gio found Mike's overprotective instinct a little curious.

So he approached. "Mr. McPhee. Nice to see you again."

Mike smiled. "Yes." He turned to his daughter. "How was class?"

"Good," said Emma. "I'll tell you about it on the way home."

"Not all of the parents pick up their kids," Gio said, trying tactfully to ask why Mike was there.

"I was working in the neighborhood. Figured I'd drop by so she didn't have to take the bus alone."

Gio couldn't decide if the bright smile and the ratty clothes made him more or less attractive. After a split second, when Mike smiled again, Gio decided they added to Mike's appeal. "What do you do?" he asked, gesturing at the paint splatters.

"Independent contractor. I'm remodeling a kitchen a few blocks from here. Well, not just me, I've got a team of guys who work for me. But, yeah, that's what I'm working on right now."

"Oh, okay," Gio said, not sure how to respond. "I know very little about that sort of thing. Is it going well?"

"It is. We should finish ahead of schedule." He smiled again, and *Dio*, but this man had a beautiful smile. "I don't know much about opera except what Emma tells me, so I guess you and I don't have a lot in common."

"Oh, I left my water bottle by the drinking fountain," Emma said. Then she dashed off.

That left Gio alone in the studio with Mike.

It was strange. Mike was not Gio's type at all. All of Gio's exes were dancers or artists or people who worked in the theater in some capacity, and yet here was this blue-collar guy who drew Gio's attention like no one he'd seen in a long time.

It was wiser to keep one's distance, Gio reasoned. Mike was handsome, but he was also the father of one of Gio's students, something that seemed ethically problematic. Furthermore, Gio had no idea if his advances would be welcome or if that would be the sure way to destroy Mike's jovial demeanor. Trying to keep the conversation going, he said, "For someone who doesn't know much about opera, you are raising quite the young singer."

"Thank you. She loves it. And she has a mind like a sponge, so she learned all about it on her own. I never wanted to force her into something she wasn't interested in, you know? My parents were always trying to make me fit in this little box, and I hated that."

"Whereas my mother sang opera at La Scala and I followed right behind her."

Mike laughed. "I'm sorry. I hope I didn't say something offensive."

"It's quite all right." Gio smiled. The truth was that he liked listening to Mike's voice. Mike probably could be trained to sing baritone, and his voice had a rich quality to it, although that Brooklyn accent kept him from sounding like he belonged in Gio's world.

Emma appeared in the door of the studio. "I'm ready to go, Daddy," she said.

"Okay, kiddo. We'll see you next time, Mr. Boca."

There weren't any other students around, so Gio leaned forward and said softly, "Please, call me Gio."

"Gio?" Mike raised an eyebrow.

"Perhaps not in front of the other students."

Mike glanced toward his daughter again. "I should go. Till next time!"

Gio watched him go, ruminating on how silly it was to develop a crush on the parent of one of his students. Except it wasn't just silly, it was dangerous.

THE thing of it was, Mike was really attracted to Gio.

It was a little strange to feel so strongly attracted to someone after a long time without dating much. Not that Mike didn't appreciate a hot guy, just that he hadn't really been looking, not after his last few relationships had fallen apart. In some ways, dating was easier now than it had been in the first years after Evan's passing, but in some ways it was harder. He didn't feel the same shame or guilt he used to, but it was hard to negotiate being a dad with dating. It wasn't just time spent away from Emma; it was that every man he'd met was perplexed—or horrified, sometimes—by the fact that he had a daughter, and that tended to scare them off.

He sat beside Emma on the crosstown bus. She sounded even more taken with the great Giovanni Boca than Mike was. "So he played us this famous aria," she said, "and it's really tough. Like, only a handful of sopranos in the whole world can sing it. And I thought, 'That will be me someday.' I want to sing that aria when I play the Queen of the Night on one of the world's great stages. I think Mr. Boca can help me get there."

"So it's going well?" Mike asked with a smile.

She grinned back. "Yeah, so far. Although, he implied that the *real* work will start in our next class." She leaned her head on his shoulder. "What's for dinner tonight?"

"Not sure. Sandy wants to come over to watch the game. I told him he could only come if he brings dinner."

"So, pizza, probably."

"Is that all right?"

She yawned. "That's fine, Daddy."

She had grown up so fast. It felt like just yesterday she'd been his little girl and he'd been crying over her starting kindergarten. She was a young woman now, starting high school in the fall. She squeezed his heart every time she called him "Daddy," because he knew the days of her doing that were numbered. He was enormously proud of her too, amazed by the person she had become.

When they got home, he put her to work on her chores, which got him a bit of whining in return, but she did them. He changed out of his work clothes, showered, and settled on the couch to watch that night's Yankees game. He picked up the remote and thought of Gio and how weird it would be to have the man sitting here with him, watching the game. Then again, Mike did occasionally put on a suit and go with Emma to the opera, so he supposed anything was possible.

Sandy showed up a short time later with a grin on his face and a pizza box in his hands. Mike let him in, and Emma, probably having been alerted to Sandy's arrival by the squeak of the door, zoomed into the room and threw her arms around him.

Sandy's real name was Alexander, but he'd been given the nickname years before because of his sunny good looks, and it had never occurred to Mike to call him anything else. They'd been best friends, brothers, since high school in south Brooklyn, seeing each other through the army, through Evan's death, and through Sandy's romantic ups and downs.

Sandy danced free of Emma and slid the pizza box onto the coffee table. "So," he said. "Yankees."

Emma sat on the couch while Mike grabbed plates and cups from the kitchen. She rattled off some trivia about the game, and Mike couldn't help but smile. That sponge brain of hers had absorbed every bit of sports knowledge he had ever imparted, and even though opera was her greatest obsession at the moment, she could talk to Sandy about baseball just as easily as she could talk to Mr. Boca about Puccini.

During the third inning, Sandy said, "So. I'm dating a doctor."

Emma perked up at the potential for gossip. "Is he cute?"

"Yes, very. Here's the issue. He's an ER doc at Roosevelt Hospital and apparently he's on call all the time. So although I like him, I'm not sure if we should really date. He doesn't have time for me."

Mike nodded. "You do need a lot of attention."

Sandy tossed a throw pillow at Mike's head. Mike caught it deftly.

Sandy sat back on the couch and sighed. "I don't know if I can be a doctor's wife. All those crazy hours. And isn't working in the ER kind of dangerous?"

"Probably not in that neighborhood," Mike said.

"Hmm." Sandy seemed to consider that. "Yeah, I guess it's not like being a cop."

A wave of panic went through Mike, cold sweat breaking out everywhere.

"Oh God, I'm so sorry," Sandy said. "I wasn't even thinking."

"It's all right," Mike sighed. "It's been more than ten years. You'd think those memories wouldn't hit me that way anymore."

"But sometimes they do," Sandy said softly.

"Yeah." He was aware of Emma staring at him, but he couldn't bring himself to look back. He had to fight not to retreat into himself, to dwell in some of the darker spaces within. He took a deep breath.

"Anyway," Sandy said. "Being a doctor also requires all that school. You know I ain't never been much for book learnin'. One of these days, he's going to figure out I'm not that smart."

"Don't need school to be smart," Mike said. It was a refrain, something he and Sandy had told each other plenty of times. Mike hadn't been college material, and he was all right with that because he'd made a good life for himself and Emma. He turned to Emma. "You're going to college, though."

She laughed. "Juilliard."

"Right. Just so we're clear."

That she didn't remember Evan was sometimes troublesome to Mike. She'd still been in diapers when Evan had died, leaving Mike a single parent to a precocious little girl. He still thought of her as their daughter, his and Evan's, even though Evan had missed nearly all of her life.

He still got angry sometimes. Those moments were becoming few and far between, but as they watched the game and Sandy prattled on about his doctor, Mike felt that wave of anger at Evan for abandoning them, for putting himself in a position that would cause harm. He knew that was irrational, that nothing Evan could have done would have made that night any less horrible, that Evan was a hero, in fact, because he'd stepped between a bullet and a kid, but, God, sometimes… sometimes he resented the hell out of Evan for leaving him alone.

"How're your singing lessons going?" Sandy asked during the sixth inning.

"First of all, it's Giovanni Boca's opera workshop, not just singing lessons," Emma said.

Sandy held up his hands. "Oh. Well, excuse me."

"It's going well. We've only had the one class so far, but I like Mr. Boca. He says our future classes are going to be much tougher, but I like the challenge." She grinned.

"Who is this Boca guy?"

"He's a famous opera singer," Emma said. "A tenor. He's sung all over the world. Now he teaches at the Olcott School."

Sandy nodded. "All right. So. On a scale of homely to dreamy, where does he fall?"

Mike put a hand over his mouth to hide his reaction, which was somewhere between horror and amusement. He didn't want to explain his attraction to the man to Sandy.

Emma raised her eyebrows. "That hardly seems like a fair question."

"Turnabout is fair play," Sandy said.

"He's pretty cute. Daddy, you agree, right? You talked to him for a while after class today."

Sandy smirked. "Oh, really?"

Mike felt the heat come to his face. "About Emma. We talked about Emma. And then I embarrassed myself because he asked me to call him 'Gio' and I didn't know how to respond, so I just… left."

Emma turned to him abruptly. "He asked you to call him Gio?"

"Yeah, I just figured—"

"Daddy, he likes you!"

Mike guffawed. "Honey, that's crazy. What reason on God's green earth could a world-famous opera singer have to be interested in a guy like me? Also, why am I having this conversation with you?"

"A couple of other teachers stopped by the workshop today. Everyone called him Mr. Boca. They seemed kind of afraid of him, actually. But he asked you to call him Gio."

"He was probably buttering me up," Mike said. "Oh, hey, look who's at bat!"

The game went into extra innings, and Mike ordered Emma to bed when it was over. Sandy helped him clean up. Mike was showing him out the door when Sandy suddenly turned around and said, "I still miss him sometimes too."

There was that wave of panic again, making Mike feel a little nauseous. "I know."

"It's been so long that I almost forget sometimes. I really am sorry for what I said."

"I know. I almost forget sometimes too. Don't worry about it."

"He'd be really proud of Emma. And you. You've done great things with her."

Mike forced a smile through the sadness that threatened to weigh him down. "Thanks. I think he'd be proud of her too."

They hugged and Sandy left.

Mike lay awake in bed for a long time that night. This was nothing like the profound loneliness he'd felt just after Evan's death, when Evan's clothes were still in the closet and his scent still on the sheets. This was a whole new apartment, in fact, in a different neighborhood, with different furniture, different linens, different scents. Evan's death didn't weigh on Mike like it used to. He missed Evan, sometimes deeply, but he'd moved on with his life. He'd raised a great daughter without Evan, built a thriving business without Evan, carved out a life for himself without Evan. Evan was now nothing more than a memory.

Mike's thoughts drifted to Gio as he finally started to fall asleep. Gio, who was alive and not eleven years dead. Gio, who was handsome and interesting and completely unlike any man Mike had ever been with. Gio, who was Emma's teacher. Gio, who was worldly and rich and not building kitchen cabinets to pay the bills.

A fantasy, in other words. But if thinking about that fantasy got Mike to sleep at night, then he was willing to embrace it.

THREE

EVERYONE at the Olcott School knew Tracy Quinlan.

The Quinlan family was widely known to be extremely generous when it came to supporting the arts in New York City. Tracy had once been a ballerina with the City Ballet. This was apparently before she caught the eye of her husband Eric and together they saw to populating all of the music and dance classes in the city with their offspring. Well, Gio acknowledged as he watched Tracy Quinlan pace in the music department's common room, that might have been a slight exaggeration, but they did have five children, including the unfortunately hawk-nosed Amelia, who was now enrolled in his summer opera workshop.

Gio hated dealing with the stage parents. He'd been dealing with people like Tracy Quinlan for most of his life, but he'd never appreciated how nefarious the overzealous parents were until he started teaching.

He took a deep breath as he walked into the common room. "Mrs. Quinlan," he said.

"Ah, Mr. Boca. A word, if you please."

"*Sì*. Come to my office."

She was expensively dressed and her heels were impossibly high, though she still walked like a ballerina as he escorted her across the common room.

"So pleasant to see you again," Gio said as he settled into his office chair. He thought he sounded rather like he meant it. He'd taught Amelia's older brother Tony during his first workshop. Tony had a decent voice but had hated opera. Gio had heard he was studying engineering in college now.

After she sat at the edge of his guest chair, she said, "I'm delighted that Amelia is thriving in your workshop."

Gio nodded, although "thriving" seemed like a strong descriptor given that she was one of the weaker singers in the class. She was still better than 95 percent of the teenage singers in the city, probably because her parents had forced talent on her by putting her in voice lessons since she'd been a toddler, but certainly in a different league from the top singers in his class.

"I saw the auditions," Tracy Quinlan went on. "Quite a lot of talent in your workshop this summer."

"I agree. One of the better groups I've ever assembled. I'm having a great deal of fun teaching them. Some of the singers need some refinement, but the raw talent is remarkable."

"I've been considering making a substantial donation to the program this year. Ms. Russini told me that donations fund most of the workshop's expenses."

"Part of them, anyway," said Gio. "I do appreciate your generosity, Mrs. Quinlan. You and your husband are both clearly devoted to the arts."

"My youngest daughter Jennifer has been taking lessons too. She wants to sing opera just like her sister."

"That's wonderful." Gio wondered what Tracy was getting at.

Tracy crossed her legs primly. "Amelia's success is very important to us. I wanted to impress that on you."

"Indeed. I imagine many parents feel that way about their children."

She tilted her head. "You do not have children of your own, Mr. Boca."

"I do not."

"Perhaps, then, you are not so familiar with the lengths some parents will go to make sure their children get everything they deserve."

Gio didn't like the sound of that. "Ah. I'm not sure I follow."

"Amelia wants to get into the Olcott School Young Musicians Program this fall. She auditioned last year but didn't make it. I hope that with your influence, she will not confront the same fate this year. She really was terribly disappointed, as were my husband and I."

There it was. Part of Gio wanted to ask to what lengths Tracy Quinlan was willing to go, but he didn't dare. He had no doubt this was a woman who was used to getting what she wanted, or at least was used to throwing money at people until what she wanted came to pass.

Gio was not especially moved.

"My colleague Ms. Russini is the chair of the audition committee for the Young Musicians Program. I don't have much of a say in who gets in." Dacia had been leaning on him to volunteer for the committee, but he didn't especially want to, so he'd been kicking that decision down the road.

Not that it mattered, because Tracy Quinlan plowed forward. "You are Giovanni Boca, and if you told the faculty you thought a student was good enough, that student would get into the program."

That was probably true. Gio sighed. "*If* a student does exceptionally well in the workshop, I will recommend her for the Young Musicians Program. But she can't rest on her laurels. She should practice as much as possible and come prepared to my class. She cannot rely on her talent alone, because she's competing with the best young singers in the region for those spots, some of whom live and breathe opera." He took a deep breath so as not to come off as combative, even though this whole conversation irritated him. "I appreciate your coming to talk with me and I will do what I can to help Amelia, but she has to do her end of the work as well." He glanced at his watch. "Speaking of the workshop, it is beginning shortly. I don't mean to cut you off, but I have to track down my assistant for the music for today's class." He stood.

Tracy mirrored his movement, rising slowly to her feet. "Thank you for meeting with me. And if I can assist you in any way…." She smiled.

He understood what she was doing. That smile might as well have been a twenty-dollar bill pressed into his palm. "I'm sure we'll be in touch, Mrs. Quinlan."

She shook his hand and then slid out of his office.

DACIA came to that afternoon's workshop—the fourth class of twelve, as they met twice a week for six weeks—to work with the female singers. She still had an amazing voice, though she preferred teaching to performing. Gio liked working with her. They came from the same place, for one thing; she grew up not far from his childhood home near Florence, and they'd met while performing together in Italy before Gio had made a name for himself. Dacia had also been instrumental in getting him this job. She'd been on the faculty at Olcott for a few years before he'd lost his voice. She had stuck with him from when he was on top of the world until he hit rock bottom, and she'd helped pull him out with the offer of another way to use his skills. He appreciated that and loved her for it. Plus, she sang like a dream.

Dacia's rich mezzo-soprano voice filled the studio as she sang the opening bars of "Habanera" from *Carmen*. He handed out music and had the kids sing some of the chorus parts from the opera. There were mixed results, although most of it wasn't good. They were butchering the French pronunciation, for one thing. One of the tenors was flat. Tiny Emma McPhee overpowered all of them.

"All right," he said when Dacia finished. "This is an important lesson. I know you aspire to greater things than the chorus, but it showed me what's going on with you all in general. A lot of you, if you're serious about singing, will get your start in the chorus and work your way up to being prima donna. That means balancing your voice with those of the other singers. That also means pronouncing the words right even if you don't know what they mean. So, let's try this."

He handed out new sheet music, a movement from a Bach oratorio, and then he had Dacia write a basic Latin pronunciation guide on the white board he'd wheeled in earlier. The rest of the class was intense and the kids clearly struggled, even Emma.

Then he broke the kids into groups and had Dacia take the girls while he worked with the boys.

The class wound down and the kids gathered up their stuff. He walked over to Dacia. "Thank you for your help today."

"My pleasure. This is a great crop of students you've got."

"I know. I made the right choices." Although he now had his doubts about Amelia Quinlan.

Dacia laughed. "Don't let them hear you say that." Then she smirked. "Did you know there is a handsome gentleman standing in the doorway?"

Gio tried not to jerk as he turned his head. Mike was there and shooting Gio an odd look.

"That's Emma McPhee's father."

"I see."

Gio wondered what Dacia saw. They stopped talking as they watched father and daughter greet each other. Both smiled and Mike asked Emma something Gio couldn't hear from across the room.

"*È bello,*" Dacia commented.

He *was* quite beautiful. "*Sì. Lo so.*"

"*È sposato?*"

Gio was curious about his history, but at least they'd established that he wasn't married. "No."

"Gay?"

"*Non lo so. Forse.*" Maybe he was. Gio couldn't really tell. It seemed unlikely that a girl would have a single gay father, but this was New York and stranger things had happened.

And now Mike was coming right for them.

"Hello, Gio," Mike said with a smile.

"*Ciao*, Mike." Gio smiled back and took a moment to appreciate being in Mike's presence again. Then Dacia cleared her throat. "*Sì.*" He threw a frustrated glance at her before looking back at Mike. "This is my friend and colleague, Dacia Russini."

Mike held out his hand. Dacia shook it and smiled at him.

"*Buongiorno*," Dacia said. "A pleasure to meet you."

"Likewise," said Mike. "I just wanted to say hi. Emma is trying to make plans with a few of the other girls and doesn't need me hovering."

Dacia reached over and patted Gio's shoulder. "I must be leaving. I'll see you at the meeting tomorrow, Gio."

"*Molto bene. Ciao*," he said.

Mike rocked on his heels as Dacia walked away.

"Girlfriend?" Mike asked.

That struck Gio as so ridiculous that he laughed. "Oh, no. Very old friend. We performed together many times, but any romance between us was kept on the stage. She's married to a choreographer."

"Oh."

"And she's, ah, not my type." He raised an eyebrow.

Mike's eyes widened. It occurred to Gio to worry that a blue-collar guy like Mike might be homophobic, but he just nodded and said, "Good to know."

Gio second-guessed himself in a way he usually didn't. He was used to going after and getting what he wanted, and he wanted Mike, but he held himself back. He got kind of a gay vibe off Mike but wasn't certain, for one thing. He thought fraternizing with the father of one of his students was probably unethical, and that it could be a thorny situation. But he had to know more about this man. Part of it was curiosity about Emma, yes, and wondering where that amazing talent came from. But part of it was just this beautiful man who seemed so unlike anyone else in Gio's life.

He said, "I don't suppose you would be interested in having lunch with me some day this week. You work in the area, right?"

"For now, yes. Lunch?" Mike's eyes went wide again, which made Gio think his instincts might have been wrong. He thought he'd sensed some mutual interest, but maybe his gut feeling was not quite accurate.

"To discuss Emma," Gio said. "She has the potential to do some really amazing things. I thought I might talk that over with you."

Mike's relief was a palpable thing. Gio couldn't tell if that was a good or bad sign. "Oh. Yes, of course. Just tell me where or when. I usually take lunch around one."

"There's a little cafe on Sixty-third." Gio gave Mike directions. "Tomorrow?"

Mike nodded slowly. "Tomorrow is good."

Emma poked her head into the studio. "Dad? I need to run by the music store on the way home. Are you ready?"

Mike smirked at Gio. "I never know who is in charge here anymore. I guess I'd better go."

"I'll see you tomorrow, Mike."

"Yes. Definitely."

FOUR

MIKE suspected an ulterior motive but wasn't disappointed to find Gio already seated when he got to the restaurant. He'd even taken the time to change clothes so he wouldn't be sitting down to a nice lunch in his old jeans and ratty T-shirt. So, wearing one of his nicer shirts and a crisply clean pair of jeans, he sat across from the man and smiled.

Gio smiled. "I'm glad you could make it. How are you?"

His voice had a rhythmic cadence to it, even with the rasp. Something about the Italian accent and that rough quality to Gio's speech was incredibly sexy.

"I'm good," Mike managed to say. He was distracted by how good Gio looked. He was wearing a dark-green shirt that looked great against his olive skin and had a shadow of dark scruff against his jaw. He had really incredible eyes, Mike noticed for the first time; they looked almost green in the dim lighting of the cafe. To keep from staring, Mike knew he had to say something. "How are you? I assume the workshop is going well, since that's all Emma has been talking about for the past week. Do you teach other classes too?"

"College voice classes at the Olcott School during the regular school year. I also teach a seminar on the history of opera in the spring. Every now and then I teach a couple of Young Musicians Program students. That's the after-school program for high school students."

"Okay." Mike felt a bit at sea. "That's… that's good. So, um, you wanted to talk about Emma?"

Gio smiled. "Your daughter is extraordinarily talented."

"Thanks. I think so too."

Mike knew he was squirming. He had a hard time accepting compliments on Emma's behalf. He rubbed his hands on his thighs and tried to calm down. He had no reason to be nervous, even if he was sitting across from a devastatingly attractive man.

Emma. They were here to talk about Emma.

"And you don't really sing much," Gio said. "Sometimes it does skip generations, as they say, but it's unusual for a girl this disciplined to come from a family with no musical experience."

Mike felt like his skin itched everywhere. He shifted his weight on the chair. "Well, I used to sing her little nursery rhymes and things when she was a baby. We always had music playing at home. The opera, though... I have no idea where that comes from. When she first started showing an interest, I managed to get some tickets to the Met. We were way up in that top mezzanine, the one that's about three miles from the stage, but she was in love. I've never seen such amazement on her face." Mike laughed to himself, trying to calm down. "As for skipping generations, well, her parents could be the most musically gifted people on the planet, but I wouldn't know. She was adopted."

"Oh." Gio tilted his head as if this confused him. "Interesting. I never would have expected."

"I get that a lot. But any resemblance is coincidental."

"I suppose genetics don't matter as much as care and love and those things."

Mike felt like he was being patronized a little. Mildly annoyed, he looked over the menu. "Did you invite me here just to praise Emma or my parenting?"

"Not exactly, and before you ask, no, I don't do this with all the parents." Gio shook his head and stared, unfocused, at something on the table. "I should be frank, then. I do think Emma is a rarity. I've been running this workshop for six years now and I've seen maybe three singers like her in all that time. Honestly, it would give me great joy to continue to work with her after this workshop is over."

"Are you serious?" Mike wanted to laugh at the absurdity of a world-renowned singer wanting to work with his little girl. "Well, I'll be frank too, and tell you that I had to scrape together the money for this class. I'm not sure I can afford—"

"We don't have to decide right now. If the rest of the workshop goes well, maybe we can work something out."

"I... okay." It seemed so unlikely. People never handed things like this to Mike.

"But I didn't just want to talk about Emma. That wasn't the only reason I invited you here. I... ah... well."

Gio laughed, although it seemed to lack humor. He rubbed the back of his head with his hand, which pushed some of his dark hair up into spikes briefly before it all fluttered back into place. Mike hadn't really noticed before, but Gio had a hell of a head of hair, thick and a bit unruly, the sort of hair one could really run his fingers through. He flexed his fingers under the table as he thought about doing just that.

Luckily, Gio didn't notice because he was too busy staring at the table. He laughed again. "*O mio Dio*, I do not think I have been this nervous since I was a teenager."

"What are you nervous about?" It dawned on Mike suddenly that Gio was perhaps on edge for the same reasons Mike was. That also seemed absurd—how could a man like Gio possibly be interested in a man like Mike?—but maybe the situation wasn't so strange if you stripped it down to its essence. Gio was worldly and knowledgeable and so very Italian. Mike had no more education than a high school diploma and came from a South Brooklyn lace-curtain Irish family, and the only reason he had ever been outside of the greater New York metropolitan area was because the army had sent him there. And yet hadn't Gio been implying the day before that he was not interested in women when he said Dacia wasn't his type? That meant Mike and Gio were just two men with some kind of attraction zinging between them, both nervous and a little awkward.

It made Mike laugh.

Gio let out a breath and looked up. "What's so funny?"

"I was just thinking, you know, here we are, two guys having a casual lunch. And yet we're both as nervous as if we were on a first date."

Gio let out a little burst of laughter. "I... yes. Honestly? I invited you to lunch because I thought that the handsome father of one of my students might be a man I'd like to get to know better. It's probably somewhat unethical, but—now why are you laughing?"

Mike tried to school his features—the laughter was almost as much humor as nerves at this point—and he had to sip his water to stop. "Emma has been teasing me for days, claiming that because you asked me to call you by your first name, you must *like* me."

"She may have been onto something," Gio said, chuckling.

"Yeah?"

"Is that so surprising?"

"I guess not." Mike found himself smiling. It was certainly a relief to know for sure that Gio was gay, at least. There was also something kind of new and interesting about this situation. Gio had been playing on his mind for days, and now it turned out the feeling was mutual. "Of course, in her little teenage mind, I'm sure she imagines us making eyes at each other and, like, passing notes in study hall."

Gio smirked. "What would your note say?"

Mike considered. He felt giddy as he thought about what to say. "You're hot. I like you."

Gio laughed. "If only it were that simple, eh?"

"Maybe it is. We're having lunch now, aren't we?"

"That's what I like about being an adult. There's a lot less *stronzate*. I teach teenagers. I see the drama these kids drag themselves through."

"Yeah. Emma and her best friend Isobel have been having a lot of very serious conversations about boys lately. I tell her she should ask for my advice. I know a few things about men, since I am one and I've been dating them for twenty years, but she says, 'No, *Dad*, you don't know what it's like.'" Mike rolled his eyes.

Gio shook his head. "I can't even imagine what it's like to raise a girl."

"She's a great kid, but it's not always easy."

Gio got up a few minutes later and went up to the counter to order them sandwiches. Before he left, he asked Mike if they should have wine as well. "Rain check," Mike said, because he had a sudden vision of an elegant evening sipping wine with this Italian gentleman and wanted to reserve that for the future. "I have to be back on the job after this."

"I will hold you to that," Gio said.

Mike hoped he would.

"Tell me your sob story," said Gio once he sat back down with their sandwiches.

Mike had no idea what to say. "What do you mean?"

Gio smiled and looked right at Mike. "If you have a teenage daughter but a young face, I imagine your age must be close to mine. Late thirties?"

"I'm thirty-seven."

"Ah. As am I. In my experience, no one gets to be our age without a little tragedy and drama. So I'm asking, what's yours? Also, sometimes you get this look on your face like you're remembering something really sad."

"I do?" Mike couldn't imagine how Gio had seen that in him. It was there, certainly, but Mike didn't like to show that side of himself, especially not to strangers.

"Here, I'll tell you mine." Gio smiled and folded his hands on the table. He leaned forward a little. "It went like this: I'd had a sore throat for a couple of days, but I kept singing anyway, because that was what you did. You drank tea with honey and the show went on. I was starring as Calaf in a production of *Turandot* in Beijing, and it was like every one of my dreams coming true."

Gio sat back a little and slid his arms off the table.

"Nessun Dorma," he said. "It is famous for a reason, you know. That aria, that was half the reason I began to sing opera at all. So there I was on stage, building up to the climax of the song. Calaf sings, *Vincerò*! It means 'I will win.' He sings it three times, and the third is this tremendous note of triumph. Calaf is confident he will win this ridiculous contest with Princess Turandot. So there I am on stage, singing the lead up to that note: *vincerò, vincerò*." He said the words like a chant.

Mike's heart ached at the realization that Gio rasped the words because he could no longer sing them.

"In the middle of the third *vincerò*," Gio said, "my voice cracked and then died. 'I will win,' I was singing, but I lost." He looked at the table. "There were polyps on my vocal chords I didn't know about. What I thought was an oncoming cold turned out to be a bigger problem. It might have been fine, but my doctor called my profession 'chronic overuse of the vocal folds,' or something like that. They did surgery and discovered that, although the polyps were healing, they left behind scars. So now I can't sing anymore."

Gio's story was delivered with the casual affect of someone discussing a trip to the beach, but the watery look in his eyes conveyed a much greater pain. Mike's sympathy was like a fist around his heart, and the emotion that caught in his throat might as well have been a softball because he couldn't form words or make sounds. For his part, Gio looked at the table, stared at his sandwich, and shook his head like he didn't want to speak anymore.

Mike took a deep breath. "I know what that's like," he said. "To have the rug pulled out from under you. To have your whole life planned out for you until someone says you can't have your plan anymore."

"Tell me," Gio said, looking up with a softness around his eyes that hadn't been there before.

So Mike told his story. He explained about how he'd finished high school knowing he wasn't college material. Not that he wasn't smart—he knew he had some brains colliding around up there—but studying and tests were not where he would excel. He and Sandy had decided together to join the army. Shortly after they finished basic training, they were shipped off to Saudi Arabia. It was there they'd met another young private named Evan. Mike and Sandy and Evan became a trio almost immediately, the greatest of friends. In one of those odd twists of fate, Mike and Evan had been alone on a patrol together one night during a week in which half the platoon was down with the flu. During a lull, Evan turned to Mike, confessed his feelings, and kissed him. Mike had likewise been harboring a crush on Evan for weeks and was delighted. They were a couple from that day forward.

"We got caught," Mike told Gio as he picked cheese off his sandwich, nervous now instead of hungry. "Before that, we'd been so goddamn discreet the CIA could have gotten tips from us, but one day we were fooling around in what we thought was an empty office and our commanding officer walked right in on us. The CO was a dick about it and invoked Don't Ask, Don't Tell. And that was the end of my army career. After we were discharged, Evan and I wound up back here in New York."

Evan had decided to make the most of his military training and went to the police academy. Law enforcement had felt like his calling. Then, a few years into his career in the NYPD and five years into Mike and Evan's romantic relationship, they decided they wanted a whole mess of kids. They set the adoption process in motion.

"The counselor we worked with at the agency told us that because we were gay, it could be years, and that was what we expected," Mike explained. He couldn't look at Gio, who must have known by now what was coming. He couldn't just cut to the chase, either. He needed Gio to know the whole story, for some reason. "I was really young at the time. I wasn't ready to be a father, but Evan was really gung ho about it, and I thought, what the hell? Let's put our names in the hat. By the time we get a child, I'll be ready. Then this teenage girl in the Bronx saw our profile and decided her baby just had to go to a gay couple. It was crazy, but bless her, wherever she is. She gave us Emma, and I will never stop being grateful to her." Mike took another deep breath. "It was an open adoption. The birth mom was supposed to stay in touch, but she disappeared shortly after she turned eighteen. Just dropped right off the radar. Stopped returning my e-mails or phone calls. I hope she's all right."

"But this is your story, not hers."

Mike nodded. "It happened when Emma was three." He knew his voice had grown quiet. Gio leaned forward, probably to hear better. But Mike couldn't say the words any louder. "Evan was on a pretty routine shift when he and his partner got called to a disturbance at a bodega. At first he thought it was a robbery, but then he saw a man screaming at a young girl. The girl was in tears. Evan's partner tried to talk the man down, but then the guy drew a gun." This was where things always got hard for Mike. He blinked to keep from showing too much on his face. "The guy was going to shoot the girl. Evan got between the girl and the bullet."

Gio put a hand to his mouth. "*Dio mio.*"

Mike sat back. "When the dust settled, I was a single dad raising a toddler in a city. So that's my sob story."

"I am so sorry, Mike."

"It's been eleven years. That kind of thing… it doesn't go away, exactly, and I still think about Evan pretty frequently, but it's not… it doesn't dominate my life the way it once did, I guess." What Mike didn't say, couldn't say, was that the only thing that got him out of bed in those days after Evan's death was Emma. If not for her, he would have had nothing to live for. He had to take care of a very young girl who had no idea what was happening, who kept asking why she couldn't see Daddy Evan anymore. He and Emma had been crucial to each other's survival.

After a long moment of silence, Mike said, "Look, my daughter is the most important thing in my life. I would do anything to make sure she's healthy and happy. I've never seen her as happy as she is when she's singing or talking about music. So maybe I'm a little uncouth and uncultured, but this is what she wants, so I'll see to it I do everything in my power to make this happen for her." He realized what he was saying as he was saying it. "Well, not *everything*. I hope you realize I didn't agree to lunch because—"

"No, I understand." Gio smiled.

"Good. Because I do like you, Gio. But that's separate from what I want for Emma." Mike looked at his watch. He had to get back to work and needed to get out of this room that was suddenly flooded with memories. He felt raw and vulnerable, a bad place to be with a man who was still a relative stranger. "I don't want to cut this short, but I've got a kitchen waiting for me."

"Yes, of course. I don't mean to keep you."

Mike smirked. "Well, maybe you do."

Gio laughed. "A little, yes."

Well, that was something. Mike supposed he wouldn't have torn his chest open and exposed his heart to just anyone, and there was something intriguing about Gio. If nothing else, they understood each other in a strange way.

There was a tussle when Mike tried to give Gio money for the lunch and Gio refused, but then they went outside. It was a sunny day, warm but not too hot. Mike paused for a moment to let the light wash over his face. Then he looked at Gio.

"Thank you for lunch," said Mike.

Gio nodded slowly. "You're welcome." He sighed and looked at something up the block. "Well, I feel like I've made myself clear. I like you, Mike, now even more than I did before lunch. I'd like to see you again. Part of me wants to say that perhaps, for the sake of propriety, we should wait before really jumping into anything. At least until the workshop is over."

"Oh." That was disappointing. It had felt like they were fumbling toward something all through lunch, and now Gio was putting the brakes on it. Mike got it—at least he'd been clear that he wasn't having lunch and contemplating sleeping with Gio just to get his daughter ahead—but it still made him a little sad to walk away.

The feeling was apparently mutual, because Gio was doing that weird staring-unfocused thing again, this time glaring at something in the vicinity of the buttons on Mike's shirt.

"Hey, Gio?"

Gio looked up.

Mike took a chance. He stepped forward as he met Gio's gaze. Then he gently cupped Gio's cheek. Gio didn't flinch or move away, so Mike didn't think it would be so bad if he pressed his lips against Gio's. When he did, he was met with a tiny whimper in the back of Gio's throat and then the full force of a kiss, a strong one tasting a little of balsamic vinegar, openmouthed but no tongues… not yet. But it would be so easy to sink into this one, to get lost in Gio's mouth, in his arms, in his skin. It would be so wonderful to let desire and instinct take over, to keep moving in search of the dazed, zippy feeling in Mike's head, to keep the blood rushing in his veins.

Mike pulled away slowly. "Something to look forward to."

FIVE

MIKE was itchy.

He didn't like the feeling. His skin felt inflamed, a remnant of wanting and a lack of satisfaction. He felt uneasy but couldn't put a finger on why. He did know that he'd rather be anywhere other than the kitchen of one of his wealthy patrons.

He made some adjustments and then slid out from under the sink. His nervous client, Elaine Hutchinson, stood there wringing her hands.

"Everything looks like it should, Mrs. Hutchinson." He stood up and pulled the walkie-talkie off his belt. "Hey, Sandy? Turn the water back on."

"You got it, boss" came the crackling response.

Mike waited a moment and then turned the handle on the new faucet. It burbled and sputtered but soon was pouring out clean water. "What do you think?" he asked Mrs. Hutchinson after he turned off the faucet.

"That's good. So what's left to do?"

Mike picked his clipboard up off the counter and glanced at it. "The tile for the backsplash is due in tomorrow. Then I just have to finish putting the hardware on the cabinets and some other small touches. We should be finished by the end of the week."

Mike's itchiness was probably due in part to Mrs. Hutchinson hovering, just like she had through the whole project, as though she didn't trust Mike and his team to finish renovating her kitchen without setting the whole building on fire. But Mike was good at this and he knew it; there was a reason he was able to charge what he did to the well-heeled Manhattan aristocrats who tended to hire him.

Sandy appeared at the apartment's main doorway, which was Mike's cue to pack it up.

"I think we're going to wind down for the day," he told Mrs. Hutchinson. "Call me when the tile is delivered, and we'll wrap up then, okay?"

Mrs. Hutchinson nodded jerkily, but was pleasant enough as she saw them out of the apartment.

Mike couldn't shake the itchy feeling as he and Sandy rode the elevator down to the first floor.

"You okay?" Sandy asked.

"Yeah." Although that was an obvious lie, and the way Sandy furrowed his brow indicated he knew it too. Still, Mike thought of a possible solution to his unease. "Hey. Let me see if I can talk Emma into staying the night at a friend's Friday. We should go out."

Sandy narrowed his eyes. "Go… out?"

"Uh-huh. Maybe to the Tides?"

"You want to go dancing?" The elevator door opened and Sandy followed Mike out. "Okay, okay. I surrender, alien overlords. You've clearly abducted Mike and replaced him with a robot, but I'm too smart to fall for your trap."

"Come on, Sandy. We should go. We never go out."

"Because you never want to."

"Now I do."

"Sure, okay. But what about your opera singer?"

Just thinking about Gio brought that itchy feeling back fourfold. Mike wiped sweat from his brow and said, "I told you, we put things on hold until the workshop ends."

"And when is that?"

"In four more weeks."

Sandy nodded. "Okay, I see what's happening."

"What's happening?"

Sandy motioned toward Columbus and they started to walk. "You're horny. You want the opera guy, but you can't have him. It's making you crazy, so you want to go out, have a few drinks, flirt with a few cute boys, and get your dance on to work out some of your frustration."

Mike didn't say anything. There was no point arguing against the truth.

"All right, big guy," Sandy said. "We'll go out on Friday. We'll go dancing at the Tides if that's what you really want. But I think you should invite this opera guy too."

"What?" Sandy was right; Mike had been hoping for an outlet. He wanted to go dance and maybe make out with a handsome stranger on the dance floor and scratch this itch that had him practically crawling out of his skin. Why was Sandy complicating that? "Did I not just explain to you that he wants to put the whole thing on hold?"

"I'm not saying fuck him. I'm saying invite him to come out dancing with us. It's a friendly thing. See if he's really worth making yourself this insane." Sandy stopped at the corner and turned back to Mike. "Although, damn, four weeks? Who gives a shit? Why bother waiting?"

"It's unethical. He's Emma's teacher."

"He's also someone with enough clout that no one will fire him." Sandy starting counting on his fingers. "It's a class that doesn't have a grade, so a parent sleeping with him can't influence anything. And you are two consenting adults. I don't see the problem."

Mike was surprised. He stared at Sandy. "That was shockingly logical. Are you sure you're not the one who got abducted?"

"You want to go out. You want to get to know this guy. Kill two birds with one stone. Or don't, but stop whining to me about the situation." Sandy pointed to the coffee shop on the corner. "Buy me a cuppa joe."

"It's not enough that I pay your salary?"

"Nope." Sandy grinned. "I want a froufrou espresso drink too, with lots of sugar. And a scone."

"I'll buy you a coffee, but don't push it."

While they waited in line at the coffee shop, Sandy's phone chimed. He pulled it out. "Oh, hey, it's a text from James."

"Who is James?"

"The doctor."

"I thought you weren't dating him anymore."

"No, I said we probably shouldn't date. But when have you ever known me to act practically."

"All right, carry on. Looks like they have blueberry or cinnamon scones."

"Blueberry." Sandy's phone chimed again. "James is free on Friday. We should all go out together."

"I'm not doing some silly double date thing with you."

"So invite a couple of other guys and turn it into a social thing. Keep it casual."

"Pretend it's not a date."

"Exactly. And then even if you don't hook up, you get to spend time with him. Which is what you want, right?"

Mike saw Sandy's logic but remained unconvinced.

MIKE didn't plan to say anything the next afternoon when he went to pick up Emma at the workshop. He was worried, in fact, that things would be awkward now, that he should not have pushed his luck by kissing Gio and then leaving him on the sidewalk. Now things were going to be weird.

He hadn't said anything to Emma and didn't intend to. For one thing, his love life really wasn't her business, no matter how often she asked about it and he voluntarily answered, and for another, she'd been in some kind of opera la-la land for the past two weeks and hadn't talked about anything else.

But she was spending Friday night at Isobel's where she could drive her best friend crazy with talk about *La Bohème* and Verdi and Maria Callas and whatever else she'd been going on about all week. Not that he begrudged her this interest and he understood why she was obsessing, but he felt ill-equipped to hold up his end of the conversation.

When he got out of the elevator and walked toward the studio, he could hear singing from down the hall. A harsh voice interrupted the singing, and then Gio's voice rang out again. "Again. Try to sing on key this time, Greg." The piano chimed a chord and then a male voice started singing something in a language Mike didn't understand. Then the sweetest sound, like a bird or an angel, came into the duet. Mike paused just outside the door but glanced in. Emma was singing. He could hardly believe that was her.

"Emma, you're a half step flat," Gio shouted over the singing.

Emma adjusted, but then flubbed something badly enough that even Mike could tell she'd made a mistake. She cleared her throat.

"Again," Gio said. "Greg, the G-sharp is this note." Gio pushed a key on the piano repeatedly. "Hit it this time. And Emma, sing from the top of your head." He quasi-sang that as he spoke, as well as he could sing with his broken voice, and he stood up straight and pointed to his head. "Now, sing on key."

The kids sang again and sounded pretty good.

Gio glanced at his watch. "All right, that's it for today. I want you all to go home and practice scales. Ee-ee-ah-ah-ah, okay? And learn the words to the pieces *before* class. Don't waste my time trying to learn the song here."

The kids in the class scattered. Mike hesitated at the doorway. Emma saw him and nodded. He figured he'd just wait and put Sandy's stupid idea of a night out with Gio and his friends out of his mind. It was a stupid idea anyway. Who could even imagine what Gio would think of Mike's friends. Sandy and Mike were cut from the same cloth, and Sandy could hold his own in a lot of strange social situations, so Mike thought that would be all right, but what if Gio met Dave or Angelo? The whole thing was a terrible idea.

Before he could duck away, while Emma talked with one of her classmates and very slowly put her sheet music into the folder that fit in her bag, Gio jogged over. "Mike. Hello."

"Hi," Mike said. He took a deep breath, trying not to overthink this and make it awkward.

"How are you?" Gio asked, leaning on the doorway.

"Uh, okay." He glanced at Emma, still chatting away with some girl. And then the words just tumbled right out of Mike's mouth. "You want to go out tomorrow night?" Shit.

Gio stared at Mike for a long moment without blinking. "I thought we weren't—"

"Not, like, a date." Mike took care to whisper so the kids wouldn't overhear, although they all seemed too absorbed in whatever they were doing to pay attention to the adults. "Some friends are getting together. Usual Friday night thing. Thought you might want to tag along, but I get it if you don't want to. No, you know what? Forget I said anything. No biggie, I'll just call Emma and get out of your way."

Gio smirked. "You're cute when you're nervous." He glanced around him. "What would we be doing?"

Mike was starting to worry for his own blood pressure. Yikes, why was this so hard? "Uh, well, usually we go to this Thai place on West Fifty-third. It's not, like, the best Thai you've ever had, but it's decent. Then we'll go to the Tides. That's a gay club on Forty-seventh. Have you ever been?"

"No, I can't say that I have."

"It's been around for a million years. It kind of attracts an older crowd. I like going there because I don't feel like a dirty old man preying on the young guys, you know? They play good music on Fridays. We'll dance."

"Yes, all right. That sounds like fun. Text me the details. Do you have my phone number?"

Mike pulled his phone out. Gio dictated the number. Once that was settled, Mike said, "This is probably also not really ethical, like what we talked about, but it seems less scandalous than, well, you know. And this way I still get to see you."

Gio smiled. "I look forward to it, then."

A couple of the kids pushed past them on their way out of the studio. Emma walked up. "All right, Dad, let's go."

Mike wondered what he had just done as he walked with Emma toward the bus stop and listened to her ramble about whatever the issue had been with class that day.

"And it's Greg's fault because he's always flat," she was saying as they waited for the bus.

"Uh-huh."

"Daddy, are you even listening?"

"I'm listening, kiddo."

She glared at him like she didn't believe it, but then went on ranting about the other kids in her class. Mike wanted to interrupt and tell her she was being a snob, but letting her talk gave him time to dwell on his thoughts about Gio.

WHEN Gio walked into the common room near the voice department's offices, he spotted Dacia lounging on one of the ancient sofas, flipping through a choral score. Kevin, a grad student who worked as a department assistant three afternoons a week, was manning the dean's secretary's desk.

"Where's Angela?" Gio asked Kevin.

"Out sick. Or her kid is out sick? I dunno, but someone's got the flu."

"Ah." Gio sat next to Dacia on the sofa.

She smiled at him. "How was the workshop?"

"Today's was difficult. Greg, he's a little rough around the edges. Needs to develop better pitch or he's not going anywhere."

Dacia nodded and went back to examining the choral score. Gio glanced over her shoulder and recognized a section of it as being from a Handel oratorio he didn't like much. He stayed quiet, though.

"Something on your mind?" she asked.

"Mike asked me to go dancing with him tomorrow night."

Kevin guffawed. "Mike? You are dating a guy named Mike?"

"I thought you *weren't* dating just yet," said Dacia.

"That was the plan. It's not even a date, though. He says it's more hanging out with his friends."

Dacia raised an eyebrow. "How old is this guy?"

"Thirty-seven." Gio sighed. "That whole 'hanging out with the dudes' thing is something guys in their twenties do, right?"

"Is he even gay?" Kevin asked.

"We're going dancing at a gay club. What do you think?"

Kevin laughed. "You? At a gay club?"

"Can we fire him?" Gio asked Dacia.

Dacia laughed. "Are you going to go?" she asked in Italian.

Gio glared at Kevin. In Italian, he said, "I told him I would. I'm not sure if I will blend in with this crowd, though. Mike is more... I don't know. Rugged? He doesn't know a lot about music or opera. What if we have nothing to talk about?"

"Has that been a problem so far?"

"I suppose not. But there's also the other thing."

"That he's your student's father?"

"Yes. You don't think that's unethical?"

"I suppose it is, but the workshop is ending soon, no?"

"You guys are no fun at all," Kevin said. "You know I don't speak Italian."

Dacia threw an arm around Gio and gave him a brief hug. "It will be a new and interesting experience for you," she said in English. "It might be nice to fall in love with someone who is not a performer for a change. Performers are so dramatic."

"*Dio.* Who said anything about falling in love?"

Dacia stood. "You would not be having an existential crisis over a man you just wanted to fuck."

As she walked away, Gio shouted, "I hate my friends."

"*Noi ti amiamo!*" called out Dacia.

Gio rolled his eyes.

SIX

OF ALL the times for a meeting to run long! Gio had gotten stuck at the most epic faculty meeting of all time. Eons passed, seasons changed, animals went extinct. He was inclined to tell everyone he'd just do whatever they wanted so he could get out of there, but no, the meeting dragged on, well past five and into the dinner hour. When it at long last mercifully ended, Gio bolted from the conference room and to his office, where he rapidly changed clothes, checked his e-mail, said something nasty to his assistant Angela, and then apologized for being rude. He took a moment to examine himself in the men's room on the way out of the building. He thought he looked passable. His hair was mussed but that couldn't be helped. He could have used a shave, but there was no time. His shirt was a little wrinkled, but maybe that would fix itself as he wore it.

He wasn't going to make it in time for dinner, that was plain, so he grabbed a sandwich on his way down Eighth Avenue and ate it as he walked. It was not a good sandwich—the turkey had no flavor and there was way too much mayonnaise—but it was sustenance and that was what mattered. He got a text from Mike to meet him and his friends at the Thai place where they were eating, and then they'd walk to this club together.

So Gio, of course, caught every "don't walk" sign as he walked. By the time he finally got to Fifty-third Street and found the restaurant, he wanted to cry.

Mike and four other men were sitting around a table toward the back. Gio walked over to them and said hello.

Mike stood and… arms. He had incredible arms. He'd been wearing sleeves every time Gio had seen him before so he hadn't really noticed, but now he was wearing a tight black tank top that showed off meaty, muscular biceps and perfectly outlined the pecs of a man who worked out or did a lot of physical labor—probably both, given Mike's profession—and Gio's mouth went dry.

He was a far cry from the lithe little dancers Gio had been dating lately.

Mike smiled. "Well, I'm glad you made it."

"Sorry, terrible meeting. If I could have left it, believe me, I would have in a heartbeat."

Mike nodded solemnly and gestured toward the table. "Here, meet everyone. The blond one is my friend Sandy. We've known each other for a million years and served in the army together until I got discharged. The handsome man in the pink shirt is Sandy's new boyfriend James. He's a doctor and we're supposed to be impressed by this." Sandy threw a napkin at Mike, which just made Mike laugh. It was nice to see Mike laughing instead of nervous, although there were several empty beer bottles on the table, which might have explained that. Mike went on, "The mustache sitting next to James is Dave. He did a tour in Saudi Arabia with me and Sandy in the late nineties. And the guy with the shellacked hair over there is Dave's boyfriend Angelo." Mike placed his hand on the small of Gio's back and said, "Guys, this is Gio."

Everyone greeted Gio with smiles and waves.

"We just have to settle up the bill and then we'll be on our way," said Mike.

"Yes, all right."

"I got this," Sandy said. "You and Gio go ahead and wait outside."

Mike pulled a wallet from his back pocket and handed a wad of bills to Sandy.

They were relatively alone out on the sidewalk, but Gio was still conscious of the people scuttling by him. And he couldn't take his eyes off Mike's arms.

"Sorry, my friends are...." Mike waved toward the restaurant, looking flustered, but didn't finish the sentence.

"It's okay," said Gio, although he had no idea what Mike was apologizing for.

"I'm glad you made it, though." Mike hopped a little, shaking out his arms. "I... this is... it's a little strange for me, I guess. You don't strike me as the kind of guy who hangs around in clubs, but I can't for the life of me think of what else I'd rather be doing on a Friday night." He put his hands on his hips, which only emphasized the whole package. Gio stared at that chest and wondered what it would be like to touch this man, to be in bed with him. Mike said, "Well, I guess I can think of a few things I'd rather be doing." He winked.

"Huh?" said Gio.

Mike laughed. "Wow. I make a joke about sex and you're not even paying attention."

Gio let himself touch, let his fingers float down Mike's chest. The tank top was soft and Mike's skin was warm beneath it. *Oddio.* "You're distracting," Gio said.

Mike caught his hand and held it for a moment. Mike's hand was rough and calloused but warm against Gio's soft skin. Gio felt weak for a brief moment. The hardest physical thing he ever did was run on the treadmill at the gym. But Mike had work-roughened hands and strong muscles, and his body was incredible. Mike let his hand go and Gio dropped it to his side.

"I'm distracting?" Mike said.

"You are… you're a beautiful man, Mike."

"Thank you."

"You go out like this often?"

"Not like we used to." Mike gazed down the street toward Ninth Avenue. "For a while there, Sandy and I were going out pretty regularly, but we've been doing much less of that lately. We've been busy, I guess."

Gio wanted to know so much about that. He wanted to know if Mike and Sandy had been an item, if Mike had gone home with a lot of strangers, if Mike was more of a party boy than he came across as. Gio didn't ask any of these questions, though, worried he wouldn't like the answers.

"I haven't been to many dance clubs in the States," Gio said.

"No?"

"When I lived in Milan, there was this little disco near La Scala that I used to love. Milan has a few gay bars, but it's not like New York. So this was kind of a refuge. It's where my friends and I went to dance and drink. I was more carefree in those days, I suppose. I had my whole career ahead of me." It was a little bittersweet, thinking back on that time. "Well, anyway, I suppose I have been feeling my age lately." Gio shrugged.

"Maybe what you need is a little dancing to feel young again," said Mike. He glanced toward the restaurant. "The guys are coming."

Gio appreciated the sentiment but felt a little skeptical. Looking at these friends of Mike's made Gio feel a little awkward and out of place. He worried he wouldn't be able to keep up or he'd make himself look foolish. But before he could get very far with that line of thinking, Mike's friends emerged from the restaurant.

When Sandy walked outside, he slapped Mike's back and signaled toward the corner. Gio understood then that the guys were a buffer. Gio had been invited into a social situation so that Mike could see him without being alone with him. It was a clever scheme given the circumstances, although Gio wished he had more time to talk with Mike.

Gio let himself be swept up in conversation with these men as they walked. They made it easy, luckily. Angelo spoke pretty good, albeit accented, Italian; his family was from South Brooklyn and Naples before that and his grandmother had spoken Italian at home, he explained. He could speak both school Italian and some of the Neapolitan dialect his grandparents had spoken. Dave piped in to talk about the vacation they'd taken to Rome and Tuscany a few years before. Gio lamented that he hadn't been home to Tuscany in a number of years. "I'm from Borgo San Lorenzo originally," he explained. "It's a large town a few miles from Florence."

"I loved Florence!" Dave gushed. "Such a beautiful city."

So that went pretty well.

Mike spoke softly to James for a moment, so Gio turned to Sandy when Dave started asking Angelo what he remembered from the trip. Sandy smiled. "You should know, Mike is my brother. Not in the blood sense, obviously, but you work the trenches together, you see some of the shit we saw when we were in the Middle East? You're brothers for life."

"You want to protect him," Gio said. "I understand that."

"I was the one who suggested he invite you out this evening. Partly because he likes you and wants to spend time with you, but partly because I wanted to scope you out. Just so we're clear."

"All right."

Sandy was a little intimidating. He wasn't quite as big or bulky as Mike, but he had some of that same strength, the same wide shoulders that spoke of working out and lifting heavy things.

"Is this where you give me the speech about how you'll hurt me if I hurt him?" Gio asked.

"No. No, Mike can take care of himself. I am a little curious about your intentions. I mean, if you just want to fuck around, that's fine with me. But Mike's last boyfriend left him because he couldn't deal with the fact that Mike had a kid. So you should be clear on what you want, is all."

Gio hadn't quite gotten past the simple fact that he liked Mike and that the attraction was mutual. He'd thought about sex with Mike—he'd have to be dead inside not to, he reasoned—but he hadn't gotten as far in his thinking as a relationship. Because that was an issue, wasn't it? Gio adored Emma, but as a teacher does a student. Mike was her father. And that added a whole layer of strange to the situation that Gio had been aware of but hadn't quite wrapped his head around yet.

"I don't really know," Gio said. "We just met."

Sandy nodded. "I know. No need to make a commitment right this minute. Just... things worth thinking about."

It was early enough in the evening that the club wasn't quite hopping yet. There were a few people milling around, most of them clustered around the bar. Music was blaring. Angelo must have spotted someone he knew because he gestured and then he and Dave disappeared into the small crowd.

"When you do go out, this your regular spot?" Gio asked Mike.

"Yeah. We come here... well, not that often. How often do we go out, Sandy?"

"Not like we used to. Once every other month, maybe."

"That's sad," said Mike.

"We're almost forty," said Sandy.

"That's sadder." Mike laughed.

"What are you all drinking?" James asked.

He took drink orders and vanished. Gio felt somewhat better now that he'd talked to everyone in the group. He fell into conversation with Mike and Sandy.

"That seems to be going well," Mike said, nodding toward James's departing figure.

"I know," said Sandy. "He's dreamy."

"I like him. Hang on to that."

Gio thought the dynamic between Mike and Sandy was interesting, particularly in the way they looked out for each other. Gio found himself hoping he met with Sandy's approval. "How long have you and James been together?" he asked.

"Not long. This is only maybe our fourth or fifth time out together."

Sandy absently bobbed his head to the music. Gio looked around the club. The music was clunky and repetitive and the décor was just this side of tacky—they seemed to be going for a kind of beachy theme, with palm trees painted on the walls and Chinese lanterns hanging from the ceiling—but the crowd was as Mike described, mostly guys in their thirties or forties, no especially raucous behavior. There was a throbbing mob of men dancing together closer to the DJ booth, though, and the dancing was unambiguously sexual and intended to attract male gazes.

"So if you don't go to clubs in New York," Mike said, "what do you do with your spare time? And don't tell me you're all work and no play."

"I go to the theater a lot," Gio said.

Mike chuckled. "When my sister says, 'We're going to the theater,' she usually means she and her husband are going to see a big Broadway musical, but somehow I don't think that's what you mean."

Gio smiled. "I like some musicals okay. But, you're right, I mostly go to see plays. Or the ballet or the philharmonic. And the opera, of course."

"Of course," Mike said with a smirk. "What else does a classy guy like you do with his off time? Do you read? Watch television?"

"Sure, some. Well, I don't watch a lot of television, but I read. I like a lot of the midcentury Italian writers. Calvino, Moravia."

Mike frowned. "Okay."

It occurred to Gio that Mike probably wasn't familiar with those authors. "Do you read much?"

Mike shrugged. "A little. I got into reading sci-fi when I was in the army. And I kind of like military thrillers. I mean, most of them get the details wrong, but they're kind of fun too. So, you know. Nothing too brainy."

Gio wished he could take back his answer. He hated that he'd made Mike feel self-conscious. "Sounds like more fun than the stuff I read," Gio said, trying to apologize. He smiled.

Mike smiled back, so that was something. Then he closed his eyes and bobbed his head. "Oh, this is a great song."

With no further explanation, Mike slipped away and joined the writhing bodies on the dance floor. At first he just bobbed in time to the beat of the song, but as the music picked up tempo and layers of instrumentation and singing were added, he started to really move.

"I probably should have warned you that Mike loves to dance," said Sandy.

Mike moved with a surprising fluidity and grace for a man as large as he was. He raised his arms and moved his hips and got into the music. He turned and pivoted and swayed. It was beautiful and mesmerizing.

A guy walked up behind Mike and put a hand on Mike's hip. Mike went with it, closing his eyes and leaning back. The guy snaked his hands up Mike's body, smoothing over the fabric of his shirt, pressing against his chest. Mike pushed his hips back and danced with the guy. Gio suspected he should have been jealous, but instead he found the scene intensely erotic. Mike dancing was maybe the sexiest thing he'd ever seen.

"That's... wow," said Gio.

"You're not... freaking out?" asked Sandy.

The first guy moved on to dance with someone else and another man came up in front of Mike. Mike danced with him too, pressing their bodies together and grinding their hips briefly before shifting into different kinds of movement. This guy's hands were all over Mike, and he kissed Mike's shoulder.

"Should I be freaking out?" Gio asked.

"No. This is how he blows off steam. He's done this for years. Whenever he has a particularly stressful week, he wants to go dancing. Then he'll make out with half the guys in the club but won't take any of them home."

"He doesn't take them home?"

"Nah. Just fools around on the dance floor. He works through his stress that way." Sandy shrugged.

Gio watched another guy come up to Mike and whisper something in his ear. They got right to the dancing, moving around each other, everything easy movements. Gio wasn't jealous so much as incredibly turned on.

James came back, carefully balancing everyone's drinks in his hands.

"So... Gio. Is that short for something?" James asked as he handed a glass over.

"Giovanni."

"And you teach voice lessons… wait. You're Giovanni Boca. I saw you in *La Traviata* at the Met seven or eight years ago. You were incredible."

"Thanks," said Gio, his gaze still glued to Mike. "You remember it was me?"

"Oh, yeah. I had orchestra seats. I remember how hot I found the male lead." James laughed. "No offense, man. Not to be creepy, but I immediately went out and bought that recording of you singing the same part. A French opera company, if I remember correctly."

"Yes." Gio remembered that recording.

James dipped his head bashfully. "So, yeah, I remember it was you. I heard what happened to your voice. What a terrible shame."

Gio normally found these conversations unpleasant, but he was so focused on Mike he barely heard it. "Um. Excuse me."

He went to Mike. If Mike had steam to blow off, if he had something to work through, Gio suddenly wanted Mike to do that on his body, not with strangers. Mike smiled when he saw Gio approach and gestured toward himself.

The music was too loud to speak over, so Gio let his body do the talking. He put his hands on Mike's waist, which was hard and muscular. Mike put his hands on Gio's shoulders and tugged him a little closer. *Dio*, but Mike was so sexy, all that gorgeous skin showing, a confident grin on his face, his very movements on the dance floor like sex. Gio slid his hands a little lower to feel Mike's moving hips, and then he reached around to cup Mike's firm ass, and—*Santa Maria*—Gio wanted to get Mike naked as soon as possible. For now, he had to settle for dancing.

Mike moved his hands down and pressed them into the small of Gio's back, pulling him closer. Gio was not an especially talented dancer, but he held his own as Mike led. The moves were mostly writhing anyway. Gio tried to copy Mike's movements, tried to undulate his body. Mike threw his head back, so Gio swooped in and licked Mike's Adam's apple. Mike lifted his hands and plunged his fingers into Gio's hair, and that felt amazing. Dancing with Mike, being surrounded by him, that was amazing too. Gio wanted more of that, wanted to get even closer. He moved, getting up on his toes, and he kissed Mike.

Mike's lips vibrated with what must have been a groan, because he held Gio's head in place and plundered his mouth. Gio opened up for Mike, slipped his tongue into Mike's mouth, tasted him, learned his flavor and scent. They kissed like no one was watching, like their lives depended on it, like they could have just devoured each other right there in a room full of people. It was one of the hottest kisses Gio had ever experienced. It was thrilling, and Gio's heart raced and his blood rushed, and everything about this was exciting and erotic. Mike pressed back into him, pressed his erection into Gio's hip, clutched Gio as if he were holding on for dear life. So Gio did all those things back and went one further, digging his fingers into Mike's sides, scraping his teeth against Mike's lip, and trying to keep the movement of the dance going.

The song changed into something a little mellower. Mike pulled back and smiled. He took Gio's hand and led him back toward his friends. Before they were in earshot of James and Sandy, Gio said, "You are the sexiest thing I have ever laid eyes on."

Mike smiled and kissed him briefly. "So much for keeping our distance."

Gio forced himself into small talk with James and Sandy but kept a hand on Mike at all times. It had been hot watching Mike dance with those other guys, but now Gio found he wanted to keep this treasure for himself. And if Mike moved in bed the way he moved on the dance floor....

Mike laughed suddenly.

"What?" Gio asked.

Mike leaned over and whispered, "You just made the weirdest face. You're thinking about us together, aren't you? I am too." He bit Gio's earlobe before he pulled away.

How on earth was Gio supposed to think about small talk now?

But Gio managed to talk about opera with James, a museum exhibit everyone had seen with Sandy, and he griped about that afternoon's long meeting with Mike, and the whole time he was practically vibrating out of his skin with the need to get Mike alone somewhere and fuck him until the world ended. Because he wanted to fuck Mike like he wanted to take his next breath, a need that made his skin sing arias; he wanted to be inside this man, to watch him fall to pieces, to make him come.

He danced with Mike again, which didn't do a goddamn thing to sate his need, but it was a joy just the same to get his hands all over the man, to press their bodies together, to move in time with the thrum of the music. Dancing with Mike felt like singing in a way nothing had since Gio had lost his voice.

WHO knew that simply giving in to one's desire to run one's hands through another man's hair could bring such breathless joy? Mike did it again and again, learning the contours of Gio's skull and the soft silkiness of Gio's gorgeous hair. He managed to move his hips and his legs so that he was doing some semblance of dancing as he dipped his head to kiss Gio again, because there was nothing better on earth than kissing Gio. The man was a live wire tonight too, writhing against Mike, touching him constantly, practically vibrating with need. All of that for him, Mike thought. He loved every minute of it.

Fuck waiting. When yet another song ended and Mike realized that ache in his thighs was his body telling him he was thirty-seven and not twenty-seven, he escorted Gio off the dance floor again and over to where Sandy and James were having some sort of contest to see who could shove his tongue farther down the other's throat.

"Sandy!" Mike shouted.

Sandy turned but tilted his head toward James and gestured with his free hand. It was the "can't you see I'm in the middle of something?" look.

"I'm out," Mike said. He took Gio's hand so Gio would know there was no way their night was over yet.

Sandy waved and went back to kissing James.

Out on the sidewalk, Mike let go of Gio's hand and gestured toward the corner of the street. Gio followed. Mike swallowed a couple of times, hoping the ringing in his ears would go away. He said, "Emma's spending the night at a friend's, so I don't have to be home at any particular time."

Gio's eyes widened. "That's… I live on West Sixty-eighth."

That was a lot closer than Mike's place across town. "Lead the way."

It was a nice night, warm but breezy, the night air refreshing and cool against Mike's sweaty skin. Hell's Kitchen was buzzing. They nearly collided with a gaggle of twinky boys coming out of one bar and then immediately turning into another. They walked past one of Mike's favorite neighborhood bars, which was so crowded there was a line to get in. Gay and straight couples walked hand in hand up and down Ninth Avenue. So Mike took Gio's hand. He really liked the way their palms pressed together; he liked the softness of Gio's skin. Gio turned and smiled at him.

Mike wondered if they'd get a cab, but Gio led him across the street, so perhaps not. He didn't mind because the weather was so nice. Once they got above Fifty-fourth Street, the crowds thinned a little, which made walking easier.

They walked in silence for a few minutes, and then Gio said, "You've got music in you after all."

"Huh?"

"You don't sing. I always thought… for me, singing was like letting the music out. It was always in me, like a butterfly flapping its wings in my chest, and singing was how I released it. You have something of that within you too. I can see it. You don't sing, but you *dance*. That's how you let your music out."

Heat flooded Mike's face. "Oh, it isn't all that. It's just something I do to stay sane."

"Exactly. Otherwise, the music gets pent up inside you. You need an outlet to express it. Some of us sing or take up an instrument. You show the music in you with your body."

The awe in Gio's voice surprised Mike. He didn't think it was such a big deal. "It's nothing, really. I just… like it."

"It's beautiful. *You're* beautiful. And so sexy. I had no idea until tonight. I mean, I knew you were sexy, because that's obvious, but tonight you showed me something else entirely."

Mike had never been good at taking compliments, but that gave him a heady rush. He squeezed Gio's hand. He wanted to return the sentiment—he had loved dancing with Gio, had been so totally turned on when Gio had pressed against him on the dance floor, had found Gio's movements poetic and sexy in their own way. But he couldn't come up with a way to say that without it sounding totally cheeseball. "I…," he tried but stopped speaking, unsure of how to say what he wanted to say. "You're wonderful, Gio."

Gio chuckled softly.

As they approached Lincoln Center, Mike heard music. It was a little late for there to still be a performance—it was well past eleven, when the opera usually let out—but soon he saw that there was a busker sitting in front of the fountain, playing a cello.

Gio tugged Mike toward the cellist. He stopped and swayed for a moment. "That's lovely," Gio said.

Mike had no idea what the guy was playing, but it was nice to listen to and obviously took some skill.

Gio said, "That's a Bach concerto. Even if I weren't familiar with it, I'd know a Bach piece anywhere. No one ever wrote music like that, before or since. The note patterns are so distinctive." When the piece ended and the cellist dragged his bow across the strings one last time with a flourish, Gio applauded.

Mike thought to pull out his wallet and give the kid a dollar, but Gio beat him to it, walking toward the man and handing a bill to him directly instead of just tossing it into the open cello case. The way the guy's eyes widened indicated to Mike that Gio had given him more than just a dollar.

"Play us something romantic," Gio told the cellist.

The guy appeared to think for a moment, and then he nodded and placed bow to string. Mike didn't recognize this piece, either, but Gio definitely did, letting out a gleeful little noise, kind of a squeak in his throat. He grabbed Mike and pulled him into his arms, and soon Mike found himself slow dancing with Gio to some achingly beautiful piece of music. The lights from Lincoln Center shone on the sidewalk and reflected off the water in the fountain, creating an effect almost like candlelight, as if there were thousands of little flames surrounding them. Gio grasped Mike's shoulders and led him in a dance that wasn't quite what Mike was used to, but he figured out how to follow. It was a little odd; Mike knew he was a big guy, and as such, he was used to leading, but Gio's hold on him was firm and confident.

"It's from *La Bohème*," Gio explained. "Beautiful and tragic. But this song is from early in the opera, when there is still hope. Oh, it is gorgeous. I have always loved Puccini."

It was possibly the most romantic moment of Mike's life. He had a handsome man in his arms, he was dancing to the music of a single cello, and it was just them at the Lincoln Center Plaza. Warmth spread through his chest, and he felt giddy and dizzy and so very happy, and then all those feelings seemed to get lodged in his throat. He wanted to tell Gio that this was amazing, but he found he couldn't make words.

Then the song changed. Mike didn't know this song either, but there was something hauntingly familiar about it. Gio knew this one of course, too, and he tightened his hands to fists, grabbing onto the fabric of Mike's shirt. His body went tense suddenly. Mike moved, encouraging Gio to keep dancing, to forget about whatever was bothering him. Gio clutched at Mike and then pressed his face into Mike's shoulder. There was an odd fluttering sensation against Mike's collarbone, but then Gio picked his head up and Mike realized he was singing softly.

It was in a language Mike didn't know—Italian, probably—but the look of anguish on Gio's face went so deep it could not have been acting. Mike kept dancing, kept moving Gio in slow circles around the cellist, tried to encourage Gio to stay with him.

Then Gio whispered, "*Vincerò.*"

And Mike understood. This was "Nessun Dorma." Emma had played him a recording of it at his request the evening after his lunch with Gio. She'd had a Pavarotti recording on her MP3 player. He recognized the song now, recognized its meaning to Gio.

The cello was rich and vibrant, ringing out in the night. Then it was silent.

Gio pulled away from Mike. Mike didn't want to let him get away, and definitely not when his hold on things was so loose. He reached forward and wiped a tear from Gio's cheek. Gio reached up and clutched at Mike's forearm.

"I still miss it so much," Gio said softly. "Every day, my soul aches because I can no longer do that. I can't sing. I'll never have that again. I'll never be Calaf shouting into the night that I will win the princess."

Mike reached for him and pulled him back into his arms. "But you've won me."

Gio squeezed him tight. "Yes," he whispered. "Yes."

SEVEN

MOST baroque concertos followed the same pattern.

The first movement was usually fast, something to catch the audience's attention. It was an *allegro* or a *presto* or perhaps a *vivace*—fast and bright. The excitement of first love, the initial rush of lust. Sex started that way, with excitement and urgency. It was grasping and pulling. It was mouths fused together, licking and biting, nails pressed into skin. It was the violin tremolo in an opera's prologue, designed to crescendo and build anticipation. It was trembling fingers and limbs, fluttering hearts, shallow breaths. It was music swelling. It was the rending of garments.

No longer able to wait, Mike and Gio tore clothes off each other as Gio pushed Mike toward his bedroom. They kissed hard and fast, sucking and pulling and pushing. Gio grabbed Mike's hair and tugged him closer, needing to be closer to him, around him, inside him. His desire was the sort of desperation only characters in an opera could feel for each other at first meeting. Gio's erratic pulse beat like a mezzo-soprano singing the opening bars of an aria that would bring the house down.

Then Mike pushed Gio onto the bed and crawled over him. His body, clad now only in a pair of black boxer briefs that left almost nothing to the imagination, was a thing of beauty. His skin was smooth, not too hairy, tan from the summer sun. He was sculpted perfectly, though he had a scar on his abdomen and another up near his collarbone. A tiny tattoo of a star on his bicep looked like graffiti on a smooth marble sculpture. So, not perfect, but lived in, experienced. Gio reached up and kissed him. He hooked a hand around the back of Mike's head and held him close while he explored that mouth. "I want to be inside you so bad," Gio said.

"Mmm, yes," said Mike. "I want that too."

The second movement was usually slow. It was an easier *adagio* or a *largo*. It was an opportunity for a soloist to show off or for the composer to pull at an audience's heartstrings. A gifted violinist could make the audience weep with just the right pull of the bow across strings, using vibrato and volume changes to express just the right emotion.

Gio pushed at Mike until Mike lay on his back on the bed. Gio reached for his nightstand. He realized he hadn't asked what Mike wanted, but as soon as Mike had enough space to do so, he stripped off his boxers and pulled his legs apart. And there it all was, Mike's hard cock lying on his abdomen, his balls already drawn up toward his body, and that space between his cheeks exposed and waiting for Gio.

Gio's mouth went dry.

He wanted to do this right. He got what he needed from the drawer and then crawled on top of Mike, who grinned and put his arms around him. Gio shifted his hips and slid his cock against Mike's, which pulled groans from both of them. Arousal moved like a shiver up Gio's spine. He looked down at Mike and smoothed some of his soft hair away from his face. Mike had beautiful eyes with long lashes, and they sparkled in the dim light of Gio's bedroom. Gio was breathless, powerless against the force of what was happening between them.

He kissed Mike and thrust against him. Mike curled his body to meet his thrusts. Everything about this was hot and electric. It was heady and mind-melting too, but Gio still desperately wanted to be inside Mike, wanted to make them both fall to pieces. He grabbed the lube and poured a generous amount on his fingers. He had to shift away from Mike a little to drag his fingers over Mike's entrance. Mike moaned.

They kissed as Gio prepared Mike. Mike somehow got a hand between them and wrapped it around Gio's cock. "Yes," Mike murmured. "Yes. I want this." He gently squeezed Gio's cock as if to emphasize what he was talking about.

When Gio was sliding three fingers in and out of Mike and Mike had hooked his hands around his knees to pull his legs back and was all but begging for Gio to just fuck him already, Gio rolled on a condom and positioned himself above Mike. He pressed the head of his cock against Mike and pushed inside slowly. It took everything he had not to rush this, not to thrust forward too much and risk hurting Mike, not to go crazy and let it all go yet. He would, he would let himself fall apart or be destroyed, but not quite… not just yet. This time was for exploring, for getting to know, for adjusting to the tightness of Mike's body and the scent of his sweaty skin and the vibrations of his chest as he groaned.

Then he was seated inside Mike and pressing Mike's knees to his chest and Mike was below him wearing an expression of delirious ecstasy, his eyes rolled back and his mouth agape. Gio wanted to make this man feel every crazy thing that Gio himself felt. He paused to get used to the sensation, to let himself feel and understand that he was inside Mike, that Mike's big body surrounded him, that this was not just a furtive sexual fantasy in the middle of the night. Then Gio moved.

The third movement of most concertos was usually fast again, *moderato* or a *presto, con brio* or *più allegro*. The tempo changed to keep the audience interested, to pleasure their ears and their hearts, to make them sit on the edge of their seats and pay attention. It was loud and beautiful and triumphant.

Gio's body seemed to move of its own accord, thrusting and grabbing and arching, moving in and out of Mike with the speed of a violin bow across the strings of the instrument during the last movement of a piece. He started losing his grasp on all semblance of grace or control and instead just let loose on Mike, giving him all he had. Mike grabbed at him, sunk his fingers into the skin of Gio's ass, tugged at his hair, clutched at his arms. Mike threw his head back and uttered nonsense. He shifted his hips to meet Gio's thrusts, telling him he needed more when Gio thought he had nothing left to give.

There was a tempo change again, everything faster, *vivacissimo appassionato*, all of it lively and fierce and passionate. Gio kissed Mike but their lips couldn't stay together through the movement of the bed and the way Mike was moaning. Gio reached down and rubbed Mike's cock, pulling a whimper out of Mike.

"I'm gonna come," Mike whispered.

Mike's moan was a long note held, the prima donna's high point in an aria, that one beautiful note that broke through space and time and mesmerized an audience. Mike tensed and let go quickly. Then he was coming, shooting across his own chest, his facial expression like nothing Gio had ever seen before.

Mike's body clamped down on Gio, pulling pleasure out of him, everything suddenly more, more… *più appassionato, più espressivo, più pazzo*.

Gio flew apart. He thrust his hips one last time into Mike before letting go, coming deep inside Mike's body and clutching him close. Mike's arms came around him, and their lips met in a soft kiss as Gio came down from the orgasm.

With one last flourish from the conductor, it was over. *Bravo!*

MIKE returned from the bathroom and slipped into bed with Gio. He was still reeling from the incredible night they'd had so far, from how surprising and sexy Gio was. But he was sleepy and content too, and he didn't want to overanalyze the situation. As soon as Mike was under the covers, Gio put his arms around him.

"We're bad at waiting," Mike said.

"I never was a patient man." Gio shifted on the bed as if he were trying to find the most comfortable spot. "Do you regret it?"

"Not even a little." He gave Gio a little hug.

"I feel the same."

Mike didn't regret the sex, but worry and doubt were starting to creep in. The edges of his mind were darkened by wondering what the consequences of this might be. In this moment, though, he didn't want to think much about anything beyond the way their bodies felt snuggled together in bed. Pretty damned good, as it happened. Gio's mattress was soft and the sheets were smooth and felt expensive. Mike felt wakefulness seeping out of him as he sank into the bed.

"It's over soon," Mike said sleepily. "The workshop, I mean. In, what, three weeks? Emma won't be in your class anymore. So no conflict of interest. We can lay low until then. Emma doesn't get a grade, right?"

"No, it's just a summer workshop."

"So I can't be accused of doing this to get her a better grade. Which I'm totally not, by the way." Mike yawned.

"I already told you I didn't think you were."

"Good. That's good. Because I really like you, Gio. Tonight was... there was something really special about it. Thank you for coming dancing."

"The pleasure was all mine, believe me."

"It was a little bit mine too."

Gio laughed, and the sound was rich and raspy. "I do agree. There's something happening here."

"That song the cellist played when we started dancing. It was from *La Bohème*, you said?"

"Yes."

"What was it?"

Gio sat up a little. "It's a duet in the opera. Rodolfo is a poet who lives with friends in the Latin Quarter in Paris. He's kind of miserable, so he stays behind when his friends go out one evening. While he is stewing at home, a seamstress named Mimi comes to the door to ask for a match to light her candle. He uses a bit of subterfuge to get her to stay, and they talk and, as can only happen in an opera, fall deeply in love in an instant. He sees her bathed in the moonlight, and he sings, 'O soave fanciulla.' Oh, lovely girl. It is a love song, but there's an undercurrent of sadness to the scene because both of these characters live in poverty and we find out pretty quickly that Mimi is sick."

It was interesting, knowing Gio had this encyclopedic knowledge of a topic about which Mike knew almost nothing. "Do you think I'm ignorant for not knowing more about opera?"

"No, of course not. I'm sure you know plenty about topics I am completely in the dark about. Sandy kept mentioning baseball tonight, for example. I don't think I have ever watched an entire baseball game."

Mike laughed. "No? I've sat through plenty of opera with Emma."

"Or the work you do. You remodel kitchens?"

"And bathrooms and living rooms and bedrooms. Anything, really. My bread and butter are kitchens and bathrooms, though. That's the conventional wisdom, right? Kitchens and bathrooms sell apartments." Mike lazily stroked Gio's arm. "I like it. I'm starting to do more of the design work and leave the heavy stuff to my crew."

"You design rooms?"

"Yeah. I mean, I consult with the client, of course, and he or she *always* has a strong opinion. I usually have to work with the existing wiring and piping too, especially in those old buildings, because the Landmarks Preservation people get their panties in a wad if you try to change anything. But I like the design work. I find it really challenging."

Gio reached over and smoothed Mike's hair back. "You're an artist."

"Hardly. I help clients choose which shade of granite to use for their countertops."

"You are far too modest." Gio smiled. "You dance like you have music in your blood and you must have an eye for beautiful things if you help people design rooms."

"I suppose." Mike hadn't ever thought of it that way. He still kind of thought of himself as a construction worker, even though he'd owned his own business for almost ten years. "I've worked hard to build my reputation, you know? I work with a lot of high-end clients these days. I want people to want a McPhee-designed room, and I want my name to stand for quality and good workmanship."

"That's incredible. What do you think of this room?"

Mike looked around. The walls were painted sort of an eggplant purple, and the bedding was all a soft gray. He tried to judge it objectively. "Too dark," Mike said. "This color on the walls just absorbs all the light. Even if you got a lot of sunlight through that window, it wouldn't do much to light the room. If it were me, I'd choose a lighter color. Something bright but masculine. A different shade of purple, or a bluish gray, maybe. Actually, what you could do is put this color here." Mike held up the edge of the sheet. "Put this on the walls and then get a purple duvet. I like these colors together, but man, those walls are dark."

Gio chuckled. "Your apartment must be beautiful."

"It's all right." Mike stayed so busy working on other people's homes that he rarely had time to do much to his own. "Well, it looks like a teenage girl lives in it. Emma's going through a phase right now where everything has to have sparkles, so she's been buying all these accessories covered in glitter and it gets all over everything."

Gio made a strange sound, like he swallowed too hard, but he immediately covered it up with a cough. "I can't even imagine being a single father of a little girl. That's amazing."

"I'm not exactly a trailblazer," Mike said, squirming uncomfortably.

"No, but she's great. It can't have been easy."

"It's strange sometimes. I mean, I knew basically nothing about girls going into it." He squeezed Gio gently. "I never quite got over my 'girls are icky' phase. But, you know, you figure things out. And my sister helps out sometimes."

Gio used his finger to trace patterns on Mike's chest. "Do you, ah, need to get back to her tonight?"

"Well, if she's at Isobel's she probably won't be back until lunch tomorrow, so… no."

"So you'll spend the night?"

Mike sighed happily. He certainly didn't want to leave. "Yes, I'll stay."

EIGHT

MIKE wasn't that surprised when Sandy showed up for dinner the next night. Mike immediately put Sandy in charge of ordering delivery in order to postpone the inevitable conversation. Then they sat on the sofa and Emma babbled on about the movies she and Isobel had seen the previous night. Sandy listened gamely while Mike got up and poured drinks for everyone.

He'd been thinking about Gio all day. He couldn't remember the last time he'd been this preoccupied with a guy. It had been a few years since he'd even spent a whole night with someone. There was definitely something about Gio, though.

Sandy gave him an odd look when he walked back into the living room.

"So how did your night go after you left?" Sandy asked.

Mike rolled his eyes toward Emma, trying to convey that he didn't want to talk about this in front of her.

Too late. "What did you do last night, Daddy?"

The tricky thing about having a teenage daughter was that she was still his little girl, but she talked like a grown-up. She'd seen enough television that she had some understanding of how grown-ups behaved when they went out. Mike had even had the sex talk with her, although his face had been on fire through the whole thing, and he'd had to get his sister Becky to come over and help explain a few things. Bottom line was that he knew she probably understood some of what he did on a night out, but that didn't mean he wanted to discuss his personal life with her. She didn't need to know anything about it, he'd always thought, unless he was serious enough about a guy, which he hadn't been since Evan. And even if he did find The One, she didn't need to know about his sex life.

"We went to dinner with James the doctor," said Mike, "and Dave and Angelo. Then we went dancing."

"I'll say," Sandy said.

"Shut up," said Mike.

"Did you meet a man?" Emma asked.

And there were images of Gio again, parading across Mike's mind like a movie trailer. There were flashes of memory: dancing at the club, dancing in the plaza at Lincoln Center, the intense sex they had when they got to Gio's, holding each other in bed, having sex again when they woke up at 3:00 a.m., showering together that morning. Mike was even a little sore, but he relished it, hanging on to the soreness like a memory.

God, Gio. Mike couldn't wait to see him again.

"Not exactly," he said to Emma.

"So?" said Sandy. He gave Mike a thumbs-up and then a thumbs-down.

Mike grunted and gave Sandy a thumbs-up.

"You know, Daddy, you've been alone too long. Isobel and I talked about this."

Well, that was alarming. "You did, did you?" Mike said, trying to use his best dad voice.

"Izzy's mom got remarried last year," Emma explained to Sandy. Mike knew that already and liked the new husband a great deal. "Izzy didn't like when her mom was lonely. You're lonely, Daddy. You should find someone."

"It's not that easy, Em. I can't just walk outside and find a man."

"Why bother?" said Sandy. "Maybe you've already found one."

Mike tried to give Sandy a death glare, but Sandy just laughed.

"I'm fine, sweetie," Mike said, "but it's nice of you to be concerned."

Halfway through their meal, Sandy got a call from James, which got Mike off the hook, at least. After Sandy left, Mike went about cleaning up. Emma followed him into the kitchen.

He could see that she was about to say something he wouldn't like, so he said, "Hey, do you have more recordings of Mr. Boca singing?"

The question seemed to take her off guard. "Ah, yeah. Not *Turandot*. That was, like, his signature role, but I have a different recording of that one. Do you want to borrow my iPod again?"

"Can you put a couple of songs on mine?"

"Sure. Are you—why do you want them?"

The skeptical look on her face—one eyebrow up, lips pursed—was almost comical. Mike would have laughed if he wasn't trying so hard not to get caught.

Instead, he tried to play it casual. "Just curious. He's your teacher. He doesn't sing anymore. I want to know what his voice was like. Those videos we watched had crappy sound quality."

Emma narrowed her eyes at Mike like she didn't believe him. But she said, "Where's your iPod?"

"On my dresser."

Emma disappeared while Mike did the dishes. When he was done, he sat on the couch and flipped on the TV. She walked out of her room and handed him his MP3 player. "I changed the filenames, so just look for 'Boca.' There are three songs. One from *La Traviata*, one from *La Bohème*, and one from *Il Barbiere di Siviglia*."

"All right." He tried not to let his surprise at her Italian pronunciation show. She sounded so odd when she said the titles of those operas. "Thanks."

"He does like you, you know. His face changes when you come to pick me up."

Mike sighed. "Yeah, I picked up on that."

"Just saying." She sat next to him. "He's a tough teacher, but he seems nice otherwise."

Mike put his arm around her and kissed the top of her head. He wanted to say that he liked Gio right back but didn't want to say that out loud.

After Emma went to bed that night, Mike stripped to his boxers and climbed into bed. He put on his headphones and scrolled through the menu on his MP3 player. He found the songs Emma had put there. The first had a musical introduction, violins playing a pretty melody, and then all of a sudden, Mike's ears were filled with a sound that took his breath away.

Giovanni Boca sang an aria, and Mike had never heard anything like it. The sound was emotional, it was rich, it was angelic. It was the sort of sound that would carry over the heads of every person in the Metropolitan Opera

House, perhaps over every person in the city. It was beautiful and heartbreaking, and Mike could hardly believe that the Gio he knew had once been capable of making such sounds. It made his plight all the more wrenching, because Mike knew Gio would never again sing like that, and it was really a crime that he couldn't.

He listened to the next song and the next. And when the songs finished playing, Mike played the first one again. He fell asleep that night with the old Giovanni Boca in his ears and the new Giovanni Boca in his heart.

"THIS place has a theme," Mike said as he sat down across from Gio.

Gio had persuaded Mike to spend his lunch hour at a café near Lincoln Center. It was kind of a tourist spot, with autographed headshots of famous opera singers adorning one wall—there was one of Gio on the bottom right— and music notes painted on every conceivable surface. Something about this place being so obvious made Gio feel safe, like they were hiding in plain sight.

Because sneaking around seemed to be exactly what they were doing.

As Mike settled into his seat, Gio said, "The one time my mother has come to New York since I moved here, I brought her here, mostly just to see her reaction."

"How did she react?"

Gio laughed softly. "Oh, she thought it was tawdry and ridiculous. The food is good and reasonably priced for the neighborhood, though."

Mike nodded and picked up his menu. He perused it for a moment and then put it down. He smiled at Gio. "So. Um. Hi. How are you?"

"Much better now that you're here."

Mike smiled widely. "God, I have been thinking about you nonstop for days. Thank you for inviting me to lunch, by the way."

"My pleasure."

Mike gave his shirt a little tug so that it fell into place. It was a rather nice white-and-green plaid with sleeves Mike had rolled up to his elbows.

"You look great, by the way," Gio said.

"As do you." Mike shot Gio a ridiculously sexy half smile. Gio got hung up looking at Mike's mouth, remembering the places those lips had touched. He busied himself sipping his water.

"I have no pretense for inviting you to lunch," Gio said. "I just wanted to see you."

"Nothing wrong with that."

"I'm glad you think so. I had sort of a rough morning."

"Tell me."

It felt so normal to talk to Mike like this. It was relaxed and easy. Gio explained how one of his college students had come by his office that morning. The boy was both a gifted singer and a gifted violinist, but his violin instructor was pressuring him to choose one to concentrate on over the other. The more the kid had talked to Gio, the easier it had been to recognize that Gio was about to lose a good student to the violin.

"I like this student a great deal," Gio said. "His voice has such an interesting quality. He's a high tenor, and I had him training to sing parts originally written for *castrato*."

Mike's eyebrows shot up. "Does that mean what I think it means?"

Gio laughed and nodded. "The practice has long since been banned, but once upon a time, boys with nice voices were indeed castrated shortly before the onset of puberty so they could maintain their ethereal voices." At Mike's horrified expression, Gio said, "It wasn't all bad. Apparently women of the day quite enjoyed looking at effeminate men. A few of the more famous *castrati* were treated like we treat rock stars today."

"Huh." Mike still looked uncomfortable at the thought.

"They're rare, but every now and then, I encounter a man who can sing high enough to perform songs originally written for a *castrato*. It's quite beautiful. Different from having a woman sing the same part." Gio shook his head. "This boy could do it. It's such a shame that he's choosing the violin. Well, not a *shame*, since he's also a brilliant violinist, but I am very sad to lose him as a student."

"It's an odd dilemma," said Mike. "A kid can play violin and sing opera, but he has to choose?"

"I don't love this violin instructor." Gio's student studied with Sam, the violinist who seemed to think the beauty of a singer counted more than her voice. "But I suppose he has a point. It's hard to really hone a talent if your focus is divided."

Mike laughed and shook his head. "I'm sure I wouldn't know."

"Nonsense," said Gio. "I'm sure you're talented at many things. Dancing, design, fixing things. These are important talents. I can't do any of those things."

Mike's sexy little half smile was back. "You did all right on the dance floor."

"Yes, but not like you."

Mike shrugged. "It's nothing. You just find the beat and move your body in time with it."

"Well, regardless, if I had a drippy sink in my apartment, I would have no idea how to fix it."

Something flickered over Mike's face. Gio couldn't quite read it, but the way he squirmed a little in his chair made Gio think it might have been embarrassment. "It's an easy thing to learn. Not like singing."

Sensing this conversation would only continue to cause Mike distress, Gio said, "Tell me about your day. What did you do?"

Mike seemed happy enough to talk about the kitchen he'd just finished. Gio could see he took pride in his work just from the expression on his face.

Over sandwiches, Mike asked, "Do you have any family here in America? You said your mother came to visit. Where does she live?"

"Mamma is in Italy, as is most of my family, such as it is. Perhaps we do not live up to the stereotype of big Italian families. My mother was an only child, and my father had a brother I only hear from sporadically." Before Mike could ask, Gio said, "My father passed away when I was a kid. So that's the whole Boca clan right there, basically."

"Oh, I'm sorry to hear that. It's... I suppose I know a little about losing a father, although perhaps I know more about how your mother must have felt."

Gio's chest ached a little, thinking about the loss Mike must have endured. "Yes, well. You could not possibly have less in common with my mother. She's... she's a piece of work. A diva in the classic sense."

"She also sings opera, right?"

"She's retired now, but yes, she did sing for many years." And had never achieved anything close to Gio's level of fame, something he had long suspected she resented him for. But that was a lot to get into with Mike. So he said, "I have a second family, friends and fellow opera singers, people I've performed with and rehearsed with over the years. So many great friends. I always appreciate it when talented people can put their egos aside. Perhaps the silver lining of losing my voice was that I discovered who my real friends were."

Mike nodded. "I can imagine."

Gio put a smile on the sentiment, though the truth was that many of his good friends were currently scattered all over the world, performing as he had once done. He was grateful for Dacia living close by, and he adored her, but he also found himself alone a lot. That had been one of the first adjustments to life outside of the opera house, where there were always people bustling around.

Mike held out his hand, so Gio took it. Mike said, "I would very much like to be a friend to you."

"I'd like that," Gio said.

"Maybe we could make this lunch thing more of a regular habit? On days when I'm working in this neighborhood and we can both get away, I mean."

Mike ducked his head, looking a bit bashful, as if he were asking Gio out on a first date. It would be laughable—they'd already had sex, for one thing—if Mike weren't so earnest about it.

"Yes," Gio said. "I would enjoy that. You can call me anytime, you know. If not for lunch, then just to chat. Or for any reason at all."

Mike smiled. He squeezed Gio's hand. "All right. I can do that."

Gio was still thinking about Mike that afternoon when Dacia walked into his office. "Auditions for the Young Musicians Program vocal performance classes are coming up," she said, leaning her hip on the edge of his desk. "Do you have any kids in the opera workshop who you think are well-suited? Emma McPhee, I assume."

"Maybe Greg Thompson too. He's not quite there yet, still doesn't always quite sing on pitch, but of all the boys in my class, he has the most potential. He's already improved a great deal. In a year or two, he will be very good."

"What is that expression?"

"What?"

"You made a face when I mentioned Miss McPhee. Is she not working out in your class?"

"No, she's wonderful. Best student I've had in a long time."

"Then what's the problem."

"If Emma auditions, I don't think I can be on the audition committee."

Dacia tilted her head, but then she straightened as if a lightbulb had flipped on. "So things with you and Mike...."

"Reached their natural conclusion." Gio closed his eyes, but all that did was remind him of what being with Mike had been like. He'd thought of Mike almost constantly all weekend.

Dacia smiled. "It's all right, you know. You are allowed to have relationships."

"Not with my student's father. Not if it looks like I'm giving her favorable treatment."

"So you are not available the weekend we do auditions. Who else?"

Gio mentally ran through his roster of students. "Amelia Quinlan will most certainly audition."

Dacia frowned. "She's the mezzo with the curly brown hair?"

"*Sì.*"

"She sings like a horse."

Gio laughed, not entirely able to parse Dacia's simile but knowing full well what she meant. "*Sì*, but the Quinlans are such dedicated contributors to the arts, and that includes putting forth their children to make beautiful music." He rolled his eyes. "She's not terrible. She was good enough to make my workshop. I'd put Amelia in the middle of the group." Although that wasn't really true. Tracy Quinlan had not heeded Gio's warning, and Amelia often came to class unrehearsed and unprepared. Perhaps she was used to being placed wherever her parents demanded, so she'd never really had to try. She often showed up without having learned the words to her homework songs and her knowledge of music theory was hazy at best; there was a lot you could do with raw talent, but the student had to want it too, and Gio wasn't entirely sure Amelia did.

He didn't really blame Amelia, though. He'd seen students like this before and doubtless would again. The blame for her situation rested entirely on the shoulders of her overzealous parents.

"All right." Dacia nodded and backed away from the desk. She sat in the guest chair and leaned back. "I imagine the Quinlans are the sort who would make trouble if their daughter did not make the cut."

"Tracy Quinlan came to visit me a few weeks ago and implied that. Or, more accurately, tried to bribe me. 'Anything I need,' she said. Money for studio space, new costumes, a piano tuner, whatever we want is ours for the taking in exchange for selling our souls so that an above-average but not great singer can get into the Olcott Young Musicians Program." He sighed. "I suppose there are worse crimes."

"We're not exactly starving, though."

"Also true."

Dacia looked over at Gio's bookshelf and nodded thoughtfully. "I came here this afternoon to talk you onto my audition committee, but I will take your point that you are somewhat biased as far as the McPhees go. I do not imagine you could be accused of favoritism, however. Anyone can see how talented that girl is."

"Still. I feel strange about the situation."

"Not enough not to get involved."

"True. In my shoes, *cara*, you would have done the same."

"*Naturalmente*. I have seen him with my own eyes."

"It's not just that. If that were all, I could put it aside. That night, though, it was… romantic. He is turning out to be not at all what I expected, in a wonderful way."

"I am happy for you, then."

Gio looked at his watch. "Well, I should get to my class. Might as well try to get Amelia up to snuff so that her parents don't feel they have to buy and endow a building to get her into the program."

NINE

GIO thought perhaps the worst part of teaching was watching the expressions on the faces of the kids when they had the epiphany that they weren't good enough.

He didn't like to sugarcoat things, though. Some of these singers did not have the inherent talent to make it to the world's finest stages. That didn't mean the situation was hopeless; one of his first students had a record deal and a pop song burning up the charts. Maybe these rejected kids would go on to sing something other than opera. But the sad truth was, the odds were good that about half of the students in any given workshop would either keep trying but never do anything better than singing at a sibling's wedding, or they would give up and do something more practical with their lives. He hated to be so harsh with teenagers, but this was how the world worked; Gio had received the same treatment when he'd trained in Italy. The students in those classes either succeeded or found another dream.

Yet when Gio dismissed half the class a little early during the penultimate week of classes, he saw the realization dawn that they would not be asked to audition for the Young Musicians Program, that they would not be pulled into Giovanni Boca's inner circle of successful voice students. It broke his heart. But better for them to find out now than to carry on with the hope that one day they'd sing at the Met.

Now he stood before his six best students plus Amelia Quinlan. He resented the latter's inclusion somewhat, but he knew better than to think she wouldn't show up at the YMP auditions anyway. He figured he'd play along for now. Not all of the other kids would make it, either, although he had higher hopes for them. Then again, he'd had a student two years before who had a voice that could bring down the rafters, but she had promptly quit singing upon leaving for college. Opera was dying, she'd told him. That was actually a more common outcome than Gio would have liked.

He didn't want to dwell in his pessimism, though. He looked at seven young faces and chose to see the future of opera instead.

"As I'm sure you know, auditions for Olcott's Young Musicians Program are coming up," he said. "There are not many slots open, but I think all seven of you have the potential to earn one of those spots, if you're interested. I wanted to keep you all behind today to discuss what the audition process is like and help you pick out a piece to sing."

And so he spent an extra hour and a half with the kids, dismissing each as they decided on their audition piece. He deliberately finished with Emma McPhee.

It was hard not to look at her in a new light given his relationship with her father. Maybe it was a quick thing, a summer fling, this situation he had going with Mike. They'd only slept together that one time, and Lord knew if they would again any time soon. But then Gio thought of that night, how magic it had been, and it was impossible to deny there really was something between them. Even just the few times they'd had lunch had shown there was definitely something between them. Gio had never dated a man with a child before, and he found himself in the odd position of not knowing how to act around Emma. He adored this girl, found her intelligent and insightful, and that voice was the very thing he had gone into teaching to find. But he also barely knew who she was outside of the class.

Because class was letting out much later than usual, Mike was unable to pick up Emma that afternoon, so Gio had agreed to escort her home. "You don't have to do that," Mike had said. "She's fourteen and capable of taking the crosstown bus by herself." But his relief had been a palpable element in his voice when Gio had pushed the point. Mike then shocked the hell out of Gio by inviting him to dinner.

It wasn't the first time he'd had dinner with a student's family, although the unspoken agreement there was that a nice family dinner was their kid's ticket into one of the special programs Gio was affiliated with. That didn't always work out for the families; Gio had become somewhat famous in the department for not being swayable by fancy meals or gifts of money. But this was hardly unprecedented. It certainly didn't stop the Tracy Quinlans of the world from trying.

And still Gio kept Emma last in class that day because he felt the need to sneak around. Mike had no interest in bribery. So maybe this was unprecedented in a way.

Gio walked with Emma one block south to the bus stop, and they chatted about her audition piece. She still hadn't settled on anything definitively, but he liked the song she was leaning toward and told her so. He knew the song was a favorite of Dacia's, though he did not tell Emma that. He was trying to keep the situation as ethical as possible, he supposed. He wanted to help Emma and thought she deserved it, but he felt like he couldn't help her *too* much.

"I'm sure you'll do splendidly at the audition," Gio said. "Do you play piano at all?"

"Only a little."

"Tell your father that, while it's not a requirement, most students in the YMP voice track are encouraged to take piano lessons. It's an added expense, but you can usually find a college student to teach you for not too much money. They advertise on the bulletin board on the fifth floor."

The bus pulled up and they boarded. Gio was not a fan of city buses and would have taken a cab if Mike hadn't specifically said they should take the crosstown bus. He'd said something about sticking with Emma's usual routine, which sounded like good advice at the time. The other patrons on the bus all stared at him as if he were an alien, however. Or maybe that was his imagination; Emma seemed totally unfazed. She directed him to a pair of seats toward the back.

"Thanks for the tip," she said as they sat, "but you're talking like I'll definitely get in."

"You'll get in," Gio said. He didn't add that half the department was already buzzing about her. Partly that was because Gio had been talking her up since her audition for his workshop, but Dacia and a number of other faculty members had heard her sing and were excited about having her in the program. The audition was mostly a formality. "That is, it's good to be worried about it because you'll try your best at the audition and do us all proud. If you sing like you did for my audition, you'll get in, no problem."

"Are you on the audition committee?"

"Not this year. But Ms. Russini will be there."

Traffic was rough, even through the park, and the bus crept along at a snail's pace. They spent most of the trip chatting about music. Gio discovered this was a girl who lived and breathed music, who followed opera singers' careers and knew the Met's schedule and saved her allowance money to go to performances. She reminded Gio a lot of himself at that age. This was good; it meant she had the drive to do well.

He was starting to wonder if she had normal teenage concerns when she got a text message. She fiddled with her phone while rambling to him about her friend Isobel and some boy—"I think he's cute, but don't tell Dad about this, because he will never shut up," she said—and Gio couldn't help but smile. At least a normal teenager was underneath all the poise.

The McPhees lived in a large apartment building on York just off Sixty-eighth Street. Emma led the way inside and escorted Gio to the elevator. Gio found he was nervous as they rose up to the twelfth floor. He and Mike had been speaking on the phone frequently and had managed lunch twice since their night out, but they hadn't been able to spend any time together otherwise. Suddenly dinner with Mike and his daughter seemed significant.

He followed Emma down the hall, and they paused in front of a door. Music floated out of the apartment, a steady beat with some terrible singing. "What is *that*?" Gio asked.

"Lady Gaga." Emma smirked. "The hazard of having a gay dad is that he likes to listen to dance music when he cleans the apartment. Come on."

The music was loud enough in the apartment that Mike must not have heard them come in. Just as they walked through the door, he danced his way across the living room with his back to Gio and Emma. Gio was struck again by the way Mike moved, fluid and graceful and confident. Music poured out of every step.

Mike noticed them and stopped dancing abruptly, but he smiled. "Hi! Come in."

Emma didn't know about their relationship, which was going to make dinner a heartbreaking exercise in restraint, because all Gio wanted to do was get his hands on this man, to dance with him and touch him everywhere and kiss the silly grin right off his face. But Emma was there. She bounded toward her father and presented her cheek for kissing. Mike gave her a peck.

"I was just finishing up," Mike said. "There's chicken in the oven and veggies on the stove, and I've got salad stuff too, if you want."

"You cook?" Gio asked.

"Dad's a great cook," said Emma.

Something in the kitchen beeped. "Oh, I should check on that," said Mike. "Em, why don't you show Gio around?"

It wasn't a big apartment. The living room walls were painted bright blue, probably Mike's choice. The room was dominated by a huge sofa and a TV and most of the walls were lined with bookcases or framed art or knickknacks. The space was clean if a little cluttered, mostly with the detritus of the people who lived there—sheet music, a baseball cap, CDs, unopened mail, a pink hoodie sweatshirt. Emma pointed out her school photos on one wall, but Gio's attention got snagged by a photo of a very young Mike standing next to a handsome man, both of them wearing military dress uniforms.

"That's my other dad," Emma said, pointing to the other man. "He died when I was little."

That surprised Gio too. It hit him just how normal Emma treated that relationship, like it wasn't at all unusual to have two dads, and her tone was so matter-of-fact it gave Gio pause. He realized with some alarm that he was basically moving into the space once occupied by someone who was now dead.

He followed her around and got a quick glimpse into each bedroom. Emma's was an explosion of pink, bright but tasteful, exactly what Gio imagined a teenage girl's room would look like. There was stuff everywhere—stacks of music books and CDs, stuffed animals, books, papers, all of it just sort of thrown around. Across the hall, Mike's bedroom was far more sedate, the walls painted a rich red color and the bed neatly made and covered with a gold blanket. That bedroom looked pristine. Did Mike really keep his space that clean or had he tidied up to impress Gio? Either way, Gio was impressed.

"Food's ready!" Mike called.

Dinner was pleasant. They sat around a small table that looked handcrafted instead of store-bought. Mike asked Emma about class, and they talked some about future auditions.

"I guess the big news for me," Mike said, "is that my father is finally retiring and offered me his old client list."

"In Brooklyn?" asked Emma.

"Yeah, but I thought maybe it's time to expand. Promote Sandy to be in charge of the Brooklyn operation if he wants it, let him handle those projects. I'm starting to think it would be better for our friendship if he didn't have to report to me every day." Mike poked at his chicken with his fork. "I certainly don't want to go to Brooklyn unless I have to."

"I thought you weren't close to your family," Gio said. He ignored the odd look Emma shot him.

"I'm not," said Mike, apparently not noticing that Gio had breached some sort of social barrier. If nothing else, it was now clear Gio and Mike had talked about things beyond just Emma's voice. It made Gio a little self-conscious, but he shoved the feeling aside.

Mike continued, "I'm the only McPhee kid who went into the family business. That's how I got my start in construction, by the way. My dad runs a construction company and has an office out near Coney Island. I worked for him when I was a teenager." He looked down at his plate and sighed. "I'm not sure sometimes if he was more upset that I'm queer or that I got kicked out of the army, but I suppose it doesn't matter if I'm the only one around to take over the business."

"Aunt Becky and Uncle Steve don't want it?" asked Emma.

"Nope. Becky—that's my sister—she could not want anything less. And her husband has an office job. He doesn't know anything about construction. Then there's Patrick. He's my brother. He's got a whole other life in Chicago."

Emma tilted her head. "Do you think this is a good thing?"

"Well, sure. It's more income for us. Your grandpa's business stays in the family. I've been trying to find Sandy something to do for a while."

"Sandy works for you?" Gio asked. "I thought you were just old friends."

"He needed a job." Mike shrugged as if that were the only explanation needed.

Emma looked back and forth between them a couple of times.

As dinner wrapped up and Mike started gathering up plates, Emma's phone rang. "It's Izzy!" she announced before running off to her room. Mike laughed when the door slammed shut.

Gio helped him clean up. As they stacked dishes in the sink, Mike said, "Thanks for bringing her home. I know she can do it by herself, but I worry."

"Of course. Thank you for dinner."

"It was my pleasure."

Gio noticed that, for the first time since he'd arrived that evening, he and Mike were in close proximity. They stood hip to hip at the sink. Maybe it wasn't the sexiest place, but Mike was right there and Gio had been wanting to touch him all night.

It was sweet and casual at first, Gio reaching over to run his hand down Mike's arm. Just touching him was nice. Gio wondered idly if it was possible to miss someone so much after so short a time as he moved his hand to Mike's waist and Mike turned to face him.

"You think Emma will be on the phone for a while?" Gio asked.

"With Isobel? Yeah."

They both leaned at the same time, their lips meeting in the middle, and it was such giddy relief to finally be kissing Mike. Gio opened his mouth and really tasted Mike, savored him, and he ran his hands up Mike's arms, over his neck, and into his hair. He clutched at Mike, pulled him closer, so desperate to finally get *something*….

"Hey, Daddy, can I— Oh."

Gio pulled away quickly, but the damage was done. Emma stood in the kitchen doorway, staring at them. Then her face relaxed and something like triumph came over it, although he didn't think she looked pleased.

"I knew it!" she said. "I knew something was going on!"

Mike bit his lip and gave Gio a sidelong glance. "Um, so…." He shook his head. "Em, it's not—"

"You should have said something," Emma said.

Gio couldn't figure out if she was happy or panicking or upset or what. Her face was now completely inscrutable.

Mike said, "Sweetie, I didn't want to say anything until I was sure that—"

"I can't believe— This is— No, I can't deal with this." Emma turned on her heel and stalked back to her room. The door slammed again.

"I should go," Gio said.

"No," said Mike in a way Gio knew really meant yes. He grunted. "I don't want you to go, but maybe that is for the best."

"I'm sorry. I didn't mean to cause trouble between you and Emma."

"It takes two." Mike frowned. "Uh, let me walk you out."

Gio grabbed his bag on the way to the door. When Mike opened the door, Gio leaned over and kissed his cheek. "Thanks, Mike. For dinner and… everything."

"Yeah. I, ah, guess this just became a real thing."

"How do you mean?"

Mike leaned on the door. "I was enjoying the time we were spending together getting to know each other without having to deal with the real world closing in on us. Because, you know, we don't have a lot in common, but I really like you, Gio. I'd like to keep seeing you. But I guess now I have to work this out with Emma. It's not a secret anymore. The stakes just changed."

"I'd say we should put things on hold, but look how well that worked last time."

Mike chuckled. "Go ahead and say we should put things on hold. Maybe then I'll get to sleep with you again."

Gio leaned toward Mike. "Maybe we should put things on hold. Especially this Sunday."

"What's this Sunday?"

"My next day off."

Mike put his hand on the side of Gio's face and stroked his cheek gently. Then he leaned forward and kissed Gio. "I won't see you Sunday, then. Especially not at your apartment. Definitely not at two in the afternoon."

"I really think that's for the best."

Gio kissed Mike. He meant it to be a quick peck, but he got stuck there, licking into Mike's mouth and really tasting him. Mike was such a wonderful kisser; just standing there with him was bliss. Then he heard a door close down the hall and became conscious of the fact that they were standing in the doorway of Mike's apartment, where anyone could see them.

"I'm really going now," Gio said. "I definitely won't see you on Sunday."

"Nope, not me. I won't be anywhere near your apartment on Sunday."

Gio pulled himself away with a substantial amount of effort. "Night, Mike."

"Good night."

AFTER Gio left, Mike walked to Emma's room. He knocked on the door. "Em, we need to talk."

"Did Mr. Boca leave?"

"He just did, yes."

She grumbled. He heard fabric shifting. Then she said, "All right. Come in."

Emma was sitting on her bed with her knees pulled up to her chest.

This was a new frontier in parenting. The only boyfriend Emma had ever met was the guy Mike had been dating when Emma was six. That guy hadn't lasted and Emma didn't seem to remember him, plus at the time, the only real explanation required was, "This is Daddy's special friend." But fourteen-year-old Emma was more savvy, understood about relationships, probably thought about sex.

Oh, dear Lord.

She'd also practically pushed Mike at Gio. He only partly understood where her reaction had come from, but why she was so upset was a little bit of a mystery. Mike sat carefully at the foot of her bed and took a deep breath.

"Okay, before we get into this," he said, "I just want to say that I am a grown man capable of making my own decisions, and at the end of the day, you don't get a say in what I do with my personal life. Understood?"

Emma nodded.

"Good. Now, I'm sorry I didn't say anything about Gio. I probably should have."

She still hugged her knees to her chest, but she sat up a little straighter. "How long?"

"Not very. We were going to wait until the workshop was over, but then we went out two weeks ago."

"When I stayed at Isobel's."

"Yeah." He took another deep breath. "So, okay, now you know. Gio and I are dating. I don't know if it's serious yet, in case that's your next question. I do know that I like him. I thought you did too."

"I do," she said. "It was just… weird. To see you together, I mean." She dropped her arms and relaxed her posture a little. "I've been thinking about it for a while, since you and Mr. Boca kept chatting whenever you came to pick me up. And I thought, yeah, how cool would it be if you dated him? Because I like him a lot and I thought he was gay too. But actually seeing it?"

"It's weird. I get it."

"I want you to be happy, Daddy. I do. It was really strange to see you kissing him, though."

Mike thought about the situation for a moment. "I know it's been just you and me for a long time. We make a good team, the two of us." Mike had told himself for years that Emma was all he needed, but that wasn't true. He still missed Evan some days, but more than that, he missed what they'd had. He missed having a companion, he'd missed the intimacy. "You know, all this talk of you going to college, and I keep thinking, 'I'll be here all alone.' I know that's a long way off, and you *are* going to college, but I'm not looking forward to the empty nest."

"I'm not leaving yet."

"I know. But... I like having you around. And it's not going to be just us forever. You'll grow up and make a life of your own." Mike sighed, trying to piece together his thoughts without having much luck. He wanted this to be okay, but her body language indicated to him that it wasn't. "I mean, it's weird, right, because he's your teacher?"

"Not for much longer."

"Still."

Emma unfolded herself and moved to sit next to Mike. She laid her head on his shoulder. "Yeah. What's going to happen?"

"I don't know."

"What if you break up and hate each other? Mr. Boca promised to help me with my audition for the Olcott Young Musicians Program, which I have to get into, Daddy, I have to. He knows a bunch of the faculty at Juilliard too. Everyone respects him. This is my ticket in."

Mike hadn't gotten much past thinking of the immediate problem of Gio leading Emma's workshop. He really had thought that once the workshop ended, he and Gio would be in the clear to see each other. But maybe they wouldn't.

And yet Mike didn't want to stop seeing Gio. "Em, I really don't think—"

"I thought it was cute that you seemed to like each other, but the more I think about it, the more I think it's a bad idea. And I know you're a grown man or whatever, but this is my future we're talking about."

"I know, sweetie." Although it was Mike's future too.

TEN

MIKE definitely didn't go to Gio's apartment Sunday afternoon and they definitely didn't have scorching hot sex, and so he definitely was not spooned up behind Gio, sleepy and sated in Gio's bed.

Well, except he totally did do all of those things.

"What did you tell Emma?" Gio asked.

Mike felt a pang of guilt for sneaking around, but he also felt like he needed to pursue this a little more before pushing the issue with Emma. "She and her friends went to see some pop singer who is giving a free concert in Central Park today, so I didn't really say anything. Just that I had to run a few errands, so I might not be home when she gets back."

Gio chuckled. "She's seeing a pop concert? That may derail my teachings."

"I don't know about that. She'll probably inform me tonight that her friends have terrible taste in music and that this singer is just so *pedestrian*." Mike sighed. "I do not know how I raised this girl sometimes. When I was her age, I was sneaking off to rock concerts. Sandy's older brother used to buy us beer. Not that I think that's what she should be doing, just I can't believe sometimes that she is my daughter."

"You're a good father."

"Thank you." Mike was glad Gio couldn't see his face, because he was certain he was blushing.

Gio slid his hand over Mike's arm. "When I was her age, I worked as a stagehand at a theater in Florence and took voice lessons with *il primo uomo*. He was the anchor of an opera company that operated out of the theater." Gio laughed. "I had such a crush on him. He was this bearish older man, maybe in his thirties at the time, with a full beard and everything. He had a voice that could break glass."

"Did anything… happen?"

"No. Nothing more than me following him around like a lost puppy. He was involved with a male cellist, besides. Although, they were the first gay couple I was ever really exposed to. It helped me come to terms with what I was feeling at the time."

"The only other gay person I knew when I was a teenager was Sandy, and that hardly counts."

"Did you and he ever…?"

"Nope." Mike tightened his grasp around Gio. "He really is like a brother. I've never even kissed him. One afternoon, when we were fifteen, I decided he needed to know I was gay—I had to tell someone—so I went to his house after school and confessed that I was head over heels for this boy in my English class. Turned out Sandy was totally infatuated with the same boy. That's always kind of been the way our relationship has been. I think it was even Sandy who first told me to go for it with Evan."

Gio reached behind him and ran his hand along Mike's naked butt. "Good. Just making sure I had no reason to be jealous."

Mike kissed the back of Gio's neck. "Are you jealous?"

"Maybe a little. I'd like to have you all to myself."

Mike laughed, liking the sound of that. He wanted Gio to be all his, as well.

He supposed that was his answer to the hovering question of the status of their relationship.

"I'm surprised," Mike murmured.

"Why?" asked Gio.

"I know I keep saying this, but you and I, we don't have much in common." Mike couldn't think of many ways for them to be any more different, in fact. The great opera singer, a European-born, overeducated, high-class man was lying here in bed with an ex-army glorified construction worker who had barely finished high school.

"We have more in common than you think."

"I'm not complaining. You're just not the sort of man I would have pictured myself with. And yet, there is no place I'd rather be right now than here with you."

"The feeling is mutual, *caro*."

Mike chuckled. "That's nice. Speak Italian to me."

Gio groaned. He reached back and pinched Mike's side. "All the boys want me to speak Italian."

"I love your voice. You could say anything and I would sit here and listen."

"*Ami la mia voce? Impossibile.*"

"Impossible, right? I do love it, though. It's so… musical. Especially when you speak Italian. Dear Lord, that is sexy."

"*E tu sei l'uomo più bello.*" Gio laughed. "Sexy in Italian is just… sexy. *Ma tu, caro, sei bellissimo.*"

"What did you say?"

Gio pressed his back against Mike's front. "You're the most beautiful man."

Mike laughed. "That's not true, but thank you."

"You are to me."

Proximity to Gio—and perhaps the sweetness of his words—was having the expected effect on Mike's body. He pressed his hips forward and said, "Perhaps we should make the most of our limited alone time."

"Mmm," said Gio, pressing back against Mike. "I do hate to waste time."

Gio rolled into Mike so they faced each other. They kissed gently, sweetly at first, but then things began to ramp up and Mike felt arousal rise through his body like fire licking up a plank of wood. Gio was hard too, pressed up against Mike and shifting his hips so their bodies moved together. Mike ran his fingers through Gio's hair. He bit Gio's lip gently and ran a hand over Gio's chest. Gio wrapped his hand around Mike's cock and started to stroke.

Mike had been hoping for something slow and leisurely for their second go-round, but as had happened earlier, his heart raced in anticipation of their coming together. That first time they'd been together, he hadn't even intended to expose himself as much as he did. He loved being fucked, no doubt about that, but it was something he usually saved, held in reserve for when he really liked and trusted a guy. Something about Gio made him shove aside a lot of his reservations.

That was what happened now, as they faced each other in bed, both of them naked and writhing against each other. Gio tilted his head back, so Mike licked up his neck, over his Adam's apple. Gio swallowed and sighed, threading his fingers through Mike's hair. Mike didn't want to stop touching Gio ever; he loved how smooth Gio's skin was, how soft his hair was. He loved the texture of the hairier parts of Gio, his arms and his chest and his legs, and he loved the odd freckle and age spot and the evidence of Gio's life and his heritage. Gio made sounds that were groans and rasps and sighs, but that voice, it still rumbled in his chest even if it was filtered through his broken throat. There was still power there, strength in Gio that wasn't evident on the surface, and Mike enjoyed tapping into it.

Mike wanted to fuck again, wanted to open himself up and make himself vulnerable to that strength in Gio, because the way they complemented each other when they came together was unlike anything Mike had ever really experienced before. That was the funny thing about them; they were like the oddly shaped blocks that Emma had played with as a baby. They looked completely different from each other but somehow fit together perfectly.

On the other hand, as Gio kissed his skin, licked, bit, tasted, Mike wondered if this wasn't moving too fast after all. Because there was a lot in Mike that he wasn't ready to show Gio yet. Mike had dark places, hidden corners, places he himself didn't like to visit.

He pulled away slightly, panicked suddenly, aroused still, but feeling distant.

"What is it?" Gio asked softly.

"It's nothing, I just...." Mike shook his head.

The darker part of Mike's soul took over, as if just acknowledging it was there was enough for it to burst open. He thought of Evan, of how this had compared to being with Evan, how Evan was not ever coming back. His erection wilted. Embarrassed, he said, "Excuse me," and he got out of bed.

He slipped into the bathroom and put down the toilet lid so he could sit. Then he leaned forward and placed his head in his hands. It was an unexpected invasion, those thoughts of Evan. It was like a hole in Mike's heart. A hole that had shrunk over the years, definitely, but a hole just the same.

He heard a knock on the door. "Mike? Are you all right?"

He wasn't, but he didn't want Gio to know that. "I just need a minute." He sounded almost calm.

"Okay. I'll be waiting."

The worst part was that Mike was still naked. He couldn't bear walking back into Gio's bedroom with everything showing. His body, well, that was one thing, but the open wounds on his heart were another. Now everything ached. Now he missed Evan, missed his family, missed the life he could have had under other circumstances. Those old thought patterns took over: if only this wasn't a man he was with. If only he wasn't gay. He wouldn't have this strained relationship with his parents. He never would have fallen in love with Evan to begin with.

But Mike knew he could never change that essential part of himself.

This should have been an opportunity: a man he cared about, a new chance at something important. He should have been able to just shut his fucking brain off and be with Gio, to have this fling. But instead, he found himself retreating—literally, in this case, since he'd backed out of the bedroom and into this bathroom—and panicking.

He took a few deep breaths. He stood and splashed water on his face. Then he steeled himself and walked back into the bedroom. He sat on the bed.

"I'm so sorry," he said.

"What for?" said Gio. "Nothing to be sorry about."

Mike sighed. "I don't know what came over me, but... yeah."

Gio sat next to him and put an arm around his shoulder. "I know you're not fine, so don't lie and tell me you are, but if you don't want to talk about it, that's all right."

Mike closed his eyes and leaned into Gio. "It's not any one thing. I just sort of freaked out. Thought about some unpleasant stuff. I don't know."

"If there's anything I can do...."

"No, I'm okay."

Gio stroked Mike's shoulder. "I can't be that terrible in bed. Surely someone would have mentioned it by now."

Gio's playful tone made Mike laugh. "No. That definitely wasn't the problem. You're great in bed, Gio. You're great, period. It was me this time. I just got kind of up in my own head."

"I don't know what that means, but it's all right." Gio kissed Mike's cheek. "Would you like to just lie down again for a little while? We can just talk."

Mike looked down and noticed that they were both still naked. Gio was half hard. That was interesting. "Okay. But maybe we won't *just* talk."

Gio laughed. "Oh, Mike. Come. Lie down with me. We will talk and do some other things. How does that sound?"

"It sounds wonderful."

ELEVEN

GIO'S mother had sometimes joked that he'd been born at La Scala.

It wasn't that much of an exaggeration. His parents had indeed been in attendance at a performance at the opera house about sixteen hours before Gio entered the world. Gio's mother, Elisabetta, had originally been cast to play Violetta in *La Traviata*, but she'd had to give up the part when the baby she was carrying had become a hindrance. Gio was sometimes not altogether convinced she didn't blame him for losing the part. To hear her tell it, her career never quite recovered, although considering she continued to sing until her arthritis prevented her from standing through an entire opera, Gio didn't see how that was true. And yet, Gio had spent a good portion of his adolescence convinced that his existence had prevented Elisabetta Boca from becoming the next Maria Callas.

She achieved local fame in Tuscany and toured around Italy through much of Gio's teenage years, all the while encouraging him to cultivate his voice. He sang in a boys' choir before puberty, listened to Verdi the way the other boys his age listened to U2, and was apprenticed to the *primo uomo* at the opera house in Florence by the time he was fifteen. As his star rose, he couldn't help but wonder if he'd become a proxy for his mother's ambition.

Of course, her fame had opened a lot of doors for him as well.

She lived now in a big house just outside Florence with her ever-rotating series of lovers. Gio's father, Gianni, had been a quiet, unassuming bank manager whom Gio had loved for his steadfastness as much as he'd loved his mother for her colorful eccentricity. Gianni had died of a chronic heart condition when Gio was a teenager, and Gio still missed him sometimes, but his memory faded with time.

His mother was deeply skeptical of cell phones, so she only ever called his landline and thus only caught him when he was home. Unfortunately, he was home one afternoon, working out the final lineup for the opera workshop final show. When he saw her number on the caller ID, he almost didn't pick up, but it had been a few weeks since they'd spoken, and she'd complained about how expensive it was to call internationally.

"*Ciao, Mamma,*" he said when he picked up the phone.

They exchanged pleasantries for a moment, and he continued to look over his notes and only half listened until she said, in Italian, "We're putting on *Maria Stuarda* this season." These days, Elisabetta was running an opera company out of a small theater.

"The Donizetti one?"

"Is there another, darling? We had auditions for Maria last week. What a paltry group of singers."

"It's a difficult role."

"I am considering taking it up myself."

Gio sighed and rubbed his forehead. She often threatened to just take the lead role herself when there was no one of sufficient talent to sing it. "Are you trying to cast a soprano or a mezzo?"

"What are you trying to say, Giovanni? I can still sing soprano."

"Yes, I know. I'm not trying to say anything. I'm just asking a question. The last few times I've seen *Maria Stuarda* put on, they cast Maria as a mezzo." Gio knew his mother was aware that the part was written for soprano originally, but that the first woman to take on the role had a mezzo-soprano voice, which had set enough of a precedent that it had become up to the discretion of whoever was casting in all subsequent productions. "You have options, I suppose."

"I do. How are you, darling? Still teaching?"

"Yes. The final show for my summer workshop is coming up."

"That's splendid."

"I've got a student this year who would amaze you. Best teenage singer I've seen in quite some time. Maybe ever."

"Oh, I'd love to hear her sing. You'll send me the recording of the show again?"

"Yes, I will."

A stray thought about Mike flitted through his head. Mike had been much on his mind since the afternoon they'd spent together, when Mike had suddenly bolted from the bed. Gio wanted to ask what that had been about, but wasn't ready to push Mike too far just yet.

To his mother, Gio said, "I have also, ah, been seeing someone."

"Seeing as in romantically?"

"Yes. His name is Mike."

She laughed. In her strongly accented English, she said, "What kind of name is Mike?"

Back in Italian, Gio said, "Short for Michael. *Michele*. But thank you for belittling him."

"Oh, I am so sorry, darling. Just these Americans have such silly names. What does he do? I assume with a name like Mike he is not a singer."

This was why he never told his mother anything. He felt like she should know that he was serious about someone, but she had always been controlling and judgmental. "He remodels apartments."

"Eh?"

Gio had to take a moment to explain Mike's job, as if Elisabetta assumed kitchens fixed themselves by shedding their skin like snakes. "He owns his own business," Gio concluded.

"That's nice, darling."

"So what I hear you saying is you won't come to the wedding," Gio said, unable to keep the irritation out of his voice. The comment was intended to be flippant and he knew his mother would take it that way, even if it was far too soon to know if this relationship would ever head in that direction.

"Is it really that serious? Because it sounds like a whim. Isn't that what you gay men like? Working-class men? For affairs, darling. You don't marry men like that."

Gio regretted that there wasn't a good Italian word for snob. "That's an outdated opinion."

"I once seduced a man who came to fix the pipes in the bathroom."

Gio was glad she couldn't see him wince. "I don't want to know about it."

"Then why must I endure this discussion of your affairs?"

"Because I'm trying to tell you that I'm entering into a serious relationship with a man. You could at least congratulate me and leave your judgment out of it. He's a good man, *Mamma*."

"As you say," she said.

"I'm working on something, so if you're done making fun…."

"I am sorry, baby boy, but you have never wanted to tell me about your relationships before. How am I to take this?"

"That I'm honestly telling you I have strong feelings for this man? Take it at face value."

"Ah. You'll tell me how it goes, yes?"

"Yes, of course."

They exchanged farewells, and Gio was thankful when he put the phone down. He leaned back on his sofa, sinking into the plush, overstuffed cushions, and rubbed his eyes. He loved his mother, he did, but she was a lot sometimes. He supposed he should be grateful she'd never given him any grief over his homosexuality, probably due to the fact that she'd spent her whole life in theaters, where gay men were not exactly scarce. But just as she'd thrust him into a career in opera—which he'd loved, so perhaps she'd made the right move there—she wanted to control his love life also. When his home base had still been in Italy, and even when he'd moved to Milan, she had been constantly trying to set him up with men she knew, mostly other opera singers. Gio had argued that two singers was too much ego for one relationship, but Elisabetta persisted in trying to marry him off to some elite tenor or baritone. The nonsense had only stopped when he made it clear he was staying in America for good.

Dio, he was tired. Perhaps he'd take a nap before finishing his notes.

MIKE maintained an office on East Eighty-third Street, though he was rarely there. It was a necessary expense, however. Some clients got squirrelly about allowing a contractor into their homes before meeting him first. Mike at least got the office space at a steep discount; he'd remodeled the building owner's house in Westchester, and the man—or his wife—had loved the work so much that negotiating down the cost of the space had been relatively easy.

Mike and Sandy sat together in the office one afternoon.

"Brooklyn, man, I don't know," Sandy said.

"Dad has a nice roster of clients, but he mostly does small projects on new buildings in Bensonhurst and Bay Ridge. I think you could change the focus of the enterprise. We have a larger vision than Dad had. I want McPhee Interiors to be the company you call to gut renovate the historic Park Slope brownstone you overpaid for."

Sandy raised an eyebrow. "And you want me to be in charge of the Brooklyn arm?"

"You can do this, Sandy. At least be in charge of a few of Dad's clients. He's got a couple of jobs lined up for the fall that I think you could do well with. And I will, of course, be around to help." Mike tapped a couple of keys on his laptop to pull up the information he needed. "One's a kitchen in Bay Ridge, but Dad says it's easy, mostly superficial changes—no rewiring or plumbing work needed."

"They always say that, and then there's a pipe so rusty and old it's about to burst."

"Yeah, well, Dad assured me he'd checked it out himself. The other job is refinishing a basement. That probably will need some work. I think they want to add a bathroom, but Dad's notes aren't that clear."

They spent a few minutes hashing out details and talking about supplies they needed to order, and generally Sandy was so on top of things that Mike sat back and said, "See? Do you see what you're doing?"

"What am I doing?"

Mike smiled. "A good job. You know all this stuff. You can remodel a kitchen in your sleep."

Sandy didn't look convinced. He shook his head and then yawned.

"Is the doctor keeping you up at night?" Mike asked.

"If only. No, I had to get up early this morning to get my fucking car inspected. Why I still have that bucket of rust is a mystery, but the mechanic says it's sound, and they gave me a shiny new sticker, so I guess I'm stuck with it a while longer."

"It might come in handy if you're working in Brooklyn."

"Don't remind me." Sandy sat up in the chair. "But, see, they have this thing called the subway. Maybe you've heard of it? You get into these giant tin cans and they whisk you away to far-off corners of the city. I can go see my parents without even getting the clunker out of the garage."

"Oh, shut up."

"My mother will be delighted that I'm working in Brooklyn now. Hell, she'll probably bake cookies and bring them to the job sites."

"So you're taking the job?"

Sandy winced. "Yeah, yeah, I guess I am. I don't know where you'll be without me, though. Who else are you gonna get to paint trim and screw in lightbulbs and tighten bolts for you?"

"Somehow I think I'll manage." Mike shut down his computer. He was glad Sandy was taking this job, both because he wanted more for Sandy and because he didn't want to work in Brooklyn. Too many memories of doing jobs for his father in those early years, when Mike was working out how to break it to his very Catholic parents that he was queer. Somehow it had never been a question that he would tell them. And here they were, twenty years after he'd come out, their relationship polite but strained. Sandy had argued earlier that Mike's dad giving him the Brooklyn business was a sign the rift was healing, but Mike saw it more as a way for his father to continue to control the company after his retirement. He wasn't really looking forward to being under his father's thumb again. So he was pawning it off on Sandy.

He rubbed his eyes, tired suddenly. He decided to focus on happier things. "Do you want to be my date to Emma's class show? Every kid gets two free tickets, and Becky can't make it."

"Sure, although I'm disappointed I was not your first choice. Just because Becky is a blood relation...." Sandy grinned. "Do I have to wear a tie?"

"Probably."

"You have time to buy me lunch this afternoon?"

Mike glanced at his watch. "I just put you in charge of an entire branch of my company. Have I not done enough for you today? Maybe you should buy me lunch for a change."

Sandy's grin widened. "We still have that appointment with the Grangers?"

"They moved it to two, so we have plenty of time to eat. Any preferences?"

"Mmm. Indian?"

"It's too hot out for something that heavy. What about that salad place on Lex?"

"Ugh, salad? We're men, Michael, not rabbits."

"Fine. Sushi?"

"That's acceptable. Let's go."

Mike locked up the office and they took the rickety elevator downstairs. Once they were outside and out of the air conditioning, Sandy said, "It's hotter than an elephant's balls out here."

Mike laughed. "What does that mean?"

"I don't know. Elephants live in, like, hot places, and it's fucking hot outside, and... shut the fuck up, okay? It's hot."

On the walk to their usual sushi place, Sandy's phone chimed. He pulled it out of his pocket. "Ah, will you look at that? Booty call via text message."

"The doctor?"

"Yep. He gets off his shift at four. And then I will get him off."

Mike groaned. "Thanks for that."

Sandy winked and turned to his phone. Mike admired his ability to text and walk at the same time. Then Sandy put his phone away and said, "By the way, James is interested in some sort of cheesy-ass double date thing. I think he's starstruck by Gio."

"Really?"

"You're fucking a minor celebrity, if you didn't know. You *are* fucking him, right?"

"It sounds cheap when you say it that way."

Sandy rolled his eyes. "Don't tell me you're *making love*."

"No, it's not that, it's just... argh, yes. I'm fucking him." He didn't want to get into it with Sandy, but it certainly felt like a lot more than fucking. He thought of the long Sunday afternoon lingering in bed, how he'd already opened up to Gio more than he'd opened up to anyone in years, how his attempts to stay away had utterly failed. He thought about how nonjudgmental Gio had been when Mike needed to get away briefly, how comforting he'd been afterward, without pressuring Mike to explain what was going on in his head. And, yeah, once Mike calmed down, he and Gio had made out and gotten each other off, but to frame it that way really did seem cheap. What Gio had done for Mike was a hell of a lot more than a few orgasms and some cuddling.

"No need to get defensive," Sandy said. "It was just a question. So, if that's still a thing, we should all go out next time James has a day off. That's all."

"All right."

"Good. Let's order the chef's special and eat some weird fish. I'm feeling daring."

WINDING down a workshop was always bittersweet. Gio was tired after six weeks of working with teenagers and putting them through their paces, but he would definitely be sad to see a few of his students go. Three were shoo-ins for the Young Musicians Program, so he might see them around. Probably Amelia Quinlan would continue to plague him. But Gio's focus that fall would be on his college students, a promising senior tenor, in particular, so he was unlikely to see most of these kids again unless they wound up at Olcott for college.

First, though, he had to worry about the final show.

The last week of class was rehearsal for the show. Gio felt good about it. He was running it like a gala performance: all twelve students would dress up in their Sunday finest and perform at Alice Tully Hall at Lincoln Center to friends, family, Olcott faculty, and random strangers who just liked the arts. He always enjoyed watching the awe on the kids' faces the first time they walked onto that stage; it reminded him of the first time he'd sung in front of a large audience, way back when he was seventeen years old. Or he'd think of the first time he sang at the Met or La Scala or the Sydney Opera House, the first time he set foot in a studio to record, the first time he brought a house down. Nothing compared to those moments, and he enjoyed experiencing them again vicariously through his students.

But now he was still in the studio, warming up with the kids and then tasking them to perfect singing their final pieces. Marie butchered the Italian, Greg couldn't quite hit the high G, Justin forgot half the words. But this was all normal and to be expected. He was hard on each kid, but in the name of trying to get them to do it right next time.

Then Emma got up to sing.

La voce. She was just... the voice. A voice like that should not have come from a girl so young, a body so tiny, and yet it did. It was a high, bright soprano, and she had the technical skill to sing coloratura if she really wanted to. She totally nailed her aria, one sung by Liu in *Turandot*. Her Italian was like a native speaker's, even though she was still mostly imitating the sounds of each syllable. She finished on a flourish, and her classmates burst into applause.

No denying it. Emma was a prodigy. She would sing on a great stage one day.

And Gio was dating her father. There was no escaping that fact. It was clear to Gio now that his interest in Mike went far, far beyond his interest in Emma. After that Sunday afternoon they'd spent in his bed, Mike undeniably had something unique that Gio wanted badly. It was obvious, too, that they'd crossed an important threshold, that Gio had done something to poke at one of Mike's sensitive places. For all he presented a calm exterior, there was a lot of turmoil in Mike, and he'd let Gio see that. It was a lot to take in, and Gio had never wanted to get that deeply involved, and yet here they were. That dark place in Mike terrified Gio, and he wasn't prepared to get involved with all of it, but he wasn't ready to step away, either.

Despite the fact that the workshop was ending soon, hence removing the main obstacle to a real relationship with Mike, the situation had begun to feel even more fraught and tangled than before. Could Gio mentor this girl and still maintain a relationship with her father? Was it completely inappropriate? Would it all blow up in his face? Did he really want any of it?

He did. *Dio*, he most certainly wanted it. He wanted to soothe the hurt places in Mike, to explore those dark places that terrified him so, to really get to know this incredible man he'd stumbled over.

Since he'd lost his voice, Gio had come to expect the worst. Nothing, not even nature's greatest gifts, lasted forever. He'd once had a voice everyone talked about, the way people would soon be talking about Emma's. Gifts like that were fleeting. One had to make the most of them.

As he wound down the class, he said sternly, "Miss McPhee, can I see you before you go?"

She walked over to him with some amount of trepidation on her face. Luckily, Mike hadn't arrived to pick her up yet, so Gio reasoned he had a little bit of time. He waited for most of the other students to clear the room before he spoke to her in hushed tones.

"You should know that I very much would like to have you as one of my personal students at some point in the future. You're enormously talented, Emma, and it would be a great honor to mentor you."

Her eyes widened. "Really?"

"I haven't said anything about this to your father, but assuming you get into the Young Musicians Program—which you definitely will, because the faculty is already buzzing about you—I'd like to do a few lessons with you. You have the raw talent, but it could use some polish."

"To my father…. You haven't said anything to Dad."

"This exists outside of my… interest in him. You, *bella*, are a rare bird, and I want to help you learn to fly." He sighed and sat on the piano bench. "But I suppose this situation can't be separated from the simple fact that I very much like your dad and would like to continue seeing him. I know he would stop our relationship in a heartbeat if you told him to, as well, and I know you don't really… approve of us, per se, but…."

"It's not that I don't approve."

"Mike—your dad—said you think it's weird."

"It *is* weird."

Gio laughed and rubbed his forehead. "The situation is complicated. For now, let us try to separate one from the other. I want to be your teacher. I also want to make your father happy, and I think being with me makes him happy. I think I can do both, but not without you." He shook his head. "Although Dacia Russini would very much like to work with you, as well, so if you find it too weird to be taught by your father's significant other, well, I can make arrangements. Dacia is a marvelous teacher, so you would still be in good hands."

She looked at him for a long moment before saying anything. She glanced toward the door as if she expected Mike to materialize there. "You're Dad's… boyfriend, I guess. Wow, that's strange. But you're also Giovanni Boca. One of the greatest living opera singers."

"Well, not so much anymore."

"Still, you once were. Before all this happened, I wanted to work with you so much, but now, I don't know. Can I think about it?"

"Take all the time you need."

Mike did materialize then. He walked right into the studio. He said, "Hi!" brightly and then reached over and smoothed some of Emma's errant hair. He kissed the top of her head. "How was class?" he asked.

"Good," Emma said.

Gio stood. He wanted to give Mike a kiss hello but wondered how smart that would be. Instead, he reached over and squeezed Mike's hand.

Emma let out a little grunt and said, "Let me go pack up."

While Emma had her back turned, Gio gave in to his desire and gave Mike a quick peck.

"I can't stay, unfortunately," Gio said, stepping back and glancing toward Emma. "I have a meeting anyway. I sometimes think half of teaching is attending meetings."

Mike laughed. "That's how some of my projects go. I spend more time arguing with my clients about tile and carpet samples than I do working some days."

Gio smiled but didn't have time to say more before Emma came back. She looked ruffled and annoyed, but she spared Gio a glance before she tugged on Mike's hand and said, "Let's go."

"Think about what I said, Emma," Gio said. "Really think. I don't want to pressure you into a decision."

"I will," Emma said.

"What is this about?" Mike asked.

"I'll tell you on the bus. Let's go, Dad."

"O… kay." He shot Gio a look of longing before following Emma out the door.

TWELVE

MIKE'S mother had been the classical music fan. As he and Sandy made their way through the lobby of Alice Tully Hall, he had some kind of trauma flashback to being eight years old and being squeezed into a suit that didn't fit anymore so his mother could take him to see the Philharmonic. He'd hated every minute of it. The music was boring. There was nothing to look at except the musicians. He'd squirmed in the uncomfortable seats until, mercifully, he was allowed to get up and leave the theater, only to find out it was merely intermission and he had to go back. He'd spent the next fifteen years of his life telling anyone who asked the, "What kind of music are you into?" question, "Anything but classical." Even the worst that country music had to offer—and he'd heard a lot of it when he was in the army—was a substantial improvement over the dreadful boringness of violins.

When Emma first arrived, Mike's mother had been convinced that the way to foster genius was to play a lot of Mozart and Beethoven whenever Emma was around, and Evan had readily agreed, trying futilely to make peace with Mike's family. Emma's arrival had actually already gone a long way toward repairing the rift—Mike's parents might not have liked Mike's homosexuality, but if there was a grandchild involved, perhaps it could be overlooked. So Emma's early years had been filled with classical music, much to Mike's chagrin, and when she developed an interest in it herself, he'd had to feign liking it. Over the years, he'd developed a grudging appreciation for it, and he liked choral music and opera all right. That is, he'd take Madonna and Gaga over Pavarotti any day of the week, but seeing classical music live was no longer the worst thing that could happen to him.

Mike and Sandy settled into their seats in the section reserved for family of the performers. Mike's mother might have made a fine guest as well, and he imagined that she'd get a kick out of seeing Emma on that stage. However, even if they had been able to have a civil conversation lately— pretty much any time he called, she yelled at him for something he was doing wrong, be it mishandling the takeover of his father's business or being too indulgent with Emma or any number of other things—she'd recently sprained an ankle and was being kind of a diva about it, not traveling more than a mile from her house. Mike was feeling pretty done with her antics, which was why he hadn't even mentioned that this performance was happening.

Sandy, who had cleaned up nicely and put on a tie and everything, looked around at the other parents. He whispered, "This feels very 'one of these things is not like the other.'"

"I know," Mike said. At the other end of the aisle, he recognized an aging Upper East Side socialite whose bathroom he had redone a few years back. It was startling to be so aware of the class difference between himself and most of the other parents, who were expensively attired and professionally coiffed. Mike was pretty good at blending in, currently in a Tom Ford suit that had cost him most of the profit from a kitchen remodel in TriBeCa, but he still felt quite acutely that this was not his sphere, and these were not his people.

The auditorium filled, and five minutes after the show was supposed to start, the lights dimmed and Gio walked onto the stage.

"Welcome, everyone!" he said. "As most of you know, I am Giovanni Boca and I am here this evening to present the gala final performance of this summer's opera workshop."

Gio's accent seemed especially pronounced to Mike. He loved the cadence of Gio's voice, but even that seemed exaggerated. Mike realized as Gio talked a little about the work he'd done with the students that he was performing. His exaggerated affect was for the benefit of the audience. Mike wondered if Gio had been performing this way for the parents all along without him having noticed.

"Without further ado," Gio said, "I'd like to introduce you to twelve very talented singers."

Twelve teenagers walked onto the stage in a single-file line and arranged themselves on the risers. Gio turned around, produced a baton seemingly from out of thin air, and the performance began.

Mike had no idea what the kids were singing, though the program indicated it was from a Verdi opera. Sandy, likewise, sat there with his head tilted, as if he was trying to decipher what was happening in front of him.

After the choral piece, the kids went backstage again, and then they returned one at a time to do their solo pieces. Mike could not deny there was a lot of talent in this group. He was particularly impressed with a tenor named Greg who had a voice that sounded far more mature than his appearance.

Emma was the last one on stage. Gio was nothing less than effusive when he introduced her, though he didn't say much more than "And, finally, Emma McPhee." He seemed giddy, though. This, Mike thought, was the star of the show. *His* daughter was the star. How strange was that?

The piece started sweet but then turned more dramatic. Emma had explained to Mike a few days before that this aria was sung by the tragic figure in the opera, the woman who loved the hero but was destined to lose him to the more beautiful princess. It was nothing short of amazing—and also kind of surreal—to see this girl he'd raised from infancy on the stage, singing her heart out and sounding like nothing short of a miracle.

He was crying when it ended.

Emma brought the house down.

He was, of course, the first one standing when she took her bow, but he wasn't the only one. Other parents and audience members got to their feet and shouted, "Brava!"

"Did that sound really come out of little Emma?" Sandy asked.

"I've been listening to her practice around the apartment all week, so I know intellectually it did, but, man, I just didn't *know*." He wiped his eyes. "I had no idea she would sound like *that* on a real stage."

Mike's chest swelled with love and pride, and he whistled and clapped until his hands hurt, and still it was not enough to convey everything he felt in that moment. His beautiful daughter had just given the performance of a lifetime. How could anything ever compare?

Gio brought the kids back out to do one final group number. It took a while to get the audience to settle down, but once they did, the kids started to sing together again. Mike marveled at how lovely Emma looked. She'd put on a purple gown he'd helped her pick out, and her rich brown hair was twisted up at the back of her head. It was one of the strange talents he'd picked up as the father of a girl—Mike's sister Becky had taught him how to braid and French twist and otherwise do a girl's hair. Gio, too, looked good today. He wore a black tux perfectly tailored to his figure, and his dark hair was a little unruly. Mike was proud of Gio as well, amazed he was capable of teaching his students to do what they were doing now.

Then he had a more upsetting thought: Emma could sing like an angel, and Gio could teach teenagers to make the sweetest music anyone had ever heard. Mike remodeled rich people's bathrooms. They didn't even belong in the same universe.

Mike didn't see Gio or Emma again until the reception in the lobby after the show. The kids came in a few minutes after the parents had been plied with cocktails and hors d'oeuvres. Emma jogged over to Mike and threw her arms around him.

"Did you see that, Daddy?" she asked.

"You were amazing, sweetheart. The show was incredible. I am so proud of you."

He felt the tears sting his eyes again as he looked at her.

She hugged him tight and then took a step back. "Hi, Sandy."

"Hi, little girl. How come you never told me you could sing like that?"

She shrugged. Mike reached over and tucked an errant piece of hair back into the twist. Then he put an arm around her and hugged her again. "I love you so much," he said.

She hugged him back. "I love you too. Where are those little pastry things Sandy's eating?"

Sandy pointed. Emma ran off.

When she came back, a few of the parents were on her trail. Emma introduced the kids in her class to Mike, although most of them knew him already since he'd shown up at the end of class so consistently. She said, "This is my dad and this is my Uncle Sandy," a few times. Mike shook a lot of hands.

One woman said, "Your daughter is amazing. What an incredible voice!"

"Thank you!" said Mike. "Not that I had anything to do with it. She has a lot of self-discipline."

The woman nodded. "Oh, how rude of me. I'm Georgina Mansford. My daughter Julia was in Mr. Boca's workshop last year. He's really outdone himself this year with the kids he picked. My Julia is gorgeous and talented, of course. She has one more year at Dalton and then she'll be ready for Juilliard."

"That's wonderful."

"Yes. Her father is a banker, you know, so at least we have the funds to put her through the best schools. No expense too high for our Julia." Georgina Mansford paused. "What do you do, Mr. McPhee?"

Mike hesitated, feeling inferior suddenly. "I'm, ah, an independent contractor. I do home renovation."

"He's too modest," Sandy piped in. "He owns his own business."

"Marvelous. We need more small business owners thriving in this city." It was clear she was acting now, though. Her smile seemed hollow.

She excused herself and Mike let out a sigh. He felt itchy everywhere with the need to escape from this place, but he didn't want to make too hasty an exit when Emma seemed to be enjoying talking with her classmates so much.

Gio walked over then. He shook Mike's hand and held it a moment longer than was probably wise. "Did you enjoy the show?" he asked.

"Very much," said Mike. He wanted to give Gio a kiss or a hug or just grab him and run out of the theater. But he remained there, standing a foot from Gio but unable to touch him, quietly going mad.

"This, *caro*, was my crowning achievement as a teacher, I think." Gio grinned. "I haven't gotten to talk to you since we've been tied up with dress rehearsal, but did Emma talk to you about lessons in the fall?"

"You want to be her teacher."

"Not right away, but I have some instructors in mind for her. You saw the reaction she got from this crowd. If she has good teachers, she can get even better." He leaned forward and cupped his hand around his mouth. "This crowd is very stuffy, yes?"

Mike laughed. "Yes."

"We should talk at some point in the future. Seriously talk. I do want to be her mentor, but I don't want the other stuff to complicate things."

Mike frowned. He hated that his relationship with Gio had been relegated to "other stuff."

"We should talk," Mike agreed.

Another very finely dressed woman appeared. Mike caught the frown on Gio's face just before he covered it up with a wide grin.

"Marvelous show, Mr. Boca," said the woman. "Really fine stuff."

"Thank you, Mrs. Quinlan." He glanced back at Mike. "Let me introduce you to Mike McPhee. He's Emma's father. She was the last girl to sing today."

"Yes, of course. Delightful to meet you." She held out her hand to be shaken. It was thin and bony and ice cold. "My daughter Amelia sang 'Habanera' in the middle."

"She was great," Mike said, although he couldn't recall which of the kids was Amelia.

"Will your daughter be auditioning for the Young Musicians Program?"

"Yes," Mike said, although he was still working out how he'd pay for it. Gio had told him there were scholarship opportunities; that was a pile of paperwork Mike didn't want to think about quite yet. Better not to taint what had been a pretty marvelous day. He was still basking in the glow of Emma's performance, so he smiled at Mrs. Quinlan.

"Amelia will be auditioning as well, so I suppose we will see you there. Or perhaps your wife?"

"I'm not married." Mike didn't like the way this woman was fishing for information. Trying to be polite, he added, "So, yes, I'm sure I will see you there. I look forward to it." He knew how to play the game with people like this, since he'd been doing it for so long.

"That man over there talking with your daughter, he's not your partner?"

Mike glanced at Gio for help, but Gio just stood there with a placid smile on his face, as if he were tuning out this whole conversation. "No, he's a family friend."

She dug into her handbag and came back with a postcard, which she handed to him. It advertised a meeting of the Upper West Side Association for the Arts. "My husband and I chair the UWSAA. We work together to fund arts projects in the neighborhood. We sponsor a choir and an orchestra that practice out of a church on Ninety-fourth."

"Okay."

"You should consider coming to a meeting. I'm sure you would make an interesting addition." Something off to the side seemed to snag her attention. "Ah, my husband is calling for me. If you'll excuse me."

When she was gone, Mike turned to Gio. "What was that?"

"Tracy Quinlan. She's… a force, to be certain."

"Do I want anything to do with these people?" Mike held up the postcard.

"No, definitely not," Gio whispered. "Stuffed shirts, all of them. A necessary evil in my profession, since their support funds things like my opera workshop, but I could do without the Tracy Quinlans of the world." He sighed. "I'd love to chat with you, but I have to make nice with the rest of the parents too. I'll see you soon, yes? You'll call me?"

"Of course."

"*Ciao*, Mike."

Mike shook his head. He was sad to see Gio go, but more than that, he felt like Tracy Quinlan had just kicked him in the shin.

"Not just a summer fling, then?" Sandy said as he walked back up to Mike.

"I guess not." Although Mike wondered if it ever had been. He'd been falling harder by the day, ever since that night they'd gone out and danced in front of the very fountain Mike could now see through the lobby windows.

Emma finished up eventually. Sandy offered to buy dinner for her and Mike—"At a real restaurant, even!"—so Sandy and Emma negotiated cuisine as Mike tried not to get too overwhelmed by everything he was feeling: pride, love, and shame, but above all, a profound sadness that descended on him suddenly, a realization, perhaps, that giving Emma everything she wanted meant that the things he wanted would fall by the wayside.

On their way out of the theater, Mike glanced back at Gio, who was deep in conversation with Georgina Mansford. Gio was a part of that world in a way that Mike would never be.

Summer, it seemed, was over.

THIRTEEN

A WEEK after the gala, Mike still hadn't called. Gio thought it strange that now that they could finally be together openly, they weren't spending any time together at all.

Of course, there was no reason Gio couldn't be the one to call.

He sat in his office and stared at his phone, thinking this was about the time Mike would have been coming to the studio to pick up Emma if the workshop were still in session. Surely he was off work about now. Maybe Gio would even catch him before he took the bus back across town and they could grab a cup of coffee nearby. That seemed innocent enough. They could just… chat. No messy emotional stuff, no sex, and no pressure. Just a friendly conversation to reinforce that they liked each other and could be good together. Yes, that was an excellent idea. He was about to dial when a shadow darkened his doorway.

Tracy Quinlan.

He stood. "Hello, Mrs. Quinlan. It is a pleasure to see you."

"Likewise. Do you have a few minutes?"

Gio glanced at his phone. "A few, yes. Come in."

She came in and arranged herself on the guest chair. Gio imagined Tracy Quinlan led the sort of life that had at some point involved lessons on how to sit like a lady, because there was something polite and studied about her posture. "About the upcoming auditions…," she said.

"Did Amelia settle on a piece? I suggested one of Rosina's arias from *Il Barbiere di Siviglia*, but last I heard hadn't decided. Maybe that's too hard. There's an aria in *Così fan tutte* that might be a better fit, actually, now that I think about it. No need to go overboard trying to impress the committee. She only needs to sing well."

"That part of the audition we have handled. The next part is up to you."

"Me?" Gio knew where this was going but opted to play innocent. "I'm not on the audition committee this year."

Tracy's eyes flared wide for a moment, like this was new information to her and it was a surprise. She recovered quickly. "You do have some influence on the committee."

"I have discussed with the committee which of my workshop students I would recommend for the Young Musicians Program, that is true. I mentioned Amelia." Perhaps not in the most favorable terms, but he *had* mentioned her. That was not a lie.

"I do hope so. She works so hard. She deserves a shot at the program. And, really, I'd hate to think she didn't get in because you favored another student inappropriately."

"I pride myself in not playing favorites. I have a reputation for being objective."

"Really?" Her tone was sardonic, which Gio did not appreciate.

"I made my recommendations based on the talent of the singers, and that is all."

"Right. Because you are not the sort of man who would promote a singer because you are having an affair with her father."

The accusation stung. Gio was so surprised by it, he sat back in his chair. "What are you—?"

"Don't bother to deny it. Amelia said Emma McPhee's father spoke to you after every class, and then I saw you kissing. Seeing you together at the gala just confirmed it. I never imagined you could be a man so easily swayed. You are right about your reputation. Everyone I've talked to has said you are not a man who could be influenced with money or sex. What a lie that turned out to be."

Gio tried to gather his wits. "It's not a lie. Emma McPhee is an extraordinarily talented young singer. And I reiterate, I'm not on the audition committee for the Young Musicians Program. I'm not even teaching any courses for the program this fall. So any decision made in that regard is completely out of my hands."

Tracy scoffed. "We both know that's not true. One word from you, and whichever students are your favorites are in the program for certain. And if you're promoting one singer because her father is providing you with sexual favors, well, that makes things look pretty bad for you, doesn't it?" She shook her head. "I suppose it would have to be sexual, wouldn't it? It's not like that man can afford to bribe you with money." There was a disgusted snarl in her voice. "I wonder if he's even gay."

Gio stood. "Do you really think you can earn my favor by insulting me?"

"No." Tracy stood as well. "My husband is close friends with Howell Laughton."

That wasn't as strong a blow as Tracy seemed to think it was, although it was cause for alarm. Howell was the head of the voice department at Olcott. He was technically Gio's boss, although the actual hierarchy became a little confusing when egos got involved. Not that Tracy would understand that.

"So you're saying you will take information you think you have to Howell and accuse me of favoritism for the purposes of ensuring that your daughter gets into the Young Musicians Program."

"Perhaps I will." Tracy took a step toward the door. "If I were you, I wouldn't be so dismissive. I have more power than you know."

Gio was tempted to tell her to go ahead and talk to Howell. He thought about what Dacia had said to him weeks before: no one could deny Emma's talent, which would keep him safe from being seen as doting on her more than the other students. Besides, there were no rules about dating the parents of students—Gio had looked into it—so he wasn't doing anything wrong. Not really.

But he also didn't want to give this woman any more fire to play with. "If Amelia practices, if she gives a solid audition, she's in. I have nothing further to say on the matter."

"All right," Tracy said. "We shall see. But know that I will do whatever is within my power to assure my daughter's success. She deserves a spot in that program."

Tracy Quinlan left without another word.

Gio sat back down. He didn't want to let this encounter bother him, though it did a great deal. It had been a point of pride to be Giovanni Boca, the Unbribable. It lent an air of authenticity to what he did; he took on students for their talent and no other reason. The situation with Mike was changing him, could affect his reputation. He could see that now, and it was a consequence he hadn't anticipated. But now, sure enough, things in his professional and personal life were getting tangled.

Perhaps it would be better to step away, or to let Mike keep his distance. He could call it a day and go back to focusing on his college students. He certainly wouldn't have to deal with Tracy Quinlan threatening him if her accusations had no substance.

And yet he missed Mike as if someone had cut out one of his ribs. It had been a week since they'd had a conversation longer than five minutes, even, and that was something he intended to fix immediately. If he was going to court trouble, he might as well really pursue it.

No one could know what tomorrow would bring, he reminded himself.

He picked up the phone.

MIKE finished washing his hands and then took a step back to admire his handiwork. He really loved the warm quality of the Spanish-style tiles his clients had picked out for their new kitchen. The pattern he'd laid out was unique, and he was happy to be providing the clients with the one-of-a-kind kitchen he'd promised. He pulled his phone out to take a picture of it so he could put it on his website.

Just after the shutter clicked, his phone rang. Gio.

After Mike answered, Gio said, "Would you like to have dinner tomorrow night?"

It wasn't that Mike had been avoiding Gio so much as taking a step back to reevaluate what was happening. He was still reeling from his encounters at the workshop final show, not sure what to make of the fact that those people had looked down their nose at him. He should have known better—he *did* know better—but he couldn't shake the idea that Gio had been looking down his nose at him too.

"I'm free tomorrow," Mike said. He wasn't sure how wise it was to go out to dinner, but he did miss Gio a lot—Gio had been nearly all Mike had been able to think about for a week—and certainly the man deserved an explanation for why Mike had stepped away.

"Good. I've picked out a restaurant." He rattled off the name and address. Mike didn't know it, but it sounded expensive. "You will love it. They have excellent seafood. Great food for this terribly hot weather we've been having."

"All right."

"Oh, I can't wait to see you. It's been too long."

"I know. But I've been working and—"

"It doesn't matter, *caro*. I will see you tomorrow, yes?"

"Yes, tomorrow."

"Seven o'clock."

"Yes. Listen, I'm at a job right now, so I need to—"

"Oh, yes. I'm at work also. I didn't mean to keep you. We'll catch up tomorrow. *Ciao*, Mike."

Mike slipped his phone back in his pocket and felt a wave of sadness. Hearing Gio's voice reminded him of all he'd stepped away from. He had definitely missed Gio, missed seeing him and speaking to him regularly, but he didn't know what to do or say anymore.

He finished up, said good-bye to his clients, and went outside. He'd been hoping to walk home through Central Park, but it really was oppressively hot. He walked a block and caught the bus instead. He came home to an empty apartment—Emma had texted him about an hour before to say she and Isobel were going to the movies—and it was a relief in a way, because he needed a few minutes alone to sort out his thoughts.

He thought of Evan. Falling in love with Evan had been so easy. They'd come from the same place, were cut from the same cloth. Well, Evan had grown up in the shadow of Wrigley Field in Chicago, but it might as well have been South Brooklyn for all their childhoods had been alike. They related to each other because of their similarities and mutual attraction, and though they'd had to sneak around in the early months of their relationship, once they were in New York and everything was out in the open, it had been… easy.

He supposed loving Gio could be that easy too, but it felt more complicated, more tangled.

Mike walked over to where Evan's picture hung on the wall. He reached over and touched Evan's likeness briefly. "You've been gone for a long time," he said. Evan had been on his mind a lot in the last couple of weeks too, probably mostly because of Emma's success. It was hard to let go of the idea that Evan should have been there to witness everything Emma did. He should have known, too, that Evan could never stay out of Mike's romantic relationships. "Emma, she's the most important thing. If getting involved with Gio does anything to affect Emma, I don't know if I could…."

He shook his head. "Am I being ridiculous? Are my fears unfounded? Is it just because I'm older now? Because I have Emma to look out for? Because meeting you absolutely changed my life, and I think being with Gio is changing me too, but I don't know if I can do it. I don't know if I can be a part of his world. I don't know if I can be with him if Emma isn't 100 percent on board. I just don't know."

He closed his eyes and reached out. He leaned on the wall for a moment. "I've just barely been holding things together since you left. Now what do I do? Do I love this man and risk everything? Do I let him love me? What should I do, Evan? What should I do?"

Mike knew he wouldn't get an answer, but that didn't make it any less frustrating when the silence was broken by the front door banging open. Emma walked in and dropped her handbag on the couch.

"Hi, sweetie," Mike said. He was seized by an overwhelming urge to hug her, but wondered if she would think that was weird.

"Hi. Are you okay?"

"Yeah, I'm fine. How was the movie?"

"Good, but kind of dumb. Izzy thought this one actor, I can't think of his name, was kind of hot, but I don't know." She giggled. "Then we went to Starbucks and I had a latte, so now I'm all wired. I'm also starving."

"Oh, good." Mike walked into the kitchen to survey possible dinner offerings. "Are leftovers okay?"

"Is there any of that lasagna left?"

"Yup. Probably enough for both of us."

"Then that's good."

Emma sat at the table while Mike heated up dinner. She rambled on about the movie, although Mike only half listened. He was preoccupied now with the impending dinner with Gio.

He slid the lasagna on plates and put one in front of Emma. Without even thinking about it, he poured her a glass of diet soda, and had a flashback of pouring her glasses of milk as she sat in her high chair at this same table in the apartment he'd shared with Evan. Now she drank lattes and went to the movies on her own. He shook his head as he sat at the table.

"Seriously, Daddy. Are you okay?"

"Yeah." Then he figured he might as well have it out. "Gio invited me to dinner tomorrow night. So you'll be on your own."

"You want me to go to Izzy's?"

"Is that okay? Or maybe you could go to Aunt Becky's? She's been nagging me about seeing you because she was sorry she had to work during your workshop show."

"Yeah, I guess that's okay."

"Are you still upset about me dating Gio?" *Might as well be direct*, Mike reasoned.

"It's not that I was upset. It's just… it's still kind of weird. Is it, like, serious?"

"I don't know." Well, it was serious, or Mike's feelings about Gio certainly were, but he still couldn't decide if he should commit to the relationship or not.

She nodded. "What about lessons and stuff? Everyone keeps saying I'll get into the Young Musicians Program, so if that happens and Gio wants to be my teacher, is that going to be weird? With you and him?"

"I don't know that either. I guess we have some things to work out." Not that he was asking her permission; it struck him suddenly that this was an entirely inappropriate conversation to be having with his daughter. "Eat your lasagna."

She rolled her eyes. "Yes, *Dad*."

FOURTEEN

MIKE'S body language practically screamed that he didn't want to be there. He sat in a chair across the table from Gio, his posture stiff, his shoulders tight. He mostly looked at the table.

"This is a nice restaurant," Mike told his wineglass.

"Yes, one of my favorites. The chef once worked at one of the finest restaurants in Perugia. That restaurant was exclusive, almost impossible to get a table. I ate there once when I was, ah, in my midtwenties, when my career was just taking off. They wanted to have *la voce di un angelo* eat at this restaurant." Gio chuckled. "Anyway. My friend Dacia knows Paolo. He owns the place and is the head chef. I recommend the seafood especially. He's a real wizard with shellfish, and they get everything fresh."

This didn't hearten Mike much. He continued to stare forlornly at the menu.

Gio reached across the table and cupped his hand around Mike's wrist. "Is something wrong?"

"No."

"Really, *caro*? Because you look so sad."

Mike put the menu down and took a deep breath. "I don't belong here."

The waiter interrupted then. Gio ordered the seafood *fra diavolo*, his favorite thing on the menu. Mike ordered a steak.

So, all right. Mike was an all-American kind of guy who liked his meat and potatoes. Nothing wrong with that. Even if it bothered Gio a little that Mike hadn't taken his recommendation.

"Mike," Gio said when the waiter was gone, "please talk to me."

Mike continued to frown and look at the table. After a long moment of silence, he said, "It's stupid."

"It's not stupid. If something is wrong, I want you to tell me."

Mike nodded. "It's just... it's a lot of things. I play worst-case scenario a lot in my head, you know? My daughter is the most important thing in my world. The Olcott School, Juilliard, singing opera, all of it is her dream. You stand in a position to help her get there, to make her dreams come true. But if I fuck things up with you, will I ruin her chances for the future she wants?"

"You couldn't possibly. She's too talented for—"

Mike held up his hand. "You say that, but say we break up. Say it's nasty and bitter. Say you're so angry with me you can't even see straight. Maybe you don't intend to sabotage Emma, but looking at her every day reminds you of me, and maybe you stop giving her extra attention. Maybe you forget to fill out a form or something. Maybe you unwittingly sabotage her because you're upset with me."

That wounded Gio, insulted him. Anger bubbled up at the accusation of potential sabotage, as if Gio would ever stoop so low. And that was not to mention Mike's pessimism. He was already writing their ending. "Or maybe you and I live happily ever after."

Mike laughed softly and shook his head. "No. I don't believe in happily ever after. I thought I had that once, but it was taken from me. There are no happy endings, Gio."

Gio sat forward a little, frustrated by Mike's attitude. He'd always been a bit of a romantic, he thought, so he always hoped for a happy ending in his future. He understood Mike's skepticism, but it was still upsetting to hear it voiced so unequivocally. It made him feel sad for Mike that Mike didn't have that hope.

"So, fine, no happy ending. But what if you and I spend the next thirty years together?"

Mike squirmed in his chair a little. "I'm not sure... that is, when Emma found out about us, she was clear that this relationship between us could not interfere with her ambitions. I told her she didn't get a say in my personal life, but if this directly affects her, that's a different situation. The more I think about it, the more I think that takes priority."

Why was this conversation like so many insect stings? All of it felt like tiny needles poking against Gio's skin. He understood what Mike was saying, but he also had more hope for them than that. "So you would end something really wonderful happening between us just because you're worried about the small chance that we break up and I take out my anger at you on Emma? That's ridiculous. We're adults."

"I know, but all these scenarios play out in my head in which Emma gets the short end of the stick because you and I are at odds, and that's not fair to her. I have to put her first."

Was Mike trying to end things? It wasn't at all clear. Gio certainly did not want to end their relationship. "Is that what you're worried about? Because let me assure you, Emma is one of the most amazing talents any of the faculty at Olcott have seen in a generation. Everyone was abuzz about her after the final show. I want her to succeed as much as anyone. So I promise, if something goes wrong with you and me and I feel I can no longer be her best advocate, I will step back. Any number of teachers on that faculty would be a wonderful mentor for her."

Mike picked up his knife, turned it in his hands, and put it back down. "That's kind of you. Very levelheaded."

"Yes, well. I may be an artist, but I can be practical as well. And you, *caro mio*, are acting strangely tonight. You're already running the worst-case scenario on our relationship but fail to see the best case. There is something here. I do not think even you can deny that. I like you and I care about you."

Mike smiled faintly and nodded. "I care about you too."

"So what's the problem?"

They received bread and the appetizer Gio had ordered, a cheese plate. Mike sat patiently while the waiter explained what each cheese was and which region of Italy it had come from. The plate also had a few thin slices of soppressata and prosciutto. Gio didn't need it all explained to him—he could have easily identified each item on the plate—and he wanted to shoo the waiter away so that he could get Mike to keep talking. And yet Mike hung on the waiter's every word, and as soon as the waiter departed, he picked up a knife and took a small slice of cheese.

"It's not just Emma, though, is it?" Gio asked. "What did you mean before when you said you don't belong here?"

"I didn't know until two minutes ago that people even made cheese from sheep's milk."

"All right."

"You are a part of a world that knows about fine things like opera and fashion and fancy food. I'm from South Brooklyn. I know rock music and comfortable blue jeans and pizza."

Gio didn't understand what Mike was trying to say. "What does that matter?"

"I don't belong with you, Gio. I'm not part of the world you live in. I… I work for people like you. I'm not an equal."

Gio suddenly understood Mike's recent silence. The inferiority complex, that wasn't something Gio expected from a man who seemed so unself-conscious.

"I don't care about that. Those things are superficial," Gio said.

"Worst-case scenarios—that's what I do. All the time, in my head, I'm imagining the worst. What I imagine with you sometimes is that you take me to some dinner party where all everyone knows is wine and, hell, sheep cheese, and I know nothing about these things. I know about tile and grout. I know about plumbing and carpentry. I can fix your sink or help you choose a good paint color for your living room. But all I really know about wine is that it comes in white or red. I like nice restaurants, and I'm sure the food here is great, but at the end of the day? I'm more comfortable eating takeout with Emma in our living room, you know? This?" He lifted his finger and spun it around, indicating the room. "This is not me. This is not my world. But it is your world, and I can't help but think that we just don't belong in the same spaces."

Gio understood Mike enough to know that simple denial would not be enough to dissuade him from his opinion. "Do you know who my last boyfriend was?" he asked.

Mike raised an eyebrow. "How on earth would I know that?" He sampled a piece of the sheep's milk cheese. "Hey, this is pretty good."

Gio smiled. He reached over and rubbed Mike's hand briefly, but then sat back on his side of the table. "The last guy I dated was Pavel Minskov."

Mike shrugged and tried the quince paste. "Okay."

"A brilliant ballet dancer. The Moscow Ballet did a three-month engagement at Lincoln Center a few years ago, and he was their star. I met Pavel shortly after I lost my voice, actually. It was the first time I'd been with someone who appreciated me for myself and not my voice. Or so I thought."

"What happened?"

"He liked that my vocal injury kept me in the public eye for a while, or at least in the public eye of the opera world. Then the Moscow Ballet continued its tour, so he left New York. And that was that."

"Oh."

"My point in telling you is that Pavel was very much of my world. Opera, ballet, these are performances admired by a specific sort of patron of the arts, if you understand my meaning. Pavel was from a family of performers very much like mine. He'd had years of dance training and had become a tremendous success, widely admired in the community. He and I had much in common. But we had nothing to talk about. Pavel is shallow and egotistical. He wanted a piece of fallen opera star Giovanni Boca but had no interest in Gio the man."

"So he was an asshole."

Gio laughed. "Yes. But, see, the point is that Pavel was from my world, as you put it, but I definitely did not belong with him. You, on the other hand, I have a real connection with."

The waiter appeared with their entrees and put the mostly eaten cheese plate off to the side.

Gio snuck glances at Mike as he arranged his napkin and his plate. He was falling for Mike and he knew it. Mike seemed to be slipping away like sand through his fingers, and that was painful and frustrating. There was so much to appreciate about Mike—he was intelligent and kind, his body moved and hummed with music constantly, and he was breathtakingly gorgeous. But more than that, he seemed to understand Gio in a way few other men had. He knew Gio the man, knew him independent of his now long-dead opera career.

"I listened to recordings of you," Mike said as he cut his steak. "Your voice—"

Or Gio had misjudged. Wearily, he said, "I know. Please don't."

Mike nodded. "I think it gave me a greater appreciation for what you lost. Listening to your old records, I mean."

That surprised Gio, but he felt like he needed to backpedal. He'd had a few years to cope with that loss, and though he still missed singing with every cell in his body, he'd resigned himself to his fate. "Really, it's nothing. You know more about loss than I ever will." Until meeting Mike, Gio had thought the loss of his voice was the greatest tragedy to ever descend on his universe, but Mike's losses had been far more traumatic. "You humble me, you know that?"

"How so?"

"I was an arrogant fool for a long time. I thought my voice was my ticket to everything I wanted in life. Money. Fame. Even sex. And then suddenly, I felt like I had nothing. But I did still have something. I had my knowledge, my reputation, my experience. I became a teacher so I could help other singers even if I can no longer join their ranks."

Mike nodded. "I felt like my whole world ended when Evan died."

"And, see, my pain doesn't even compare. I'm still alive and well. I lost a skill, a talent, but I didn't lose someone I loved like that."

Mike leveled his gaze at Gio. "It's not a contest."

"No. And I don't think of it that way. But this is how we relate to each other, *caro*. We both understand about loss."

Mike nodded, but he didn't seem quite present anymore, like he was drifting back to a darker place. "When Evan died, I had to pull myself together for Emma. She was so small and she needed me. But that loss… it still pulls at me sometimes." Mike stared off at something in the distance.

Gio could see things were pulling at Mike now. He took a moment to savor his food and process everything Mike had told him. There was only one conclusion. "You're afraid to love someone because you're afraid things will end again like they did with Evan. You're afraid to get your heart involved if someone can yank it away from you."

Mike closed his eyes. He put his fork down for a moment and rubbed his forehead. "I… yeah, I guess that's part of it. But it's not just me I have to worry about. I come as part of a package deal. And I can't risk breaking Emma's heart too."

This was the darkest corner of Mike's soul laid bare, and Gio understood that now. Under all his calm, Mike worried and fretted. That made Gio nervous, but it was intriguing too. There was a depth to Mike that Gio hadn't seen when they first met. Gio thought perhaps he could bring some light to those dark places, help Mike just as surely as Mike was helping Gio.

"Maybe there are no happy endings," Gio said, "but isn't it worse not to try to see if there are? To live in hope that maybe this time everything will work out?"

"I don't know."

"You and I have both known loss. Our lives turned out very differently from how we thought they would. But that's no reason to throw away what could be a very good thing. You deserve a shot at happiness, if nothing else."

"Maybe."

Mike's ambivalence cemented Gio's certainty. And suddenly, he saw it. He saw years of them together, he saw Mike laughing, he saw good meals, good wine, good music. He saw casual evenings at home. He saw a whole life together that he could never have imagined for himself, but it was wonderful and he would not let it slip away. He said, "I think you and I have more in common than you think. And I believe we owe it to ourselves to see if what we've been searching for can be found in each other. Maybe it doesn't survive the summer. Maybe we fall passionately in love and are together for decades. But it's not fair to cut it off just because we're afraid."

Mike ate quietly for a moment. "You really dated a ballerina."

"Pavel is technically a *ballerino*, but…. Yes, I did."

"If nothing else, staying with you will be interesting."

Gio laughed. "Yes, I think it will be."

MIKE'S head was swimming. It had been difficult to just come out and say everything that had been on his mind, but Gio had not laughed or mocked him, had merely accepted his words. Mike appreciated that.

What Gio had said about loss, that too had rung in Mike's head. Maybe they did have a few things in common.

What Gio had said definitely did a lot to comfort Mike. He still worried about what could happen, but Gio's words had gone a long way toward convincing him it would be foolish to end things before they even got started. After all, the source of Mike's anguish was that he wanted this relationship, he wanted Gio, very much, but felt inadequate.

But Gio had chosen him. Mike thought he owed it to both of them to honor that choice, to let himself feel everything he could feel instead of holding back, to care for Gio the way Mike thought he deserved to be cared for and to let Gio care for him as well. It was a terrifying step forward. It was exciting, too.

Mike followed Gio back to his place after dinner. He still felt a little shaky and uncertain as Gio paced around his living room, putting things away and keeping his hands busy.

"Gio," Mike said.

It was soft, just a breath of the man's name in an attempt to get his attention, but Gio moved quickly and soon Mike found himself face-to-face with the object of his desire and affection. Something fluttered in his chest as he gazed at Gio, and he settled more firmly into his decision.

"Gio, I… I want to try. To be with you, I mean. I want to see where this goes. I want you."

Gio smiled and put his hands on the sides of Mike's face. "I'm glad. I truly am. But I should tell you, something happened at work yesterday that may be relevant."

"What is it?"

Gio ran his hands over Mike's shoulders. "The parent of one of my workshop students—do you remember Tracy Quinlan? You met her at the final show."

It rang a bell, but Mike couldn't picture the woman's face. "Maybe."

"She's a real piece of work. She and her husband contribute piles of money to the school and into arts programs all over the city, and she feels this gives her license to dictate to us which programs her children get into. She's been popping into my office all summer to reiterate that it is my sacred duty to make sure her daughter gets into the Young Musicians Program at Olcott."

"All right. What does this have to do with me?"

Gio slid his hands down Mike's torso and rested them on his waist. The move seemed a little inappropriate for the conversation, but Mike had to admit he was having a hard time keeping his hands off Gio. He gave in and touched Gio's back.

Gio said, "She knows about us, or she thinks she does. She threatened to take it to my boss if the auditions for the YMP don't go her way."

Gio said this glibly, but the statement made Mike's heart stop. He immediately dropped his hands and took a step back. "What?"

"Ah, yes. This is one of those instances where I probably should not have said anything."

"A parent is threatening you because she saw us together?"

"It's not really a big deal."

Mike begged to differ. "What can she do?"

"Nothing. She's just being a bother because her daughter might not get into the program. Heaven forbid the girl should actually have to audition instead of just getting in because her parents paid for it."

That didn't provide much relief. "Can she do anything about Emma?"

"No. Absolutely not. The whole department is on Emma's side. I'm not on the audition committee, so I don't get a say in who gets into the program, either, so there's no bias on my part. And what you and I are doing is not against any rules. Everything will be fine, *caro*. There's no need to worry. I just wanted to let you know what happened. For the sake of honesty."

"But she could get you in trouble."

"Maybe. I doubt it, though. I'm worth a lot to the school. Having my name on that opera workshop gets the summer programs a lot of attention and money. She can't prove any favoritism. I'd like to mentor Emma, but I have no involvement with the Young Musicians Program next year, so it doesn't matter."

"But this is what could happen, isn't it? Your involvement with me could make it look like you're giving Emma a leg up against her competition."

"So I won't mentor her. She works with Dacia and still has access to every opportunity being a student at Olcott opens up for her. I want her to succeed, Mike, I genuinely do. I won't put her in jeopardy. You have my word on that."

That made Mike feel a little better, although the complexity of politics at the school left him reeling.

Not to mention that it was too late. The best course of action would have been not to get involved with Giovanni Boca to begin with, but here they were. Mike hadn't been able to stay away, and even now, standing a foot away from Gio, he missed Gio's touch.

"I don't know what to do anymore," Mike said. "I want you, I really do, down in my gut I do. But I'm so terrified of everything. I'm worried you'll get to know the real me and won't like what you see. I'm worried this will have consequences for Emma. I'm worried this will end."

Gio tilted his head. "You know what I know from thirty-seven years of listening to and performing opera? I know that life is about risk and reward. Great passion is risky. It can burn you, it can destroy you, it can rip out your heart. But it is also one of the greatest things we will ever experience. We risk our hearts when we fall in love, but is the reward not worth it?"

Was it? Mike had been in love only once before, and look where it had left him. Still, eleven years after Evan's passing, he had to agree that for all the pain, he had a lot of happy memories, and there was Emma. He could never regret the decisions that had brought Emma into his life.

"It's worth it," Mike whispered.

"I would be willing to risk a lot for you, Mike, my heart included. It must be plain to you by now how much I care. I have never met anyone in my life quite like you, and I'm certain beyond anything there could not be a man more perfect for me. So get all of the nonsense about not belonging in my world out of your head. All of that is just window dressing. You and I are but two men in a large city who found each other by some miracle, and there is a spark of something between us that cannot be denied."

Mike closed his eyes. "You say these things. Your words are so beautiful. I don't have words like that." Mike had so much to say, but no idea how to say it. He felt all of those things in his heart, though, and he knew he was falling for Gio just as surely as Gio was falling for him.

"It doesn't matter to me. You have music in your heart as surely as I do, and that is all that matters. That we make music together. So we run into adversity? We find a way around it." Gio laughed softly. "Listen to me getting all dramatic. You'd think I was singing an aria."

"No, it's… it's wonderful, what you're saying."

"*O tesoro mio*, this is where you kiss me."

So Mike did. He leaned forward and claimed Gio's mouth with his own. He pulled Gio into his arms. And it was like his skin was on fire, desire aflame suddenly in his heart, in his mind, in his body. Maybe what Gio had said, maybe those beautiful words were just words, but they meant something to Mike and felt important.

Mike broke away from the kiss. "I must be losing my mind."

"The feeling is mutual."

Gio kissed him and their lips slid together, their tongues met, and Mike took a moment to slow down and really taste Gio, to savor the texture of the kiss. He ran his hands through Gio's hair, touched his face, pulled him closer.

He thought perhaps the real source of his uneasiness for the past couple of weeks was the idea that he couldn't have this for some reason, and perhaps it was better to pull away now rather than to really put his heart on the line. But that was stupid; wrapped up in Gio as he was now, he couldn't imagine denying himself this.

So they would make music together. Mike kissed Gio again and steered him toward the bedroom. A siren wailed outside and Mike was suddenly reminded of a symphony he'd heard at Emma's urging that was supposed to recreate the sounds of the city. There were honking trumpets and clanging metallic drums, and those were the obvious sounds, but the city had its own sort of rhythm and music to it. For Mike, the sounds of the city were as steady as the thrum of the beat in the house music they played at his favorite dance clubs. The sounds he and Gio made as they kissed and maneuvered around the bedroom involved pounding heartbeats punctuated by sighs and groans. The city, the music of it, was about sirens and construction noises, yes, but it was about beauty and sex too. The music Mike and Gio made together would have to incorporate all of those things.

When they were naked and writhing together on the bed, the sound became stranger. Mike kissed Gio and rubbed against him, but then lifted his head. "What's it called in music when two notes are played at the same time and they sound kind of harsh together?"

Gio furrowed his brow. "What are you... do you mean discordant?"

"Yes, discordant. I was thinking about us making music together, and I thought it must sound discordant."

Gio put his fingers on Mike's lips. "No, *caro*. We make beautiful, melodic, soulful music together."

Mike laughed. "I didn't mean it in a bad way. It's like modern music. It sounds weird because we're used to the way songs have always been, but the composer is creating something brand new, you know, so of course it will sound weird. But it's beautiful in its way too."

Gio smiled. "I like the way you think."

"Mmm." Mike kissed Gio. He pulled away slightly again. "I want you, Gio."

"How do you want me?"

"Inside me. Always inside me. You... you fill up the silence in me."

Mike was embarrassed by his clumsy attempt at poetry, but Gio's lips parted and he blinked. "And you said you had no beautiful words." Gio ran his hand down Mike's cheek and smiled. "You are so much more than you realize. Let me show you."

But Mike didn't need demonstrations. He'd spoken his own sort of truth. He had dark spots in his psyche, holes in his heart, missing parts of his soul. He'd experienced enough loss and heartbreak to last anyone a lifetime. And yet something in Gio filled all those places in Mike, made him feel hope again for a happy future instead of resignation to the status quo. Mike likewise wanted to fill the empty places in Gio, give him the music he needed, the voice he'd lost. It was a difficult thing and Mike wasn't sure he was up to the challenge, but he would give it his all.

Once Mike was ready for Gio, Gio lay on his back and stroked his cock. Mike rolled a condom on him and poured a generous amount of lube over it. Then he hovered over Gio, nipping at his lips, trying to let the anticipation build even more. Mike was hard, arousal zipping through his blood, through his system, but this was about more than just getting each other off. This was about creating a new sound together.

Mike positioned himself and sank onto Gio's cock. Gio held Mike's waist tightly, digging his fingers in and throwing his head back in ecstasy as he sank into Mike's willing body. And that was it right there, that moment Mike loved, when Gio first pressed inside and their bodies adjusted to each other and they were connected in this marvelous way. Mike closed his eyes and just let himself feel it, felt Gio moving within him, beneath him. Gio ran his hands over Mike's body as Mike set the pace and they moved together, making notes that collided with each other's sounds, with the noise of the city outside Gio's window. All of it came together to make a sort of breathless, triumphant music.

Maybe Mike didn't know much about music, but he knew he loved *this* music.

He kissed Gio, who hooked an arm around Mike's neck and held him still. Gio pushed up into Mike and it was so deliriously wonderful, the sensation of sliding in and out, of pressing together. Gio used his other hand to stroke Mike's cock, and all of the nerve endings were firing, making sparks in Mike's brain. Soon there was nothing but him and Gio, no outside noise, no outside turmoil or conflict, just two people growing to care about each other deeply and expressing that with their bodies, and soon Mike was crying out with the joy of it. He came hard, triumphantly, against Gio's chest. Gio practically cheered, he seemed so overjoyed, and then he bucked his hips and sank his fingers into Mike's biceps and was gone.

A little while later, as they lay together in bed and Mike tried to understand what was happening between them, Gio said, "That is what they mean by making beautiful music together. Discordant, perhaps, but no less beautiful."

"Yes," Mike said, though he had no other words to describe what he was feeling. He kissed the line where Gio's hair met his forehead. He closed his eyes and leaned into Gio. One last time he whispered, "Yes."

FIFTEEN

MIKE opened the door and let Gio into the apartment. He'd invited Gio to dinner as a way to make the relationship seem more normal and less like a secret. It seemed like these were important steps toward normalizing something that still felt far from normal for Mike.

Emma was being a good sport, although it was clear she was still not quite sure what to make of Gio and his place in Mike's life. That made Mike nervous as Gio leaned over and gave him a quick kiss. Mike smiled and escaped to take dinner out of the oven. He glanced at Emma on the way, but her expression told him nothing.

Normal. There was no reason for this not to be normal.

Mike had made a baked chicken dish, which he pulled out of the oven while Gio awkwardly spoke to Emma. He placed the baking dish on the table, and Gio made a show of inhaling and commenting on how good it smelled. Mike thought he was a decent cook, although he'd learned, as with many things he knew how to do, as a result of needing to do things for Emma. Gio and Emma settled in at the table as Mike put out a salad. He grabbed a bottle of wine for him and Gio—he'd asked for advice at the local wine store—and a can of diet soda for Emma. When he finally sat, he took in the tableau of his daughter and his boyfriend sitting down to a meal and was struck by how domestic, how normal, this seemed. That was good.

For the first few minutes of the meal, no one spoke. Everyone helped themselves to food and the silence was punctuated only by the sound of flatware scraping against plates. Mike racked his brain for possible topics of conversation, but it was Gio who broke the stalemate.

"Emma, have you decided on what you will sing at your Young Musicians Program audition?"

She perked up a little. "I was thinking about 'Sì. Mi chiamano Mimì.' from *La Bohème*, but I'm not sure if that's the right thing to sing. What do you think?"

It was a relief, in a way, to realize Gio could be a resource for Emma in a way Mike couldn't. This was how the two of them would connect, find common ground.

"I had a thought, although you certainly do not need to do what I say," Gio said. "It should be your choice. But I was thinking the real role for you is Violetta from *La Traviata*. Similar to Mimi in a lot of ways, but, hmm. *Non lo so.* I think Verdi is prettier than Puccini in some ways. I brought you some music, if you want to look it over after dinner."

"Oh, thank you. I don't know *La Traviata* very well."

"I think the difference is that Mimi is often hopeless, but Violetta is full of hope."

And then they were off, discussing various opera plots and voice parts. Mike had a hard time following most of it, but they were talking to each other, so he wasn't bothered. He was content to eat and listen to the conversation.

After dinner wound down, Mike offered everyone ice cream, which was a big hit. Gio and Emma were practically best friends by then.

Gio offered to do the dishes, which Mike tried to talk him out of, but they compromised with Mike putting the food away while Gio got out his sheet music.

Mike overheard Gio say, "This is my favorite part of *La Traviata*. It's part of the finale of Act I. Violetta is a courtesan, used to being treated poorly by men. Then Alfredo comes into her life and declares his love. She's so beautiful that men declare their love for her all the time, so at first she doesn't think much of Alfredo, but then she decides there's something about him. '*Ah, fors'è lui*,' she sings. Maybe it's him. Maybe this man is the one. He is, of course, though there are complications in Act II. It's...." Gio hesitated for a long moment. "Really, the end of *La Traviata* is unbearably tragic. It's this wonderful love story wherein Alfredo loves Violetta despite her past, and she loves him in return, but then she dies of tuberculosis. But this is opera, no? Not many happy endings."

Then Gio hummed.

It didn't have the same force that his voice had in recordings, but he started to sing softly, and there was certainly something there. He finished and said, "Well, two octaves higher, obviously, but what do you think?"

"I like it," Emma said. "I'll definitely consider it."

Mike walked back into the living room and saw them sitting close together with several pages of sheet music spread out on the coffee table. Mike sat next to Emma and said, "How's it going, kiddo?"

"Good." Then Emma's phone rang, preventing further conversation. She hopped off the couch and ran into her bedroom. Mike heard her say, "Hi, Izzy!" before her bedroom door closed.

Mike reached over to Gio and tugged on a lock of his hair. "I appreciate you working with her."

"Of course. I want her to do well. She would have to really screw up at her audition not to get into the program at this point. I don't see that happening—she's too much of a perfectionist—but it's an opportunity for her to shine as well." Gio put a hand on Mike's knee. "At first, I wanted her to get into the program so I could work with her, because I wanted to have my name attached to such a wonderful student. But now I want her to succeed for your sake as well. I want… I don't know. I want lot of things."

Mike leaned over and gave Gio a soft kiss, not a prelude to anything so much as a demonstration of his affection. When he pulled away again, Gio was smiling.

"So, *caro*, what do you usually do on a weeknight like this?" Gio asked.

"In the summer? Well, a lot of the time, Sandy comes over and we watch baseball."

"Baseball?"

"Mm-hmm. Yankees are playing Tampa Bay tonight, I think."

"All right. Then that is what we will do."

"Are you serious?"

Gio nodded, so Mike picked up the remote and flipped on the TV. He found the Yankees game.

"Now, I only know the basics of the game. I never played as a kid. In Italy, everything is *calcio*, or what you call soccer."

"Right. Well, ask me anything."

"Did you play baseball?"

"A little, but mostly just with the kids in my neighborhood. I played football in high school, but the team was really terrible, so I'm not sure that counts."

Gio laughed. "I will admit that I was not athletic at all as a child." He turned toward the TV. "So you are a Yankees fan, I assume."

"Yup."

Mike put his arm behind Gio on the couch. Gio moved closer and then leaned his head on Mike's shoulder, so Mike lightly wrapped his arm around him. He was a little concerned about Emma bursting back out of her room, but as far as public displays of affection went, this one seemed pretty tame.

"What do you like about the game?" Gio asked.

Mike considered the question for a moment. "Well, the thing with a professional game is that it feels tense sometimes, because it's difficult. Like, the whole point is to hit the ball and run around the bases, right? But a good batter only gets a hit about a quarter of the time. An excellent batter only does it about a third of the time."

"Really? It seems like they hit the ball more often than that."

"Well, a hit only counts if the batter gets on base, so he has to do three things when he's at bat. He has to hit the ball, he has to hit it in a way that makes it difficult for the other team to catch it, and he has to make it to first base before the other team gets control of the ball. It's not an easy game, baseball. I think that's what I like about it. And when you put two really great teams against each other and you don't know who will win? I love games like that."

"I see."

They watched the rest of the inning play out, with Gio occasionally asking questions about what was happening, and they were chatting through a commercial break when Emma reemerged. She sat in the armchair.

Gio sat up, leaning away from Mike a little, which Mike appreciated, although he immediately missed the proximity.

"How is Isobel?" Mike asked.

"Good," said Emma. "So, um, the Metropolitan Opera is doing a show in the park on Friday. Can we go?"

"Who is 'we'?"

"Me and Izzy. And you and Gio, if you want."

Mike was touched that she would think of it. "I... yeah. Gio?"

Gio smiled. "Yes, I would like that. Is this Isobel also a singer?"

"No. She plays violin."

"Ah, I see. So she is still musical."

"Yeah. Let me call her back. I think we'd have to get to the park at five. Is that okay?"

"That's fine, sweetie," said Mike.

And she was off again, but Mike felt like peace had been achieved.

GIO tried to discern what was happening in the baseball game. Each time he thought he understood the rules, something would happen on the screen and Mike would react to it in a way that ran contrary to Gio's understanding. After the third time he asked about it, he gave up and just sat back to watch. He was amused how Mike leaned forward during the last inning and seemed to hang on every moment.

After the game ended, Emma hopped up, gave Mike a kiss on the cheek, and announced that she was going to go read in bed.

"Thanks, sweetie," Mike said. "Sleep tight."

Gio wondered if he was thanking her for leaving them alone.

Spending the night was out of the question. Even if Mike would allow it, Gio felt strange about it. Their relationship was too new, too untested to bear anything too intimate with Emma close by. He supposed he could argue his way into sleeping over, but he didn't think he could withstand a night in bed with Mike without touching.

He looked at Mike, who smiled and looked back at Gio. "So," Mike said.

Gio laughed. "Yes. This is a somewhat unprecedented situation."

Mike lifted his hand and lightly ran his fingers across Gio's shoulder. "I wish you could stay, but I think under the circumstances—"

"I know, *caro*."

"Someday, maybe."

Gio leaned closer to Mike, close enough to smell him. Mike had a warm, complex scent that lately Gio had found irresistible. It was part sharp soap, part musk, part mint, but it was all Mike and Gio loved it.

He hooked a hand behind Mike's head and pulled him forward until their lips met in a spectacular kiss. He'd been wanting to kiss Mike, really kiss him, all night and this was the first real opportunity.

Mike pulled away. The room was flooded with the sounds of the sportscasters talking about the game, and Gio suspected Mike had left the TV on to mask any sounds they made. Mike smiled. He leaned back and rested his head on his arm. "I'm really tired."

"Do you want me to go?"

"Not just yet." Mike took Gio's hand. "I like having you here."

"I like being here."

"Do you think it will be weird to do family things with me and Emma?"

Gio considered. "Well, it will be going to see opera. That's right up my alley."

Mike grinned. "You know, you're the first guy I've dated who had anything to talk to Emma about."

"Really?"

"Yeah. Most guys I've met haven't known what to do with a girl. But, hell, she talks about singing most of the time. I can't keep up. But I'm glad that you can."

"You do a better job than you think. It's clear she adores you."

Mike closed his eyes and nodded. "It's just been the two of us for so long. Sometimes I think she raised me as much as I raised her."

They were quiet together for a moment, just gazing at each other and occasionally touching. Mike had that sad expression on his face, as if perhaps he was thinking back on his sob story, on the circumstances that led him to be a single father to Emma. This man was amazing, Gio decided. To have overcome everything he had and still be this hard-working, beautiful, wonderful man was not something to be taken lightly. "You know what's remarkable about you? You seem so well-adjusted for someone who has been through as much as you have." Gio had his own set of trauma, but what Mike had experienced—getting kicked out of the army, disappointing his parents, losing his partner, raising a daughter alone—that was a lot for one man to bear.

Mike smiled ruefully. "Other people have said that. I think I'm better at looking well-adjusted than I am at actually being it."

"Men have been felled by lesser traumas than you've experienced."

Mike shrugged. "I try to keep it together. I don't know. I keep busy, I guess. I don't like to dwell on the past. I have to hold things together, at least for Emma's sake. I can't…. Falling apart is not an option."

Gio leaned over and ran his knuckles gently down the side of Mike's face. "Maybe what you need is someone to help hold you together."

There was a small smile on Mike's lips. He leaned into Gio's touch. "Maybe."

Gio was overcome by the conviction that he wanted to be that person, wanted to hold Mike and help him and make all of his pain go away.

Ah, fors'è lui, he thought. Maybe Mike was the one, the man so completely different from all who had come before that Gio could not help but fall in love with him. If his life were an opera, he'd sing an aria now about how everything was changing and the future looked bright. He could only hope this was not a tragic opera.

SIXTEEN

CENTRAL PARK in the summer was a revelation sometimes, a place out of time and space, an area of the city that didn't belong in the city.

It was a hot August night. On the streets, it was muggy in the way only New York could be, particulates of dirt and grime sticking to the skin. But in the park, everything was clean and green again.

Sort of. Mike followed the path to the meadow with Emma and Isobel, the two of them chattering and not paying attention, periodically needing to be steered out of the way of a dog or random detritus on the walkway. And then there was the meadow, already covered in a mass of people and blankets. Mike took a moment to extend sympathy to the poor, thinning grass of the meadow for having to withstand this crowd. He hadn't been expecting so many people, but he supposed he should have been less surprised that the opera would be such a draw. That, and any free concert in New York was bound to be an attraction.

"Uh, Gio got us a spot, right?" Emma asked.

"He said so." Mike pulled out his phone to see if he'd missed any texts. He saw one from Gio indicating he was up near the right side of the stage. There sure as hell seemed to be a lot of people between where they currently stood and the stage. "We're never going to find him."

"You're calling him Gio now?" asked Isobel, her voice dripping with skepticism.

"He said I could. He *is* Dad's boyfriend."

"I still can't believe that."

"Girls?" said Mike. "I'm right here. You want to maybe not discuss my personal life so loudly around me?"

"Sorry," said Isobel. Then she and Emma started whispering to each other.

"Still right here," Mike said. "Make yourselves useful and keep an eye out for Gio."

Mike led them around the right side of the mass toward the stage. Feeling helpless, he pulled out his phone and called Gio. When Gio answered, Mike said, "Could you stand up and wave or something?"

Gio laughed. "Where are you?"

"I don't know. Right side of the stage."

"Stage right or your right?"

Mike groaned. He wasn't even sure what stage right was. "Uh, my right if I'm facing the stage."

"You must not be far."

They spent a good two minutes trying to wend their way through the crowd, until finally Emma said, "There he is!" and, yes, finally, there was Gio, standing and waving. He grinned when Mike made eye contact.

He'd snagged a pretty good spot and had spread out a blanket that was being held down by a black plastic bag from a bodega and his overstuffed leather messenger bag. When Mike reached the blanket, Gio pulled him into a hug, which was nice. Mike closed his eyes and savored it for a moment before he backed away and introduced Isobel. Emma decreed the spot acceptable and sat down on the blanket.

They all got settled. Mike held up a plastic bag. "We got sandwiches and cookies. I hope turkey's okay."

"It is. I bought some sodas, like you asked."

Mike nodded. "So explain to me what we're watching."

"It's a bunch of stuff," said Emma.

"Yes," said Gio. "Sometimes they do a whole opera, sometimes they just do highlights. This year, they're doing 'The Best of Puccini.' I know one of the baritones singing tonight, so I asked about what they'd be doing. He didn't know for certain, but he implied they didn't want to do a whole opera this year because the audience sometimes loses interest."

"That's dumb," said Emma.

"I know, *cara*, but opera is not as popular as it once was, which you well know. I continue to be surprised so many young people audition to be in my workshop each summer." Gio laughed softly. "But then, this is New York City."

Emma and Gio speculated about which arias the performers would sing while Mike started to fish through the bag of sandwiches and figure out which belonged to each person. None of them were labeled, which was frustrating, so Mike had to open each one. Isobel was going through a vegan phase, so he'd gotten her a portabella mushroom sandwich, and that one at least was easy to identify. But Gio's turkey versus Emma's chicken? Who knew?

Then Emma said, "Do you think they'll do 'Nessun Dorma'?"

Mike froze.

"Undoubtedly," said Gio as if this were no big thing.

"Will that be all right for you?" Mike asked.

"*Carissimo*, I would lead a very difficult life as an opera instructor if I spent the rest of it avoiding that aria. It is perhaps Puccini's most famous composition."

Mike didn't believe it would be that easy for Gio, but he let it go and distributed the sandwiches.

The show began a short time later. It opened with some long orchestral piece that Mike thought sounded vaguely familiar. Then singers trotted onstage, sometimes solo and sometimes in groups of two or three, always in elaborate costumes or ball gowns and tuxes. Gio quizzed the girls on their knowledge of each song, asking Emma to name the opera it came from or the song's context in the story.

As the night went on, they shifted positions on the blanket. Gio sat next to Mike, within touching distance, though he kept his hands to himself. Emma and Isobel sat close and had a series of hushed conversations. From what Mike could pick up, the topic bounced around from the show to the cute boy sitting three blankets over—and he was cute but also way too old for a couple of fourteen-year-old girls to be gawking at—to how gross the vegan cookies were. Mike rolled his eyes at the last bit—the cookies were sort of flavorless, but they were the best Mike could do on short "Izzy is still vegan and can't have anything with dairy and eggs, remember, Dad?" notice.

The performances bored Mike a little, if he was honest. It was hard to pay attention to words he didn't understand. At least at the Met, they showed the English translation on the little screen in front of each seat, and most of the time, he could follow along that way. Here, there was a screen above the stage that had the lyrics, but the glare of the setting sun made it difficult to read. Still, once the sun started setting, the humidity seemed to thin out as well, and it was a nice night, all told. The girls were enjoying themselves, a nice breeze wound its way through the crowd, and he was sitting next to an intriguing, attractive man who was, against all odds, capturing his heart. Mike leaned back on his palms, closed his eyes, and let it all drift over him.

And then there was a change on stage, and Mike looked up. A man in a tux walked onto the stage, and a hush descended on the audience. Mike wondered if the singer was someone famous.

"Gianni Robelleschi," Gio said.

"What does that mean?" asked Mike.

"He's a famous tenor, Dad," said Emma. The "duh" was implied.

Mike glanced at Gio, who looked uneasy. Mike took his hand and held it in the space between his and Gio's thighs. Gio laced their fingers together.

"*Buona notte*," the man on stage said. "Before I sing, I wanted to pay a brief homage to the great men who have sung this song before me."

And Mike got it.

On stage, Robelleschi said, "Many recordings have served to make this song one of the most famous in opera. Domingo, Pavarotti, Boca. Each man put his own spin on the song, and each recording demonstrated such aching emotion. It's an odd song to have become so famous, as it makes little sense taken out of the context of the opera, but it is so beautiful that it is no wonder it is one of the best-loved arias in all of opera." Robelleschi paused and looked down. "A little birdie told me Giovanni Boca is in this very audience somewhere."

A murmur went through the crowd, and everyone started looking around. Gio bowed his head. Luckily, the waning twilight made it difficult to see anyone's faces, Gio's included, so he seemed relatively safe.

"Gianni, no," Gio whispered.

Mike squeezed Gio's hand.

On stage, Robelleschi laughed. "Well, if he is here, I certainly hope he does not laugh me off the stage. So now, I give you 'Nessun Dorma.'"

The little orchestra on the side of the stage started up softly and rose up. Robelleschi took a step back from the microphone and then opened on a strong note, one Mike had now come to recognize.

As the song progressed, Gio's grip on Mike's hand became firmer, until a break when an off-stage choir sang an interlude, when Mike pulled away and put an arm around Gio instead. Mike wasn't sure how Gio felt about public displays of affection, but as it seemed Gio was about to lose his grip on his emotions, the situation seemed to warrant it. Plus, from Mike's casual observation, they were definitely not the only gay couple in the audience.

By the time Robelleschi got to the "*Vincerò*" part at the end, Gio had buried his face in Mike's neck.

Mike rubbed Gio's back when the song was over. It wasn't until the next singer was a few bars into her aria that Gio lifted his head and said, "That was harder than I thought it would be."

"I'm sorry."

Emma, bless her, said, "Hey, Daddy, can we go find the ice cream cart?"

"Sure, sweetie. You need some money?"

"Yeah, that would be good."

Keeping one arm around Gio, Mike managed to fish his wallet out of his back pocket, pull out a few bills, hand them to Emma, and put his wallet back. Parenting—all about multitasking. "But I thought Isobel is vegan?"

"Maybe they have Italian ices or popsicles," Isobel suggested.

"Don't wander off too far, and call me if you can't find us again," Mike told Emma. "I'll send up a flare."

When the girls were gone, Mike pulled Gio closer.

"Thank you for holding me together," Gio said, lifting his head a little.

"Not a problem. It's what I'm here for."

"Ha. Did I not just promise to do the same for you?"

Mike's heart warmed at the memory. "Then it's your turn next time."

There was a brief silence before Gio said, "It's quite something to have the worst moment of your life reenacted on stage."

"I can't even imagine."

Gio leaned on Mike's shoulder. "Thank you," he whispered.

"Believe me. I know better than anyone how your life can just completely change in an instant. You lost something important to you. You don't have to pretend that's a small thing. I know it wasn't. So, you know, you need something, I'm here."

Gio sat up. The singer on stage hit a high note that made the moment seem more dramatic. The music swelled, the singer bellowed, and Gio gazed at Mike with tears in his eyes.

Mike fell irrevocably in love in that moment.

"An instant," Gio murmured.

Mike smiled, for once feeling like everything would be all right. "But maybe life can change for the better in an instant too."

Gio kissed Mike. It was a surging kiss, their lips meeting in a rush, the huge crowd of people around them, a few stars poking through the city haze above them, a soprano belting out her passion on the stage. It was up there with the most romantic moments of Mike's life. He raised a hand and ran it through Gio's hair, wanting to touch him more, wanting to pull him closer.

"Dad, that's gross."

Gio and Mike pulled apart abruptly. Gio laughed. "I imagine this is what having children is like. Perfect moments disturbed by pesky teenaged girls?"

"That's about the sum of it," said Mike.

Emma and Isobel sat back on the blanket. "Here," Emma said. "I got you guys some ice cream sandwiches. We rushed back so they wouldn't melt."

"That was nice of you, Em," Mike said.

The show wrapped up after a few more arias. When it ended, everyone stood, and Gio said, "Hey, Emma, are you interested in meeting some of the singers?"

Emma's eyes widened. "You can do that?"

"Sure."

"Gather up all the trash, girls," Mike said. "Then we can go meet the singers."

"Wow, you're tough," Gio said with a laugh.

A few minutes later, Gio led them to an area behind the stage. He had a few quiet words with the security guards. One of them disappeared and came back a few minutes later with one of the singers. He was a tall, barrel-chested man, still in his tux from his performance. Mike couldn't remember which aria he'd sung, but he had a surprisingly deep voice when he spoke.

He gave Gio a fierce hug, which Mike did not appreciate.

"Ah, Robert, how are you?" said Gio.

"Even more delighted now that you're here!" This Robert had a British accent. "What did you think of our little summertime gala?"

"Marvelous. *Bravissimo.* But you don't need me to tell you that. I mean, what should I say? Some of the best singers in the world just did a free concert, but, you know, it was just all right."

Robert laughed. "Yes, well. Would you like to come back?"

"I would if I can bring my entourage with me."

"Of course. Come on back."

They all followed Robert into a backstage area. Some of the singers and musicians milled about. A woman spotted them and squealed. She ran over and gave Gio a hug.

"Gio! So you *were* in the audience!"

"I was."

"It's so wonderful to see you!" She stepped back and looked around. "And who have you brought with you?"

Mike looked down at Emma, whose face was all naked awe now.

"You're Rita Martinez," she said, her eyes huge. "I have the CD of you as Mimi in *La Bohème*. It's so great."

Gio put a hand on the small of Rita's back. "Rita, this is Emma McPhee, a bright young opera student. Remember that name, because in ten years, you will be competing for parts with her."

Rita shook Emma's hand. Emma still looked completely starstruck.

"This is her friend Isobel, who is a violinist. And this is Emma's father, Mike." Gio looked at Mike with a soft smile on his face. To Rita, he said, "*Lui è il mio innamorato.*"

Mike guessed what Gio said both from context and from the look on Rita's face. She smiled brightly and shook Mike's hand. "It is wonderful to meet you," she said.

Gio took them around and introduced them to a number of the singers. Emma was in heaven, asking for autographs and gushing at the singers she liked. Mike found it gratifying that Gio continued to make it clear that they were together, although he wondered at the wisdom of that in light of the fact of that parent who said she'd make trouble for Gio. Still, these were opera singers, associated with the Metropolitan Opera and not with the Olcott School, so Mike told his doubts to take a break so he could just enjoy being with Gio. It was quite nice being introduced as Gio's significant other and made their relationship tangible in a way it wasn't always, as if telling strangers about it confirmed it wasn't a fantasy.

They ran into Gianni Robelleschi, who looked like he was about to have a stroke as he greeted Gio. They did the introductory song and dance once again, although this time, Gio put his arm around Mike's waist and held on through most of the conversation. Mike thought perhaps he was seeking strength or reassurance.

"I hope I did the song justice," said Robelleschi. "I've been wanting to play Calaf since I was at university."

"It was lovely," Gio said, which Mike thought was charitable of him.

"Yes, marvelous," Mike said to be polite, even though he barely remembered the performance. "Gio, we should probably get the girls home before it gets too late."

Gio nodded and mouthed "thank you" and then shook Robelleschi's hand before departing.

They walked out of the park together, despite Mike pointing out that Gio lived on the west side but they were walking east. Gio said, "I want to spend as much time with you as possible."

Mike wanted to invite Gio back to his apartment, but didn't think he should, under the circumstances. For one thing, Isobel was sleeping over, and having Gio over just seemed inappropriate. So when they got to Fifth Avenue, Gio said he'd get a cab back across the park and Mike pulled him into his arms and hugged him tightly.

"Thank you for a wonderful evening," said Gio in Mike's ear.

"It was good for me too."

Very quietly, Gio said, "When can I get you alone again, *caro*? When can we spend a night together?"

"Soon. I'll try to work something out."

"*Dad*," said Emma, a plea in her voice.

"All right, all right." Mike pulled away from Gio. "Soon," he said.

"Soon," said Gio with a smile. Then he hailed a cab and was gone.

SEVENTEEN

SOON was impeded somewhat by the pending Young Musicians Program auditions. Gio was so busy prepping for his fall classes and attending department events that he couldn't make time for Mike, who was likewise occupied with his own work and getting Emma ready for the audition.

Gio wrestled with whether it was a good idea to pop into the auditions. He was in his office that morning anyway—why did no one tell him when he agreed to teach how much nonsense paperwork there would be?—so when Dacia stopped by and said, "I'm headed to the studio," he thought to himself that perhaps he could just say hi to his workshop students and then disappear. Well, and he'd see Mike, of course.

About ten minutes before auditions were supposed to start, he popped his head into the classroom where all of the singers and their parents were gathering. Naturally, the first person he ran into was Tracy Quinlan.

"Mr. Boca!" she said brightly. "How nice of you to stop by! I thought you didn't have anything to do with these auditions."

That was certainly a leading statement. He took it for what it was and said, "I don't. I just wanted to stop by and see which of my students were here. I thought I'd wish them good luck."

Over the top of Tracy's perfectly coiffed head, Gio spotted Mike talking with Emma in the corner of the room. He looked up and made eye contact with Gio. He smiled and went back to his conversation.

This was frustrating. In an ideal world, Gio could just stroll right into the room, greet Mike in a way that was appropriate but still indicative of the sort of relationship they had, wish Emma good luck, and stand on the sidelines with the parents. Instead, he had to make nice with Tracy Quinlan and the parents of all of the rest of his students who had come to the audition. Not only that, and he was probably paranoid, but it seemed best to stay away from the audition room for fear of feeding into any false perceptions.

Tracy said, "Amelia's a little nervous. We prepared an aria from *La Bohème*."

"Oh? Which one?"

"Sì. Mi chiamano Mimì."

"Excellent choice," said Gio, glad he'd talked Emma out of that one. The song was also out of Amelia's range; she was really more of a mezzo but was, as many naïve but ambitious girls were, always gunning for all the prima donna soprano parts. Not to mention, it was not one of Gio's favorite arias.

"I know it's cliché, but I've always loved *La Bohème*," Tracy said. "You are also a big fan of Puccini, are you not?"

"Yes." He refused to elaborate. There were no words for how much Gio wanted this conversation to be over.

Tracy crossed her arms primly. "Amelia, darling, come say hello to Mr. Boca."

Amelia trotted over and said hello.

"Wasn't it nice of Mr. Boca to drop by your audition? Do you have any words of wisdom, sir?"

"Relax," Gio said. "When you tense up, you tend to go flat, and you'll want to be as on-pitch as possible."

"Easy for you to say," Amelia mumbled.

"Be polite," her mother admonished.

"I'm sure you'll do fine," Gio said.

Tracy gave him The Look that all parents did when they wanted to ensure he got them the right outcome. He supposed coming down here wrecked his plausible deniability.

Howell Loughton, the head of the voice department, strolled in. He walked right up to Gio and slapped him on the back. "For a man who so vociferously protested placement on the audition committee, it's a little odd to see you here."

Gio felt like he'd been caught in a lie, although logically he knew he'd done nothing wrong. "I was just saying hello to a few of my workshop students."

"Ah, yes. Where is this prodigy you were telling me about?"

Tracy gave Gio a stern look.

Gio said, "Well, I wouldn't want to say anything to bias the committee while they're still in earshot, so we can discuss it later." He gestured toward Dacia, who was chatting with Greg from the workshop. "Are you staying for the auditions?"

"I have a few minutes to spare. I thought I might watch a few."

"Mr. Laughton," Tracy said. "It is delightful to see you again."

"Likewise, Mrs. Quinlan. How is your husband?"

"He's doing well. He had to work this afternoon, unfortunately. But, oh, we did enjoy having you to dinner last week. We must do it again!"

It took a lot for Gio not to roll his eyes.

Howell chuckled. "Yes, definitely. Well. Good luck with your audition, Emily."

"It's Amelia," said Tracy.

Gio excused himself to say hello to his other students, though he paused for thirty seconds to figure out the best route through the crowd. He talked to Marie first, and then Greg after Dacia had moved on, and then at last walked up to Emma and made a big show of shaking her hand.

"Well, this is awkward," said Mike.

"I'm sorry," Gio said sotto voce. "Both my boss and my nemesis are currently watching me, so I can't do anything that would seem to be favoring Emma. Although once she opens her mouth, it won't matter, hopefully."

"Your nemesis?" asked Mike.

Gio didn't feel like he could elaborate. He tilted his head toward Tracy Quinlan, hoping to convey the relevant information through body language and telepathy. Mike nodded, so maybe he understood.

"I decided to go with 'Ah, fors'è lui' after all," Emma said.

"That is the perfect choice, because Amelia Quinlan is singing 'Sì. Mi chiamano Mimì.'"

Emma's jaw dropped. "Are you serious? She was the one who suggested I sing it. Said it was perfect for me. She was going to do something from *Tosca*."

As sabotage attempts went, this was an odd one, and sure to fail given that Emma would undoubtedly outshine Amelia. "Interesting," Gio said. He glanced back at Amelia, who stood next to her chattering mother and looked bored. Gio supposed the blank expression on her face also could have been caused by nerves, but Gio suspected Amelia cared a lot less about this audition than her mother did.

"Is something going on with that woman?" asked Mike quietly, his gaze on Tracy.

"I'll explain later," said Gio, trying to think of a way to gracefully bow out of the room. "Good luck with the audition, Emma. Not that you need it. Remember to sing from the top of your head."

Gio wanted to watch the auditions but thought better of it. He shook Mike's hand, which felt like both the most appropriate and most absurd thing he could do. Then he turned to the room. "Best of luck, everyone. *In bocca al lupo.*" He walked back out into the hall.

Dacia followed him out. In rapid Italian, she said, "You are crazy. You shouldn't be here. Mrs. Q has you in her sights and intends to blame you if her daughter doesn't get into the program."

"I wanted to see—"

"I know who you wanted to see." She grunted. "I overheard the girl in question warming up about an hour ago. She's fine, but she's not as good as most of these other singers."

"What would you have me do? What will *you* do? She'll come after you and the other committee members next. She's already spoken with Howell. She made a big show of mentioning how the Q family had dinner with him last week."

"She knows about you and Mike." Dacia spared a glance toward the classroom. "She knows you and I are friends. If she goes to Howell and exposes your affair, Howell could look at it as favoritism. She'll tell him something that will put you in a bad light. That means either disciplinary action for you or Emma getting kicked out of the program."

"He wouldn't throw Emma out of the program."

"He might. You don't know what he would do. You know as well as I do that the Quinlans are ruthless. Howell might be persuaded by the great sum of money they are no longer contributing once their daughter gets rejected from the program. But I, not to mention this committee, will not admit a girl who doesn't deserve a spot. We've got six spots open and thirty students auditioning for them."

"I don't mean to put you in a difficult position." The words sounded weak to Gio's ears. He didn't want to cause trouble for Dacia, but he knew he was anyway so he could have Mike.

She crossed her arms over her chest. "I love you, Gio. You know that. I want you to be happy, and if this man makes you happy, then that is good. But you've created a mess. Mrs. Q will use your relationship as a weapon against you if she does not get her way. I do not wish for bad things to happen to you, but I know how this girl performs. She barely even wants to be here. How can I admit a student like that to this program in good faith? But her family keeps this school afloat. If she pulls out funding, programs will get cut. Your opera workshop will probably be the first thing to go."

"You know I would never ask you to compromise your integrity."

"I still won't."

"Shit." There was just nothing else for Gio to say.

"Howell's around today," said Dacia. "You can't let him see you talking to your boyfriend. Just in case."

Gio kicked the wall, which was not at all satisfying. Maybe he'd been cocky, but it hadn't ever seemed like a possibility that Emma wouldn't get into the program. She was too talented by far to get rejected. He'd been wagering with himself that Tracy Quinlan didn't really have the guts to go to Howell, but if she and her husband were inviting him over to dinner, maybe she was capable of more than he thought. Still, he imagined he'd be reprimanded but keep his job, since there was no rule against dating a student's parent, and more to the point, Emma was no longer technically his student.

Now he wondered just how much trouble Tracy Quinlan could cause for him.

"I am so sorry, Dacia."

"Knowing what I know puts me in an untenable position," Dacia said, still speaking Italian. "And even if I did go against my conscience, the other committee members could, and probably will, still reject her."

Gio glanced back at the classroom, where Tracy Quinlan was lingering near the doorway. The *her* in question was so clearly Amelia, and Gio wondered how much Italian—if any—Tracy could comprehend.

"It is out of our hands, then," he said.

Dacia bit her lip and looked toward the classroom. "I just do not know what to do or what we can do. Perhaps I'm wrong and nothing will come of this. Perhaps this girl will give a fantastic audition and get in with no problem. Perhaps Howell can see right through everyone's bullshit. But we should be prepared for certain consequences." She sighed. "I love you, but I cannot help you now."

Gio nodded. "Nor should you have to. I understand, Dacia." He looked down the hall and contemplated hiding in his office for the rest of the day. But then he added, just so Dacia would understand, "I think I'm falling in love with him."

The hard look on Dacia's face softened, but she said, "You better be sure before you put your ass on the line."

WHEN Emma's name was called, Mike walked with her to the studio room where they were holding the audition. "I'll be right out here, okay?" He hugged her tightly. "I love you so much."

"I love you too, Daddy."

"You'll do great."

Mike waited outside the room as she went in and someone closed the door. After a moment, there was muffled speaking and then the prettiest sound drifted out of the room. He had been hearing her sing around the apartment all week, but just as with the final workshop show, it was another thing entirely to hear her sing for other people. Her voice was light and airy, like a bird singing, but there was strong emotion behind it too. Mike had no idea what the words meant, but it sounded like pain and love and hope all rolled together, and he marveled that a girl as young as Emma could reach into herself and act out those feelings. He leaned against the wall and closed his eyes for a moment. He didn't have the vocabulary to describe it, but it was beautiful and he could hardly believe the sound came from Emma.

Gio appeared down the hall. He gestured toward the studio and Mike nodded. Gio looked around and then walked right up to Mike and pecked him on the lips.

They both just listened for a moment. Gio closed his eyes and briefly conducted her with a few sweeping hand motions, but then he stood still and smiled. Mike wasn't quite sure what to make of his presence. He was glad to see Gio, although perhaps not at the expense of whatever trouble it might cause if that nemesis woman was around.

A man appeared at the end of the hall and walked right toward them. He stopped next to Gio and listened for a moment. "Is that the girl you were telling me about?" the man asked quietly.

"Yes," Gio whispered.

Mike wondered who the man was, but he also knew there couldn't be much more to the aria. They all stood there listening until she finished singing. And even then, once the song ended, everyone just stood there and savored it for a moment. Mike was too impressed and surprised to speak.

"Quite a lovely voice," the man said, looking dazed. "What was her name?"

"Emma McPhee," said Gio. "This is her father, Mike. Mike, this is Howell Laughton. He's the head of the voice department here."

Mike shook Howell Laughton's hand.

"I have to run," Gio said, panic etched all over his face. "Good luck!"

Gio left so fast he almost literally was running. *This is bad*, Mike thought. He wondered if Gio was in trouble and if there was anything Mike could do.

Now, however, he was left standing in an empty hallway with the head of the voice department. He didn't want to make small talk with Howell Laughton. He wanted to kiss Gio. He wanted to rescue Emma at the end of her audition. But, no, he found himself explaining what he did for a living and how much Emma loved opera to a strange man while he waited for Emma to finish talking with the audition committee. Then, finally, she emerged with a grin on her face.

"Sounds like you bombed," Mike said with mock gravity.

She rolled her eyes. "Ms. Russini said it was one of the best auditions she's seen all day!"

Mike put his arm around her and gave her a quick hug. "I'm so proud of you, sweetie." He glanced at Howell Laughton, who rocked on his heels. "Do you know Mr. Laughton? He is the head of the voice department at Olcott."

She shook her head but extended her hand to him. He shook her hand and said, "I have been hearing about you all summer, Miss McPhee. I believe you will make a fine addition to our program."

Emma beamed. "Thank you!" she squealed.

Mike held back a laugh. She was so serious about her music it was hard to remember sometimes that, at the end of the day, she was still a fourteen-year-old girl. And still, he could see the baby she'd been, the toddler, the girl. He was enormously proud of her.

Laughton smiled. "There are cookies and juice back in the classroom where you were waiting. Help yourself." He patted Mike on the shoulder and then went into the audition studio.

Mike escorted Emma back down the hall. "So how does it feel to be the singer everyone is talking about?" he asked.

"It's not like that."

Mike chuckled. Then his phone buzzed in his pocket, so he checked it. It was a text from Gio: *Tell the little songbird she is a star and I'm proud of her.*

Mike showed Emma the message. She grinned. "Don't let it go to your head," Mike added.

As they walked back into the room, Emma said, "This is probably not the time to ask, but, like, you really like him, right?"

"Yeah, I do."

"So is it, like, serious? What are your intentions?" She gave him a stern face.

He ruffled her hair. "It is serious, but I don't know yet. Don't be a pest."

They each had a cup of juice and a couple of cookies. Emma chatted with the kids she knew, and Mike chatted with a few of the parents. Now that most of the auditions were over, the atmosphere in the room was a lot more relaxed. After about an hour, Dacia came by the room and knocked on the doorframe.

"Ladies and gentlemen, thank you so much for coming today. This was a spectacular round of auditions. Final decisions will be made over the next couple of days, and we will let you know next week. *Buona fortuna, ragazzi.*" Then she turned around and left the room.

Something wasn't quite right. Gio had told Mike they'd post who got into the program that afternoon. But no one else seemed bothered, so he ordered Emma to gather her things. The change in procedure nagged at Mike, but as there was nothing he could do about it, he figured it was better to get out of the school.

EIGHTEEN

WHEN Mike opened the door, Gio stood there wringing his hands.

"Are you all right?"

Though Mike moved out of the way to let Gio in, Gio continued to stand in the hallway outside Mike's apartment.

"Gio?"

"It's my fault."

"Okay. Are you going to come in or just stand in the hallway?" He had no clue what was going on, but he figured he could get to the bottom of it better if they were sitting.

Gio looked around and then nodded and walked into the apartment. The TV was on low, the din of a baseball game filling the small living room with sound. Mike had been looking through a catalog, trying to figure out which samples to order for a bathroom job on Eighty-sixth Street while he waited for Gio to arrive. Emma had gone off to Isobel's for the night, so Mike had called and invited Gio over.

It was the day after the auditions, and Mike still hadn't heard if Emma had gotten in. He'd been hoping Gio might have heard something, but he didn't want to press the issue. He'd been looking forward to a quiet, relaxed evening with Gio all day.

But Gio looked seriously troubled now, his brow furrowed as he fidgeted and tugged on the hem or fiddled with the buttons of his shirt.

"What is your fault?" Mike asked after he felt like he'd given Gio sufficient time to explain himself on his own.

Gio frowned. "Amelia Quinlan was not chosen to be admitted to the Young Musicians Program."

Something about that pinged Mike's memory, but he couldn't quite figure out what the issue was here. "How is that your fault? You weren't on the audition committee."

Gio held up his hand. "Thirty-one students auditioned for six slots, and Amelia was middle of the pack. There's no way she could have made it. The other singers were just far more talented."

"Gio, just tell me what happened."

Gio began to pace. "Even though the list of admitted students has not been released, Tracy Quinlan found out about the results somehow, probably through her husband's friendship with the department chair, and now she's livid. I think I already mentioned that she donates a lot of money to the school, to arts all over this city, and she thinks that should get her some special dispensation. It doesn't matter that sixteen other kids gave better auditions than Amelia."

Mike still wasn't able to follow. "What—"

"Tracy Quinlan is causing trouble. She told my boss that she had scandalous news that would change the outcome of the auditions. She knows about us, Mike, and she's been holding that over my head for weeks, threatening to go to the school with evidence that I'm helping Emma in exchange for sexual favors from you."

Then Mike got it. He sat on the couch. "But that's not true." He turned over what Gio had said in his head. "You think she went to your boss about it?"

"I'm not certain, but it seems that way. She spent an hour in his office this afternoon. I asked him about it afterward, and he told me he had some things to think about but he'd speak with me on Monday." Gio pressed his fist to his mouth for a brief moment and then said, "I'm so, so sorry."

Mike looked up at Gio, who had such a frantic expression on his face it was all Mike could do to stay seated and not try to touch Gio or make it go away. He felt, though, that there was something he was still missing. "Why are you apologizing?"

"I don't care about me. If I get fired, well, there are other schools. Dating the parent of a student is not technically against the rules, but I don't always have the best understanding of employment rules in America. It's not illegal, but perhaps it is frowned upon, and if Tracy throws her money around and makes enough noise, maybe there will be tangible consequences for me. Maybe I become persona non grata. Maybe I never get a job in this city again. That's fine, there are other opportunities. I can go to LA, I can go back to Italy. It is not me I'm worried about. But she could cause real problems for Emma."

That made Mike's heart stop. So much ran through him at once, like there were wild horses running across his chest. First Gio had implied that leaving New York was an option, but that was a terrible option in Mike's estimation, because it would take him away. And then Gio had said Tracy Quinlan could do something to Emma. Both possibilities took Mike's breath away.

"What could she do?"

"Get Emma kicked out of the program, for one. I didn't think that was a possibility, because even Howell—my boss—heard her audition, and her talent is undeniable. I mean, you were there, you saw him listening. But Dacia implied money might overcome talent in this case, and if Tracy makes a big enough imbroglio…." Gio sighed and dropped his arms to his sides. "The school does not want any appearance of impropriety, especially if it means losing one of its biggest donors."

A wave of panic went through Mike, making bile rise up his esophagus. He swallowed and said, "What can we do?"

"Nothing." Gio walked over and sat next to Mike on the couch. "There's nothing to be done. I suppose we could lie and say there's no affair. I am tired of lurking around, though."

"I would lie for Emma's sake."

"And stay away from me for a while too, I'd wager." There was a tinge of bitterness in Gio's voice.

"Emma's my daughter. She is my priority."

"And what of me, *caro*? Would you leave me if it meant your daughter would get what she wanted?"

Mike was struck by the unfairness of the question. "You can't ask me to choose."

Gio nodded. "You would choose Emma, as is right. You do not have to try to appease my feelings."

"I'm sorry." God, this was an awful situation. He didn't want to choose between his daughter and Gio. He didn't want to lie, and he was tired of sneaking around as well, not that they'd even been that sneaky lately. He shouldn't have to do any of those things. He hadn't done anything wrong. Had he?

He didn't have a lot of money, that was true. But Emma deserved a shot.

"It may be moot," said Gio. "Maybe we lie, maybe we separate for a while. Maybe we wait a few weeks for the scandal to blow over and then resume our relationship, although we saw how well that worked out last time. Maybe nothing will come of this. I can't imagine what evidence Tracy thinks she has."

"But if she pays the school enough money, her daughter will get into the program and Emma will get kicked out."

"That is a worst-case scenario, but it is possible." Gio frowned. "I'll tell you this. It's breaking my heart, do you know that? I keep thinking, if I had resisted temptation, if I had just stayed away, none of this would matter and Emma would get into the program with no controversy. She really is the best singer anyone has seen in a long time. She deserves that spot."

Mike grunted. He didn't blame Gio for this mess. "I asked you out, as I recall."

"Jeopardizing Emma was never my aim."

"I know."

"I want her to be successful. *Dio.* I want to continue to work with her. She is *la mia stella*, and she will soon be a star for everyone. She should be. I hate to think I might have done something to put that at risk."

Panic morphed into anger. Mike looked at Gio and seethed a little, both at the position he'd been put in by Gio, whom Mike understood was now forcing him into a decision of some sort, and by Tracy Quinlan and her fucking money, because money could always elevate the mediocre over the talented but poor. Wasn't that the story of Mike's life?

He and Emma shared this tiny apartment on the far East Side of Manhattan, and he'd been working tirelessly for eleven years to build his business up to the point where he could squirrel away enough money to pay for private voice lessons. Now that Emma had, hopefully, gotten into this program, he would have to save more money to keep her there. He was willing to put his own life on hold to make her happy, to work harder and make sacrifices, and it had never occurred to him to live any other way.

But now there was also Gio, who had come into Mike's life and made him see that his own happiness was within his grasp, who had filled up the empty places in him, who made him want even more. When Mike was with Gio, he felt like more things were possible. He had always prioritized Emma over everything else in his life, but giving up the man who had come to mean so much to him was not a sacrifice he was willing to make.

Mike rubbed his face and mulled it over. Perhaps all of it was for naught. Everything Mike had done, every sacrifice he had made, every penny he had saved, every goddamned thing he had done or chosen for a decade could have meant nothing. All because some woman had more money.

He stood up with a groan. He felt Gio's gaze on him as he paced in front of the TV. "Is this what the delay was about? Emma and I both thought they were going to announce who got in the same day as the audition."

"I imagine so. I don't really know, though. Usually Dacia is my main information source, but she won't talk to me about this. Said it's better if I don't know too much."

It was an enormously frustrating situation. "I can't just sit here and wait for the call from the school telling me that Emma didn't get in after all. When Dacia called me yesterday, she all but assured me Emma was in."

"She called you?" There was a serious amount of distress in Gio's voice.

"Yeah, she… she said there was some kind of delay with the decision while they waited for everyone who auditioned to get all the right paperwork in. But she told me that Emma was pretty much in. Now you say she might not get in because of this Quinlan woman. So that's it, right? That's the delay."

Gio put his head in his hands. "It is my fault. I got cocky. And now I've fucked things up for you. I will never forgive myself if Emma doesn't get into the program."

Mike was pretty steamed, but it was clear Gio was agonizing over this. Mike took a deep breath and tried to calm down. This situation wasn't Gio's fault. It was too late to change it. Because even if they broke up right this moment, it wouldn't stop Tracy Quinlan. And, besides, Mike didn't want to end this relationship, not now. He couldn't do it.

He sat back down on the couch.

"*Mi dispiace*," Gio said.

"What does that mean?"

"I'm sorry."

Mike reached over and ran his hand over Gio's head. He gently moved Gio's hands away from his face. Then he caressed Gio's face with his thumbs. "It is not your fault."

Gio looked at Mike for a long moment and then pulled away abruptly. "Bah," he said. "Stage parents. I have had to deal with them from the moment I started teaching. Tracy Quinlan is not unique. But this... this hurts me. This problem, it is getting to me like no stage parent has before. Why do you think that is?"

"Because of me." What other explanation was there?

"Because of Emma. I do genuinely care for her. I want her to succeed. I have had protégés before, but none like this, none I felt this way about."

It was like Gio had wrapped his hand around Mike's heart and squeezed. "Gio, I—"

"*Ti amo*, Mike. I love you so much, and Emma too. It rips me up inside that something bad could happen to her because of something I did."

Mike's eyes stung. His heart pounded. His insides churned. He put his palm on Gio's cheek and then leaned forward and kissed Gio gently. Against Gio's mouth, he said, "I love you too. I...." He wanted to say more, but there was nothing more to say. So he kissed Gio again. And again.

It should have been a joyous moment, but it was bittersweet, tinged with anger and frustration over the situation they'd found themselves in.

"So what do we do?" asked Mike.

"I'll talk to Howell. I'll figure this out. I'll quit if I must in order to keep Emma in the program."

Mike pulled Gio close. "And then would you leave New York? Would you leave me?"

"No. I don't know what I'd... but, no. Not like this, *caro*. That is, if another opportunity came up in another city, perhaps I would consider... ack, I don't know." Gio took a deep breath and clung to Mike. "Sometimes, when I'm lying alone in bed, I imagine what it would be like to have you as my family. Both of you. I like that vision. I want it so much. It's a lot to ask of someone, to let me into his life that way, but you have. How could I give that up?"

Mike closed his eyes and pictured that. He could imagine the three of them eating dinner together, traveling together, spending lazy weekend afternoons at home together. It was so easy to picture that Mike could practically reach out and touch the image. He wanted to. He wanted that badly. He held Gio and knew his anger was not for Gio, but for the people who would dare try to take this rare, precious thing away from him.

Gio put his arms around Mike, and they held each other for a long moment. Then Mike, feeling inspired, said, "We should go dancing."

Gio laughed. "What?"

Mike pulled away slightly and looked at Gio, really looked. What he saw were lines etched into his face from stress and fatigue, red around his eyes, flushed cheeks, ruffled hair. He looked beautiful and he looked tired, and that went a long way toward convincing Mike of Gio's sincerity. And, truly, how could Mike give up this man who loved him, and whom he loved? Mike hadn't thought he'd ever love anyone as much as he had Evan, but this was something akin to that. Gio could never replace Evan, and that had been a different kind of love, one borne of stolen moments and desperate youth. This was more mature, but no less intense. Mike hadn't realized how lonely he'd been without someone until having to face the prospect of giving up Gio.

"Let's go dancing," Mike repeated. "Sitting around here is just going to make us worry. Let's get rid of some of this nervous energy."

Gio laughed. "That first night we went out, Sandy said that dancing was how you let off steam."

"It is." Mike smiled. "And I really loved dancing with you."

Gio kissed him. "Then let's go."

THEY took the subway down to the East Village and found a gay club Mike knew. It was playing tremendously loud music. Gio didn't quite understand the appeal of the throb of bass and the pounding of drums—the sort of music that made one's chest vibrate—but Mike seemed to be in his element. He'd dressed for it too; he'd changed into a sleeveless T-shirt that displayed his amazing arms before they left. He'd lent Gio a T-shirt that fit well enough that Gio wondered how tight it was on Mike.

He was struck by how different their bodies were. Gio had been starting to feel his age lately, particularly as Mike took his hand and pulled him past all of the young men in the club. Gio's hair was graying, his body wasn't as firm and strong as he would have liked, and he was starting to notice crow's feet near his eyes. Mike, who was the same age, looked five or more years younger, his hair still dark, his skin still smooth, and his body strong and muscular. It was a body hard fought for, and Gio knew that; Mike's fingers were calloused, his skin rough to the touch in places, and he had scars and the tiny tattoo of a star on his bicep to commemorate his time in the army. To Gio, the flaws made Mike better, made him a more complete person. An incredibly sexy complete person.

And so they danced. Mike's movements had a fluidity to them that no man his size should have had. Gio was reminded of the way Mike expressed the music within him, that the dancing, the movement—the slide of his feet, the wave of his hands, the undulations of his body—were manifestations of the music trying to break out. Mike could say things with his body that he couldn't say in normal speech. It was a marvel, a miracle, and Gio struggled to keep up.

Mike didn't seem to mind. He danced with Gio, steered him through dances, touched him everywhere. They danced closely and ground their bodies together. Mike ran his hands over Gio, so Gio ran his hands over Mike, savoring his slick skin and his strong body. They kissed during a particularly sexy song, and that was thrilling, with an energy behind it that Gio had never experienced.

After a couple of hours, when Gio was tired but Mike's energy still seemed boundless, they hailed a cab and went back up to Mike's apartment. Mike didn't even pretend to stall; once the door was closed, he grabbed Gio's hand and pulled him into the bedroom. There Mike kissed Gio, and it was just as heady as it had been in the club, only more sexy, more full of promise and urgency, because here they were alone instead of in the middle of a club.

"Did you work out whatever you had to?" Gio asked breathlessly as Mike started divesting him of his clothing.

"Almost." He kissed Gio hard, biting into Gio's lower lip. Then he laughed suddenly.

"What?" Gio asked.

"I was just trying to come up with a classy way to tell you what I want. Like, 'make love to me,' or something. But that sounds so hokey."

"What *do* you want?"

Mike grabbed Gio by the hips and then tilted his head, considering. "I want you to fuck me. Hard. But, like, tenderly. Like the way we were dancing."

Gio's pulse was racing, but he laughed. "All right. I'll see what I can do."

He pushed Mike toward the bed. Together, they wriggled out of their clothes until they were a naked tangle of limbs. Mike sat on the bed and pulled Gio down with him. They kissed and pressed their bodies together, Gio on top, and Gio closed his eyes to sink into the feeling of his skin against Mike's, everything slick and smooth and hard and soft. He thrust his hips against Mike's thigh, Mike's hard cock hovering nearby, a delicious temptation.

Gio planted kisses down Mike's chest and took note of the texture: the hair on Mike's chest tickled his face but was also arousing, masculine. Gio traced the lines of it with his tongue, following the pattern down Mike's tight stomach. Mike smelled amazing, of sweat and mint and Mike. Mike squirmed under him and whimpered softly, but this was just the beginning of Gio's adventure across Mike's body.

Like the way we were dancing, Mike had said. Gio thought of club dancing, of the raw quality of it, of how it was completely different from ballet or other more traditional kinds of dance and yet the same. Mike's movements had the same beauty and poetry as the most poised ballet dancer. And dancing with Mike in the club with the bass from the music thumping in his chest had an animal quality to it. It was improvised and erotic. It was sexy and fun. It was one of the best parts of being with Mike, certainly; Gio loved to watch the music flow through him. And it didn't matter that Gio loved opera and Mike loved thumping club music, because in the end, it was all the same. The crescendo of drums was like the roaring of a singer's voice, like the buildup to a toe-curling orgasm.

So Gio danced with Mike on the bed, in the ways Mike had taught him, by running his hands over Mike's body and thrusting his hips, but also by watching Mike's reactions and responding. He kissed the area around Mike's belly button, dug his nails into the soft flesh of Mike's ass, licked along the line of hair that led to Mike's cock. He then licked from the base of Mike's cock to the tip, and it felt like the beginning of something important. Mike sucked in a breath and writhed beneath him.

Gio took Mike's cock into his mouth and sucked on it gently. Here, too, the texture of Mike's body was different, exciting, smoother, and harder, tasting of salt. Mike touched Gio's head lightly, then the side of his face, then Gio's fingers at the base of Mike's cock, at the side of Mike's hip. Mike bucked against Gio's mouth, so Gio held him down until Gio could get his fill of all this magnificent flesh. If there had ever been any question about what Gio really desired, this resolved it, because Mike tasted divine and fit into Gio's mouth so well this was clearly where Gio was meant to be.

But Mike had wanted to be fucked, too, so this would not be enough, and Gio wanted to be inside him intensely. His own cock was throbbing, and the tingles on his skin were like cries for release. Gio wanted to sink into all this lovely flesh, to become part of Mike, to be with him always.

He continued to suck on Mike and pull all manner of sounds from him now—hisses and grunts mostly, but occasionally a soft moan that Gio felt in his spine—and gently let his fingers wander to the crack of Mike's ass. Mike spread his legs wide in invitation, so Gio continued his exploration, getting to know the textures and scents of this part of Mike's body. He ran his thumb over Mike's balls, then licked them, took one in his mouth while continuing to jerk Mike with one hand and find Mike's hole with the other. The smell was intoxicating, like Mike always smelled, but more intense.

Gio spit on his fingers and pressed one into the tight muscle of Mike's entrance. Mike hissed and wriggled. Gio heard a drawer open and felt Mike's weight shift, but he was too absorbed in what he was doing to look up, and Mike certainly hadn't said to stop. He went back to sucking on Mike's cock when Mike pressed a bottle of lube into his hand.

Aha. Gio poured some on his fingers and touched Mike anywhere he could. Mike spread his legs wider, like it was open season on that part of his body, and Gio took advantage, smearing lube at the entrance to Mike's body and then pouring more and sliding a finger inside.

He sucked on Mike's cock and licked his balls and tasted skin and hair and everything that was available while he prepared Mike for their coupling, and by the time he deemed Mike stretched enough, he was so anxious and aroused it almost hurt.

He crawled back up Mike's body. Mike handed him a condom. As he rolled it on, Gio said, "I do love you, you know."

"I know," Mike said with a smile. "I never expected to feel this way, but I love you too."

It was hard to remember what the resistance was between them as Mike pushed Gio onto his back. Mike was so goddamn beautiful, so sexy, flawed and yet perfect. He poured more lube on Gio's cock and then straddled his hips. He took a moment to position himself and then with painful slowness, he lowered himself.

Gio sank into Mike at last. The grip was tight, but it was smooth going, and the blissed-out look on Mike's face told Gio all he needed to know. Mike threw his head back once he was seated and then started to move. The sensation of finally being inside Mike was a relief in a way, but it felt too charged up, too urgent. Gio thrust his hips up to meet Mike's movements. Mike threw his hands up in the air, stretching all that muscle, letting his body ripple, and for a few glorious moments, he seemed to dance on Gio's cock. Gio had never seen or experienced anything like it. This man, this strange, humble man, had become a crucial part of Gio's life. Now Gio's pulse pounded and his body arched and he loved every moment of being a part of Mike. If only it could last forever.

He reached over and grabbed Mike's cock. He poured lube on it and then stroked it slowly. Mike was all in proportion, his cock generous but a good size for his body. It was familiar, now that they'd had sex a few times, now that Gio had put this part of Mike in his mouth, but it was new and interesting too. It was part of Mike, the man Gio loved, and it was a pretty great part. Gio could not make himself stop stroking, stop touching, not even when Mike said, "Jesus, if you keep that up, I'm going to come too soon," not even when Mike put his hands on Gio's chest and ground harder against him and groaned, not even when Mike panted, "Holy shit, I'm gonna come." Gio kept stroking as ribbons of cum streaked his abdomen.

Watching Mike come was maybe one of the great wonders of the world.

It was so erotic Gio marveled that he couldn't grow harder, that the grip Mike's body had on his cock only got more intense, that the electricity pulsing through him had only one place to go. The orgasm must have started at the tips of his hair, and it traveled over his face, to his neck, down his spine, from his toes up his legs, and then everything met in the middle and with one more deep thrust, he came inside Mike. Mike was already a little limp from his orgasm, so Gio put his arms around him and held him tight as he thrust and emptied and everything went still and quiet for a moment, and then there were sparks and his brain stopped working. He held Mike tightly because doing so brought him more pleasure, but also because he loved Mike, felt like he did so with his whole heart, and he wanted to be as close to this man as he could for as long as it lasted. As the pleasure waned, Gio planted kisses all over Mike's face until their lips met in a powerful collision.

They kissed and kissed, frantic still, running their hands through hair and over skin, until Mike shifted and Gio slid out of him, and even then, they still kissed for a few moments, at least until it started to get uncomfortable. Without a word, Mike got up and offered Gio a hand, and they kept touching each other on their way into the bathroom, where they cleaned each other up and kissed some more. Gio couldn't get enough of this, couldn't get enough Mike, and didn't think he ever would.

NINETEEN

GIO woke up in the middle of the night. At first he wasn't sure why. It took him a moment to put together that he was not home but was instead in Mike's wide and delightfully comfortable bed. The air conditioner in the window cycled on suddenly, so Gio supposed the change in sound could have woken him up, but then he rolled onto his side and saw that Mike was awake and staring at the ceiling.

"*Caro*," Gio whispered.

Mike sighed and put a hand over his eyes.

Gio reached over and put a hand on Mike's chest. "What is it?"

"I don't… it's nothing."

"Clearly it's something. You look troubled."

Mike sighed again and shook his head, but then he said, "Nightmare."

"Tell me about it. Maybe that will help you fall back to sleep."

"No, I… no. I can't."

"Why not? Do you not remember?"

Mike turned his head slightly and looked at Gio. "I remember."

"Mike. Talk to me."

Mike pursed his lips and looked at the ceiling again. "It's… I haven't had this dream in a very long time. But in it, I'm there when Evan dies. Like, standing right next to him, where his partner was when it really happened. And I see the other dude pick up his gun, and every time I warn Evan not to jump, but then he does it anyway. Sometimes the girl dies too, so Evan put himself in harm's way for nothing." He lifted his hands and rubbed his eyes.

Gio's heart seized. He'd been wondering how long it would take the specter of Evan to make an appearance. He'd been thinking about it since Emma had shown him that photo in the living room of her "other dad." He'd known Mike had loved before, but then, so had Gio. A lot of time had passed. And yet it was clear that at least a small part of Mike still mourned his late partner and probably always would.

Mike said, "I think it's been more than a year since I've had that dream. I used to have it all the time the first couple of years after he died, but then it became more rare. But now I keep thinking, well, last time I really cared about someone, he was taken from me."

Gio took Mike's hand and murmured his name.

"I rationalize it," Mike went on. "You're not in a dangerous profession. You can't be taken in the same way."

Trying for levity, Gio said, "Well, *caro*, I do work with teenagers. They are pretty ruthless."

"That's not funny."

Chastened, Gio murmured, "*Mi dispiace*." He squeezed Mike's hand.

Mike grunted. "I've been thinking since last night, since you told me you love me, that love is so risky. But we can't help it. I can't change how I feel about you any more than I can make the sun stop rising in the east, and Lord knows not spending time together or ending this relationship won't do any good beyond making us both miserable. I know that. But then there's my irrational fears and this tangle with the school authorities."

"Why are we talking of ending things? Do you want to?"

"No. Not at all. I want to be with you like I want to take my next breath. Just… I guess all these things were on my mind and that was what caused the nightmare, and I thought…." Mike shook his head again. "I thought I couldn't go through that kind of loss again. If I lost you, I wouldn't survive it."

Gio curled up against Mike. He was satisfied when Mike put an arm around him. He laid his head on Mike's shoulder. "I'm not going anywhere."

"I never got to say good-bye," said Mike. He let out a soft breath that moved the tips of Gio's hair. "I just got a phone call. Not even a visit. You know, for most spouses of fallen police officers, their superior comes to their door to deliver the bad news. For me? Evan was dead before the ambulance even got to the scene, and I got a phone call two hours after it happened to tell me he was gone." He coughed. "Because of our experiences in the army, Evan was very open about me and our relationship with his squad. Not everyone liked that. So when he died, I got a phone call, not a visit."

"That's awful." And it truly was. Gio could not imagine carrying around that shame and pain for a decade, but this was a part of Mike too—this darkness, this loss.

"We sort of alternated childcare responsibilities," Mike said, staring at the ceiling again as if Gio weren't even there, as if Mike were somewhere else. "At the time, I was working for a contractor who worked mostly downtown, but my schedule was flexible, so I took care of Emma during Evan's shifts, and he took care of her during mine. So I was home that day. We had lunch together. Then he put on his uniform, kissed me good-bye, said something sweet to Emma, and I never saw him alive again."

Mike sounded so desolate. It was dry, in a way, a retelling of facts, no tears or obvious anguish, but Gio could sense the tension below the surface, all the tears Mike had already shed over Evan and this situation he'd been put in.

And here at last was Mike's breaking point. Gio had marveled at how well Mike coped with everything, but here was his damage, his loss, his sob story. Here was the dark place in Mike's heart, the place he retreated to when his life started becoming too good, his inner turmoil over falling in love again. Gio had wondered when they would tap into it, and it seemed that moment had arrived.

"I am so sorry, *caro*. I am devastated for you that you had to endure that."

"I... thank you."

"I suppose I cannot make the promise that history will not repeat itself, but for you, *per il mio bell'uomo*, I would do nearly anything to ensure your happiness."

Mike squeezed Gio's shoulders. "Just keep... doing what you're doing."

"Is that all you need? Is there something I can do?"

"No." Mike curled toward Gio. "This is something I have to work out for myself."

"I will do whatever I can to take your pain away. Anything."

"You already are."

MIKE felt a little shell-shocked as he cooked eggs the next morning. He felt spent, both sexually and emotionally. There'd been a lot of satisfying lovemaking—which, despite his dislike of the term, was the best name for what they'd done early that morning, after Mike had cut his heart open for Gio to see—but Mike was still reeling from the nightmare and from talking to Gio about Evan, something he'd never really meant to do.

Evan's death still hurt and probably always would. It wasn't the raw pain of a recent cut, but it was like an old injury that ached when it rained—it was fine most of the time, but every now and then there was a tingle or a throb, a reminder of the wound. That was pretty much how Mike felt overall. He was fine, good, even, with a satisfying life and people who loved him, but that loss still struck him hard sometimes.

But it wasn't all bad. He'd talked all of it through with Gio and had felt better for doing so afterward. Really, there wasn't much to work out. He loved Gio and wanted to make this relationship work. If Gio was willing to do anything in his power to make Mike happy, Mike wanted to do the same.

Gio flipped through the *Times* he'd pilfered from Mike's across-the-hall neighbors, whom Mike was pretty sure had gone out of town for the weekend, and periodically commented on a story he came across. Mike made him breakfast because there was something gratifying about doing so. He loved cooking for his lovers and didn't get the chance to very often because he was so frequently trying to herd them out the door before Emma came home. But now that everything was out in the open and Emma seemed okay with it, he was content to let Gio stay as long as he pleased.

It was nice, the morning, and Gio smiled brightly as Mike slid a plate of bacon and eggs in front of him. Mike took his own seat at the table and asked for the sports section.

"Yes, sports," Gio said, his eyes narrowed as he handed over the paper. "There are balls and… sticks."

"Why do you think I like sports?" Mike grinned.

Gio laughed.

Mike liked this easy camaraderie a great deal. It was fine that Gio read the arts section and Mike read the sports section. They could simply sit at the table together and enjoy each other's company.

A moment later, there was a key in the lock. Emma came in with a commotion. She dropped her overnight bag, her keys, and her little purple purse on the sofa and then walked over to the table.

"Hi, Gio," she said.

"Good morning, *cara*. How was your night?"

"Good. Isobel and I went to the movies last night and saw that new one about Catherine the Great. The story was kind of stupid, but the costumes were really pretty."

Gio chuckled. "I feel that way about most of the Zeffirelli productions at the Met. Some operas have ridiculous plots, eh?"

"Yeah. I still don't really get *Turandot*. No offense."

"None taken. The plot is very strange."

"You want some eggs, Em?" Mike asked.

"Okay."

Gio and Emma chatted as Mike got up to make another plate. That was nice too. He happily pictured them forming a family of sorts. He felt a pang of jealousy that he'd never have the same cultural knowledge Gio did, that he and Emma would not have the same kinds of things in common. But then Emma climbed out of her chair, walked over to Mike, and wrapped her arms around him. She hugged him tight.

He ruffled her hair. "Thanks, sweetie. These will be ready in a couple of minutes. Go put your stuff away."

"Okay. I love you, Daddy."

Mike was a little embarrassed that he got a tiny bit choked up. "I love you too, kiddo."

TWENTY

GIO braced himself and took a deep breath before walking into Howell's office. He wished he had a good-luck token or at least something to squeeze; he often put one of those squishy stress balls in his pocket before he went to the doctor. He found himself thinking of Mike, wanting Mike nearby somewhere, but of course, he had to face the firing squad alone.

Because Gio was pretty sure he was about to lose a job that he liked a great deal.

He walked into the office and was greeted by a stern-looking Howell. "Have a seat, Gio."

Gio sat, although it was hard to get comfortable.

"So, you probably know, we have a situation," said Howell.

"Yes."

Howell nodded. "I'd like to hear your side of it. I know you and I do not know each other that well, but it's hard to deny that your presence on the faculty here lends a certain amount of prestige. And your colleagues all speak very highly of you. You've been accused of some terrible behaviors, and I... I want to take your side, Gio. I do. But I can't just ignore these accusations."

Gio nodded. "Tracy Quinlan."

"You know I can't confirm or deny that."

"What are the accusations?"

Howell frowned. "The most mild is that you were receiving money and other favors to advance certain students in your opera workshop. That the favors you received led to your making specific recommendations to the Young Musicians Program audition committee."

"That's not true," said Gio. He tried to keep his voice even. He cleared his throat. "You can speak to the committee. Except for Dacia, who I talk with all the time anyway, I never spoke to anyone on the committee about any students."

Howell didn't acknowledge that. "The other accusations are a lot more troubling than that. The worst is that you're having an affair with one of your students, a Greg Thompson?"

It was a punch in the face, how surprising that was. "That is certainly not true. I have never behaved inappropriately with any of my students."

"Not even Emma McPhee?"

"No, absolutely not." Heat came to Gio's face. He was angry now. It was one thing to imply Mike had used his sexuality to get Emma ahead, which was what Gio had expected. Gio's guilt would have lain in accepting the favors. But to imply Gio had been involved with a student? "I would never get involved with a student, not in the way you're implying. And there's no impropriety here. I recused myself from the audition committee. Anyone in the department will tell you that Emma is a standout talent, very much deserving of a spot in the program."

"Why did you recuse yourself?"

Perhaps "recuse" had been the wrong word to use. Still, Gio didn't think his personal life was any of Howell's business, but honesty was the only way to get out of this. "I've grown quite fond of Emma. As a teacher, not in an inappropriate way. I didn't think I could be impartial."

Howell leaned back in his chair and steepled his fingers. The furrow in his brow indicated to Gio that Howell was skeptical.

"And I've been… dating Emma's father."

Howell's eyes went wide at that. "What?"

"We've been seeing each other all summer. Perhaps that's frowned upon, and in retrospect, maybe it would have been better not to have gotten involved." *Dio*, that was hard to say. And a lie, to boot; Gio couldn't imagine not having gotten involved with Mike, nor did he want to contemplate that alternate universe. "There's no policy against it, though, in my defense. And when it turned serious, I took myself off the Young Musicians Program admission committee to avoid any improprieties. Or, I was never on the committee, but Dacia wanted me. I told her no. I couldn't do it."

Howell shook his head. "You're having an affair with Emma McPhee's father."

"Yes. Well, 'affair' sounds tawdry and scandalous. I'm in a relationship with him. And I'll be perfectly upfront now, all right? Tracy Quinlan found out somehow and threatened me with that knowledge. She said she'd use my relationship against me if Amelia didn't get into the YMP. It seems to me that is exactly what she is doing now."

Howell frowned. "You should have come to me, Gio."

"I didn't think my personal life was a matter that the school needed to be concerned with."

"No, you should have come to me when Mrs. Quinlan threatened you. If I had had some warning…." He looked down at his desk and flipped through some papers. "Look, she's made a formal complaint. It's a huge mess now, and I have to investigate. You've been accused of acting inappropriately with your students, and regardless of how ridiculous I find those charges, the school can't be seen as a place that condones the abuse of children. The school administration is launching an investigation. That's why I called you in to speak with you. If I had known, though…."

Gio sat, shocked, staring at the desk. Of all the things to have happened, this blindsided him. "She accused me of *abusing* students?"

"Greg Thompson is a minor. He was one of your students, yes?"

"Yes. He was in my opera workshop."

"He's on the list for one of the slots in the Young Musicians Program."

"Mrs. Quinlan made accusations about Greg?"

Howell's face softened. "If I had known, I could have put a stop to this before it got started. I'll be honest with you. Mrs. Quinlan came in here during the auditions and gave me holy hell because you'd been allowed in the room downstairs at all. Said that you were accepting money and sexual favors to advance certain students. That she'd caught you in a compromising position with Mr. McPhee and that she'd heard you were also behaving inappropriately with his daughter. If what you say is true, that would probably be an easy matter to clear up. But she also implied that you'd been having a sexual relationship with this Greg Thompson and that you were advancing him into the program for that reason."

"Oh, just because I'm gay, I must also be a pedophile."

Howell sucked in a breath. "I didn't say that, Gio. I like you. Your colleagues like you. I don't want to believe this accusation—I don't believe most of what you've been accused of, frankly—but I have to take it seriously. And Mrs. Quinlan went above my head to the administration, so now it's a more serious issue. But I wish I could have headed her off at the pass."

Gio took a few breaths, trying to calm down. His heart raced now, anxiety mounting as he tried to figure out the worst-case scenarios. "Emma and Greg are exceptional singers who deserve their spots in this program. Is the holdup in making final decisions because of me and this investigation?"

Howell nodded.

"They do not deserve a negative outcome because of a decision I made. I appreciate the position you've been put in, but I swear, Howell, I never touched those kids, nor did I recommend them to the audition committee. The only person I discussed those students with was Dacia, and that was because she was a guest teacher at a few of my classes and, well, we're friends. I don't think there's anything inappropriate about that. But like I said, I took myself off the audition committee to avoid this very problem." He let out a breath. "Greg might lose his spot too?"

"I honestly don't know. But I've been forbidden to post the results of the auditions until after the administration concludes its inquiry."

"What will that entail?"

"I imagine they will ask you and your workshop students questions, try to find out if there was any inappropriate behavior. Mr. McPhee may also be called in to testify." Howell closed his eyes for a moment. "This is not the first time this has happened, unfortunately. Some parents are ruthless. One manufactured an affair between her daughter and one of the teachers. Produced all kinds of evidence. The teacher resigned before we could fire him, but then it turned out she'd made up the whole thing."

"Did you hire him back?"

"He didn't want to work for an institution that wouldn't believe him. So that's what I'm doing now, Gio. I want to believe you. I'll back you up during the investigation. Losing you would be a great loss to the Olcott School."

"Thank you. I appreciate that."

"And I need you to be honest with me. Don't withhold details that could come out later and embarrass both of us."

"You know everything now."

Howell grimaced.

Gio leaned forward, wanting to ask the obvious question but not knowing if it was within his rights. Still, he swallowed and said, "This is at least in part about money."

Howell shrugged. "Tracy Quinlan has not explicitly said she'd pull her money or stop donating, but through her organization, the Upper West Side Arts Association, she still funds several summer programs. If she decided we were no longer worthy of that money?"

Gio crossed his arms and sat back in his chair.

"So, yes, I imagine money is a factor for the administration. It's not fair, but that's the way this world works. You must know that as well as anyone."

"I do."

Howell sighed. "So here we are." He shook his head. "The father of a student?"

There was something lighter in Howell's tone, so Gio said, "I know, but... I don't know what I can say in my defense. He's very handsome and he asked me out one day and that was that."

"I didn't know you're gay."

Gio shrugged. "I figured everyone did. I don't keep it a secret. It's on the Internet. The Wikipedia page about me has a section called 'Personal Life,' in which my romantic failures are recounted in stark terms."

Howell laughed, so that was something. "I think I just lost a ten-dollar bet with my wife."

IT WAS odd getting a call requesting that you testify against your boyfriend.

But that was what happened as Mike and Sandy were tiling a bathroom on Seventy-sixth Street. As Mike hung up and slid his phone back into his pocket, Sandy raised his eyebrows.

"The school is investigating whether Gio inappropriately advanced Emma to the Young Musicians Program in exchange for sexual favors from me," Mike said. "Apparently Gio is also accused of inappropriate relations with a male student."

Sandy made a surprised sound that wasn't quite a gasp. "The fuck?"

Mike explained about Tracy Quinlan and trying to get her daughter into the program.

"What are you going to tell the administration?"

"The truth?"

"Which is?"

Mike put the grout aside. His hands were starting to shake. "That Gio and I started dating just before the end of the workshop, and we're still together, and Emma got into the program on her own merits and not on Gio's recommendation."

Sandy scoffed. "A likely story."

"It's the truth."

"I know, but think about it from the perspective of the grouchy school board. A major donor is threatening to pull out all of her money if her daughter doesn't get into the program. Of course, the only reason her wonderful, amazing daughter is not in the program is because someone cheated, because why else wouldn't she get in?"

"She's not very good?"

"Psshh. You're not that naive. Emma's been in this world for a long time, Mike. You know how this works. Sometimes it's not about who is good, it's about who can afford to succeed."

Mike resisted the urge to kick the side of the tub. "And so the wealthy elite win yet again and I get nothing."

"It's not nothing, Mike. First, you don't even know how this thing is going to play out. And Emma, well, maybe she'll keep her spot in the program, but even if she doesn't, she's still got you and she's still got a mountain of talent. She'll make it. I know she will."

Mike wasn't convinced everything would be tied up so neatly. He felt helpless and impotent. As her father, he wanted to do something, but he was damned if he could see what. "You're not suggesting I lie, are you?"

"No. That would probably do more harm than good. I was just trying to temper your expectations. I don't think this is one of those situations where saying, 'We're in love!' is going to work well in your defense. It's not a Disney movie."

"Ugh. Like I'd ever say something like that."

"I dunno. You've been pretty starry-eyed lately." Sandy started unpacking a new box of tile. "Look, tell them what you need to. Maybe it'll help to explain that you put off getting involved precisely to avoid the relationship looking like something inappropriate. And a teacher and parent getting involved is not unprecedented or outside of the rules. What did I tell you in the beginning? There was no grade for the workshop. Gio took himself off this young musicians audition committee. There was nothing sketchy going on. Right?"

"Right."

Sandy stopped what he was doing and looked up at Mike. "It might help if you sound like you believe it."

Mike grunted. His hands still shook too much to be any good at laying tiles. He braced himself on the sink.

Sandy stood. "Hey, Mike. Hey. It's going to be okay."

"How can you know that?" Mike threw his hands up in the air. "Isn't this how the whole fucking universe works? All I've ever done is work hard. I got out of South Brooklyn, I fought in the army, I scrimped and saved to provide for my daughter, and what does that get me? Shit. It gets me shit." He did kick the tub that time. His work boot left a smudge.

"All right, big guy." Sandy grabbed Mike's arm and pulled him out of the bathroom. "Let's calm you down before you do some actual damage."

Mike tried to gain control of his emotions. He took several deep breaths and pressed a hand against the wall of the hallway. Sandy stood back and looked at him.

"Say whatever you're going to say," Mike said.

"You're a pessimist. You know that?" Sandy said. "You assume a little bit of adversity is going to make your whole life go pear-shaped. But I've got news for you, buddy. Things are not as bad as you think."

"Uh-huh."

"You've got your health. You own your own company. You have a great daughter. And you've got a good man in your life. What more could you want?"

Well, sure, when Sandy put it *that* way. "I don't know. More. Emma's so talented, Sandy, and I'm not just saying that. She works so hard. She deserves this opportunity. It kills me that she might lose it because some woman with a lot of money—"

Sandy held up his hand. "Yeah, yeah, I get it. I know. Believe me, I *know*. My whole life is the same shit, different day. We come from the same place, remember? I get it. But you have to trust that things might actually work out in your favor every once in a while. Maybe they will this time. If they don't, you'll figure something else out. You always do."

"I'm so tired of this."

"I know."

Mike dropped his hand and stepped away from the wall. He looked at Sandy.

Sandy took a step forward and wrapped Mike up in a hug. "Oh, Mikey. I hate to see you like this."

"I'm sorry."

"Don't you fucking apologize. You have nothing to be sorry for." Sandy squeezed him and then took a step back. "It's not like you to give up the fight this easily."

Mike rubbed his forehead. "I know. But everything is so tangled this time. And Gio… well."

"You love him."

"I do. I really do. But I just don't see how this works out unless we get really lucky."

"Maybe the universe will surprise you."

Mike took stock of himself and realized he'd stopped shaking and his breathing was back to normal. "Thanks, Sandy. You're a good friend."

"No big," said Sandy. "Let's get back to work, eh?"

TWENTY-ONE

EVERYTHING was done in secret. Gio had been picturing a trial of sorts, where he'd get to face his accuser and more than one person decided his fate. Instead, he kept running into former students, colleagues, and parents in the hallways at the school. They'd give him sheepish looks, say hello, and then scurry away.

The worst was the day Mike was called to meet with the school administration. He came by Gio's office first, and he was ghastly pale and shaking so badly that Gio didn't know how to help him calm down. He kicked his door closed and hugged Mike tightly, hoping his embrace would make the shaking stop.

It didn't.

"I'm sorry," Mike said. "I'm about to go fuck everything up."

"You won't."

"I will. I... I can't shake this idea that we'll lose. You'll get fired. Emma will get thrown out. I'm a terrible failure as a parent."

"You are not. Stop that right now." Mike was in his bad place, that was certain, and Gio didn't know how to reach in there and pull him out. He stroked Mike's back. "You are a great father. I know you love her tremendously and want good things for her, and you do everything you can for her. Including this."

Mike nodded, his cheek rubbing against Gio's hair. "I don't know when I've ever been this nervous."

"I know, *caro*. Come back here afterwards and I'll take you to get a beer."

Mike backed away and reached for the door.

"I love you," Gio said. "I feel like I've been saying that three times a day for the past week, but I can't seem to stop myself."

Mike smiled briefly. "I don't get tired of hearing it. I love you too."

"Good. Now go."

Gio spent a nerve-racking half hour at his desk, pretending to work but actually fretting about what might be going on in the administrative offices upstairs.

It felt strange to be worried more about other people than he was about himself. As a performer, he'd always been selfish, wanting his own success more than he wanted that of his friends. He figured the only reason he and Dacia were still close friends was because they'd never had to compete with each other for a part. Lord knew enough of his romantic relationships had ended when his lover had accused him of caring only for himself. He could admit that was true; when he'd been young, the most important thing had been his voice. Now that he had no voice, he supposed that was no longer true. But there was more to it than that, as well.

As he analyzed possible outcomes, he realized he didn't care much what happened to him—he'd be sad to lose the job if that was indeed what the administration ruled, but he was certain he'd find something else. However, he did care a great deal about what happened to Mike and Emma. He was shaken by how upset Mike was. He would have been angry on Emma's behalf if she lost this spot she deserved over the girl whose mother was bullying the school. He wanted good things to happen to these people he had grown to love so much in such a short amount of time.

Perhaps that was what love was really about. He cared about what happened to his loved ones more than he cared about himself.

Just as he had this epiphany, Mike reappeared at his doorway. He wasn't shaking any longer, but his eyes were wide and he was frowning.

"How did it go?" Gio asked, standing.

Mike motioned for him to sit back down, and then he slid the door closed. "It was… well. Not the easiest thing I've ever done."

"What happened?"

Mike sat in the guest chair. "Before or after they accused me of seducing you to get my daughter accepted at the Olcott School?"

Gio's heart went out to him. "Oh, Mike."

Mike grunted. "I told them the truth. That, yeah, it looked strange that you and I are dating, under the circumstances, and I understood why they were suspicious, but that my intentions were honorable. I pointed out that you took yourself off the audition committee so your relationship with me wouldn't influence the outcome. And I argued that Emma totally deserves a spot in the program, because she's really, really good. That guy who's head of the voice department? Mr. Laughton?"

"Yes."

"He said he'd heard Emma sing himself and he could, uh, 'vouch for her talent' is what he said. So I think it went okay. Not a complete disaster, anyway."

"Still. I'm sure it was not pleasant to be accused of using sex to get your way."

Mike rubbed his forehead. "You know what would be nice? If just once sex didn't matter. My sexuality has been this thing hanging over my head my whole fucking life. It alienated me from my family, it got me kicked out of the army, and now it could jeopardize my daughter's future. But it shouldn't matter. My desires have nothing to do with any of those things."

Mike sounded completely exasperated. Gio didn't know what to say. He agreed, and he felt for Mike, but he couldn't figure out how to comfort him.

He stood and walked around his desk. Mike stood too. So Gio hugged him, because that seemed like a thing to do. Mike hugged him back.

"This is the only way it *does* matter," Mike said. "With the door closed. With you in my arms."

"It will be all right," Gio said. He almost sounded like he believed it.

"I don't…." Mike sniffed. "You know what I realized when I was sitting up there? All week, I couldn't stop obsessing over this and how, you know, it's always the Tracy Quinlans of the world who win. She can afford to win. I can't. But you know what? I'm sick of losing to people like her. And I decided that I couldn't let her win. I couldn't let her just come in here and tell these lies and get her way. Emma deserves this. She's worked really hard to get this far and she should have that spot."

"I agree, *caro*. She deserves it."

"I can't let her beat you, either. You deserve this job. You deserve your good reputation, your integrity, the life you have now. She shouldn't be able to take that away from you."

Mike tightened his grip on Gio. It was a little overwhelming, being held in a grasp like that, but it was wonderful too. Gio could feel all of the emotion pulsing through Mike, could feel his muscles practically vibrate. He could feel Mike's indignation, his anger, his frustration. He felt all those things in his chest as well.

Gio had been bred for this life, practically; many of his first opportunities had been handed to him because his mother had once been a prima donna. But he and Emma had one thing in common, which was the gift of a talent so remarkable it could take them places not everyone could go. Gio had been around elite musicians long enough to know that often talent triumphed, but sometimes money did too.

"If something happens," Gio said, "we'll figure it out. I will do whatever I can to help Emma. All right?"

Mike leaned his forehead against Gio's. "I know. Thank you."

Gio sighed and leaned into Mike. Then, with some reluctance, he pulled away. "I bet you'd like that beer now."

THE beer was at a gay bar on the northern end of the Theater District that didn't serve food, which was maybe a mistake, because Mike realized as he finished his first drink that he hadn't eaten all day.

Gio had only had a few sips of his vodka tonic, and he kept staring at it as if it tasted funny but he couldn't figure out why.

It had been that sort of day. But Mike reasoned that now that his brain was starting to swim around in his head, maybe he could stop reliving that half hour he'd spent talking to the Olcott School administration.

Because a lot of shitty things had happened in Mike's life, and generally he preferred not to dwell on them. Pushing all of it aside left Mike with a lot of anger sometimes. This situation was maybe the worst, because Mike's ethics and integrity had been called into question. Always in the past, he'd felt like he'd had that on his side. The army policy was wrong, Mike's father was a bigot, Evan had saved the life of a child at the expense of his own. Mike could deal with these things and still stand tall. But those administrators had shamed him, had implied he'd done something morally wrong. He still didn't believe that he had, but doubt had crept in. What if he had? What if it was his own fault for setting his sights so high? What if he was at fault for wanting things he couldn't have? There was a moment during the questioning when he'd felt no better than dog shit on the bottom of the school president's shiny polished shoe.

Was it worth it? He was putting his core beliefs on the line for… what? For Gio? For sex? For love?

He turned to Gio, whom he'd come to love so much so quickly, and he reached for his hand. Gio took Mike's hand and smiled.

"My name still counts for a lot, you know," Gio said. "That is, if the school does not take Emma, I will coach her. I will teach her to be *la prima donna*. If she doesn't get into this program, maybe next year she auditions for Juilliard. They have a similar program for teenage musicians."

Mr. Laughton had escorted Mike out of the room as the hearing had ended and whispered softly, "I believe you. I've heard Emma sing. I'll do what I can." Mike had found that somewhat comforting. But it wasn't a guarantee.

He looked at his own hand, wrapped around Gio's, and then he looked up at Gio. Their eyes met. He asked himself again if it was worth it. Was having to endure being accused of something vile—of being shamed into thinking there was something bad or wrong with his relationship, or that he'd used his sexuality to get what he wanted, that he was just as bad as Tracy Quinlan because he'd used his assets to advance his kid—worth the reward? Was having to get through that half hour when he felt like the very foundation under his feet had been pulled out from under him worth this moment here with Gio?

He couldn't speak for a moment, couldn't find a way to articulate what he was thinking and feeling, didn't know how to get answers. He looked into Gio's dark, intense eyes and started to say, "Gio, I need…." Although he didn't know what he needed.

Gio kissed him. And there. That was it. This was what he needed. He had to know this connection with Gio was a real thing, that he loved and was loved in return, that maybe a half hour of shame was worth a lifetime of happiness if only he could find a way to make all the moving parts in his life come together. Maybe all this would work out and Emma would keep her spot and go on to great things. Maybe she'd get kicked out but get into another school. Maybe Gio's teaching would be enough to get her where she wanted to go. And, of course, there was always the possibility that she'd get to college and decide to be a doctor or a lawyer or some other thing and leave singing behind.

Was it selfish to say that, yes, being with Gio was worth all of it?

"Mike," Gio whispered against his mouth. "I feel like I'm losing you."

"I'm sorry. How do you say that in Italian? *Mi dispiace*." Mike was probably totally mispronouncing it, but he wanted to try the Italian, thought maybe it would bring him and Gio closer if he learned it. He leaned back. He squeezed Gio's hand. "I was trying to decide if I'd change anything that happened this summer. If all this could have been avoided if I'd made different decisions. Like, maybe I shouldn't have come to the classes every day. Maybe I shouldn't have asked you out so soon."

"*Caro*, it would not have made a difference. Tracy Quinlan's daughter would have gotten a rejection and she probably would have found some other reason to go after Emma or one of the other students in the class. She would have found some way to ruin something to get her daughter ahead."

For the first time all day, Mike found himself really smiling. "Gio. I would not have changed a thing."

Gio laughed softly and kissed Mike again.

Mike wasn't sure if the wave of wooziness was due to the heady feeling of kissing the man he loved, or the alcohol, or the lack of food, or all three, but he suddenly got very dizzy. He pulled away from Gio and put his hands on the table. "Maybe I should get something to eat," he said. "Do you have to go back to school?"

"Not really. I wouldn't get anything done anyway. Too much on my mind."

"Right. So?"

"There's an Italian place across the street. It's not quite *authentic*, and they drown all of their dishes in marinara the way all Americans do, but—"

"Gio." Mike laughed. "Let's just go there. I'm the sort of uncouth American who likes a lot of red sauce."

Gio laughed too. He kissed Mike's forehead. "All right. Have it your way, *amore mio*."

TWENTY-TWO

MIKE woke up to a phone ringing. He felt movement beside him in bed. Mike stretched and looked over in time to see Gio grab his cell phone off the night stand. He greeted the caller groggily and then said, "Yes, that's all right. Of course, sir. I will see you then."

Gio hung up and grunted as he put his phone back on the table.

"What is it?" Mike asked.

"That was the president of the Olcott School. He'd like to see me later this morning."

"What time is it now?"

"Almost eight."

Mike groaned. It was later than he would have liked. He had given himself the day off to spend with Gio, but now it looked like that time would be cut short. He reached over and pulled Gio into his arms, determined to savor things while they lasted.

"When is Emma getting back?" Gio asked.

She was at Becky's place. Mike felt bad for continuing to ship her off so he could spend more time with Gio, but Emma didn't seem to mind much. Becky certainly liked having Emma around. She had two boys under the age of seven who absolutely worshipped Emma, and Becky appreciated having some help with them.

"Late morning, probably. We were talking about going to the Met today. The one with the art, not the opera."

Gio chuckled, which Mike appreciated.

Mike explained, "There's an exhibit about musical instruments or something that she wants to see."

"Ah, yes, I heard they got a new Stradivarius."

Mike had no idea what that meant, but he nodded. "She said she wanted to go with you, but if you can't make it, maybe we'll do something else." It meant a lot to Mike that Emma was now deliberately including Gio in her plans. It gave Mike some hope that everything might work out, at least as far as this relationship went. He was overjoyed that Emma had come around, at any rate.

"Perhaps we can still go to the museum," said Gio. "I suppose if I'm just going to get fired, it won't take very long."

Mike smoothed the hair away from Gio's face. He supposed that was a possibility. "Do you really think that's what will happen?"

"I don't know. I really don't know what to expect."

"At least come back here for dinner tonight?"

Gio smiled. "As if I could stay away." He sighed. "*O caro*. I am worried about today."

It was the first time Gio had ever explicitly admitted that. He'd been obviously agitated for a few days, but kept brushing it off whenever Mike asked him how he felt about what was happening. It wasn't that Mike was glad Gio was worried, but he was reassured in a way to see that Gio was expressing more plainly some of what Mike had been feeling as well. Mike kissed Gio's forehead. "I'd tell you it's going to be all right, but I can't really be sure of that myself. All I can say is that I'll be here when it's over."

"Assuming Emma doesn't hate me forever because she was thrown out of the program."

Mike's heart sank. "Do you really think that will happen?"

"No, but I can't be certain."

Mike was worried, but he felt oddly optimistic for a change. Maybe it was the high of waking up next to Gio after a good night spent together. He wanted there to be many more nights like that in their future. It seemed like that was in his grasp. If only he could hold on to it....

Gio lightly touched Mike's face. "Whatever happens, we're in it together, right? I'll get the news and we will figure out what to do with it. It's you and me now, and we'll... figure it out."

Mike liked the sound of that. Perhaps that was why things didn't seem so dire. "Yes. Together." He took Gio's hand and squeezed it.

Gio smiled. "I love you, *caro*."

"I love you too." Their proximity to each other was intoxicating, and Mike reveled in it. "What time do you have to be there?"

"Eleven."

"Oh, good. We have a couple of hours together, at least."

"Indeed." Gio slipped his hand under the covers and ran it over Mike's ass.

"Perhaps I can take your mind off the meeting before you have to go to it."

Gio smirked. "Perhaps."

THE administrative section of the Olcott School building smelled like old paper and chalk, which was a safe thing to focus on as Gio walked down the hall to the president's office. It felt like he was a dead man walking.

Maybe he was.

He knew he was being too dramatic—he was still an opera singer at heart, he supposed, and thus prone to be over-the-top—but he dreaded this meeting. He hadn't been dealing well with the uncertainty about the outcome of this situation, so much so that he'd admitted to Mike that he was nervous. He hadn't intended to do that; he hadn't wanted to burden Mike with his own feelings on the matter when Mike had so much to deal with himself. Then again, telling Mike had been a relief in a way, and Mike had comforted him.

Mike continued to humble Gio with his big heart and the way he dealt with adversity. And now this amazing man loved Gio. Gio held that close to his heart as he walked into his appointment.

The president of the Olcott School, an austere man named Lou Vanderbrandt, sat at his desk. Howell was in one of the spare chairs. The other was vacant, waiting for Gio.

"We do have a situation," Vanderbrandt mused as Gio sat down.

"I realize that," said Gio. "And I appreciate the position you've been put in, but—"

"Let me speak first," said Vanderbrandt. "First, regarding the accusations that you acted inappropriately with students. We take such accusations very seriously."

Gio's stomach dropped. He'd nearly forgotten about those charges. It seemed like he should be able to easily defend himself from the patently false accusations, so he'd spent most of his energy worrying about what he had done and how that could affect the outcome of the situation. "Yes, I—"

"No need to defend yourself. It became clear to us pretty quickly that the charges were spurious." Vanderbrandt fingered his wedding band. "Look, Gio, I'll be honest with you about this one. Mrs. Quinlan stood in this very office and rattled off a viciously homophobic diatribe about how the gay teacher was obviously molesting his students. My husband was just outside the office, waiting to take me to lunch, when this happened, and I can tell you that he was not appreciative." He shook his head and leaned forward, toward Gio. "I was already predisposed not to believe that particular accusation, I admit. But I had to follow procedure. When no students offered anything to support the charge, and indeed most of them found it completely unbelievable, the administration considered the charges dismissed. I mean, even the boy you were accused of molesting had no idea charges had even been made. We had to follow up, though. You understand."

"Yes. But—"

"I'm not a fool. I know how this game works. When a woman with a clear agenda makes charges against a teacher about whom there have been no complaints, you have to wonder. So you've been acquitted of those charges. Just to get that off the table."

Gio decided to stop trying to get a word in edgewise. He nodded and mumbled, "Thank you."

Vanderbrandt was not finished, however. "We've decided to let Amelia Quinlan into the Young Musicians Program."

And there it was. Any relief he felt at the dismissal of the false charges vanished in an instant. It wasn't just that this wasn't an outcome he wanted; he hated that Tracy Quinlan had won after all she'd put him, Mike, and Emma through.

"Not the outcome you wanted?" Vanderbrandt asked.

Gio hated that his feelings must have been so apparent on his face. "It's not relevant what I think," he said. "She's a fine singer. If the school has decided to accept her, I hope she takes every advantage of the amazing opportunity she's been given."

"But you don't think she deserves the spot."

"Again, it's not relevant what I think."

Vanderbrandt nodded. "Yes, it would appear that, in this situation, that is true. Look, Gio. I believe that there was no impropriety on your part, and if there was, you took the correct steps in taking yourself off the audition committee. I know of your friendship with Dacia Russini, but even without her on the committee, Emma McPhee would have been accepted and Amelia Quinlan probably not. But the problem here is that, if the Quinlans take their money away, the school will lose a large enough endowment that it will affect the fall semester in a profound way. We'd have to cut classes or let a few teachers go."

Gio took a moment to process that, and then said, "So you're accepting Amelia to keep the endowment?"

"Yes."

It was astonishing that Vanderbrandt seemed to have no compunction about that. Then Gio realized what this could really mean. "Emma McPhee gets to stay?"

"Yes."

It was an odd sensation to fret about the unfairness of Tracy Quinlan winning while also feeling relief that Emma got to stay. It was unfair, but probably the best outcome he could have hoped for.

There was a long silence, after which Vanderbrandt said, "I'm surprised you haven't inquired after your own employment."

That almost seemed beside the point. "I suppose you will tell me what your verdict was."

Vanderbrandt nodded toward Howell, who said, "We considered asking you to take the fall semester off, but that wouldn't be fair to the students you've already made commitments to. You will continue to work with those students, but your schedule is restricted otherwise. No new students, no additional classes."

Gio recognized that this was kind of a token punishment—he hadn't anticipated taking on new students in the fall semester except perhaps for Emma, whom he could easily work with outside of the school—but the stern look on Vanderbrandt's face indicated that perhaps this was not a widely known fact.

"All right," Gio said. "I can accept that."

Howell walked him back down the hall a few minutes later, and Gio found that his feelings were more mixed than he would have anticipated. The Amelia thing aside, this was really the best possible outcome. Why was he not more elated?

"I'll call the McPhees," Howell said. "They might appreciate knowing nothing has changed regarding Emma's place in the program. And I suppose we can finally post who was admitted to the YMP. Then maybe the parents will stop calling me, at least."

"Yes," Gio said, though he intended to call Mike soon as well.

"I apologize for putting you through this, but you know how these things go."

Gio shrugged. "I will not be teaching any YMP classes next semester, and probably not for a while, I'm guessing. So it is immaterial to me."

Howell stopped near the elevator and crossed his arms over his chest. "You care a great deal more than you're letting on, but all right. I will take you at your word and carry on with my day." He shook his head. "But I don't like it much either."

Gio closed his eyes for a long moment and tried to get his bearings. "I am grateful that you and the administration are letting me keep my job and also keeping Emma in the program. I am. And maybe I do care, but enough of my personal stuff has been aired because of this mess, so you'll understand if I'm not eager to share my thoughts."

Howell pressed the down button. "I understand, Gio. I was there when Vanderbrandt questioned Mike McPhee. My heart went out to him. To both of you. That can't have been easy." He took a step back from the elevator. "He seems like a nice man, for what it's worth."

"He is."

"Maybe the two of you would like to come over for dinner sometime soon. Bring Emma. My wife is a great cook."

"All right."

Howell bid him farewell and went back to his office, leaving Gio standing near the elevator wondering what had just happened. He pulled out his phone and texted Mike: *Emma's in and I keep my job.*

When he got back to the first floor, his phone buzzed. Mike had texted him a smiley face.

You spend too much time with teenagers, Gio texted back.

I know. Come over tonight and we'll celebrate.

Gio smiled. Together—that was what they'd agreed to that morning. Maybe life wasn't completely fair, but Gio had Mike, and that felt like a victory. He texted, *I will see you soon. I love you.*

Mike texted back, *Love u 2.*

EPILOGUE

GIO reached behind him, so Mike took his hand as they walked to their seats. It wasn't the first time Gio had gotten them orchestra seats to the Metropolitan Opera, but it felt different this time. For one thing, Mike was still partial to the balconies because he loved the theater's architecture, which you couldn't see as well from the orchestra section. Also, he was nervous in a way he never had been before.

"This is intense," Sandy said as they walked across a row to their seats. Mike turned around and saw Sandy gawking and looking around.

Behind him, Sandy's boyfriend rolled his eyes and said, "Stop staring. You're so uncouth."

Sandy grinned. "You like that about me."

They were cutting it close to performance time. Mike had needed a glass of wine before the show to calm his nerves, so Gio had bought him one from the bar just outside the theater. It had made them all run a little late. The lights dimmed briefly, so Mike took his seat.

Gio reached over and intertwined his fingers with Mike's. "Calm down, *caro*."

"I know, but—"

Then the lights dimmed for real and abruptly the orchestra began.

Mike tried to concentrate on the story, reading the subtitles and watching the costumes on stage. They were attending the Julie Taymor production of *Die Zauberflöte*, and as often happened when Mike went to the opera, no amount of Gio—or sometimes Emma, although not tonight—

explaining what was going on could make him understand the story clearly. It didn't help that he was distracted.

But then... then. A lovely eighteen-year-old singer named Emma McPhee came out with the chorus and graced the stage with her presence. Well, she was part of the chorus. Not quite Queen of the Night, but still, Emma's first time on this stage—definitely not the last, Gio kept saying—and here she was in this famous theater right here at home.

She'd been talking about applying to schools in Europe, which Mike didn't think his poor heart could handle—the thought of Emma in a foreign country made him feel faint—so, really, that she was right here and starting Juilliard in the fall, these were good things. She was less thrilled when Mike pointed out that the apartment they shared with Gio on West Eighty-fifth Street was awfully convenient to the school, so she didn't *have* to move to a dorm. That was a battle he sensed he was about to lose.

He squeezed Gio's hand, thankful he didn't have to face the empty nest—and his forties, since *that* birthday had happened the previous year—by himself.

At intermission, Gio leaned over and kissed Mike's shoulder, a gesture lost somewhat in the fabric of Mike's suit jacket, but one that was appreciated just the same. After four years together, Mike didn't need the grand gesture to be convinced of Gio's love, but that didn't mean he opposed such moments, big or small.

"Our beautiful girl looks quite at home on the stage," Gio said.

Mike was trying really hard not to cry. He swallowed and nodded.

"I'm proud of her too, Mike." Gio paused and sat back in his seat. "This will happen every time she performs, won't it? We will always be awed by it."

"No. Well, yes, probably." Mike sighed. "She looks so beautiful in the costume. She...." He pressed the heels of his hands to his eyes.

"Let me buy you some more wine," said Gio.

"No, I'm all right." Mike turned and looked at Gio, trying to find some solace in his patient gaze. "I'm not ready for her to grow up. I'm not ready for her to go off to college."

"She's not going far."

"I know, but... she'll be on her own, and I worry and...."

"She will always be your baby."

"Yes."

When the opera ended later, and Mike, Gio, and Sandy had shouted, "Bravo!" and "Brava!" until they were hoarse, they all walked out to the fountain in front of Lincoln Center. Mike held Gio's hand. He still remembered fondly the first night they'd spent together all those years before, when they'd danced to a solo cello in this very spot. Now it felt like they were coming full circle in a way, standing here as part of a family.

Gio made small talk with Sandy and his boyfriend, but Mike focused on looking around the square, waiting for Emma to walk out. They waited a good twenty minutes before she appeared, walking beside a man Mike recognized as one of the actors who played a secondary character. She giggled and clutched at the man's arm, which got Mike's hackles up. Her personal life wasn't helping his blood pressure much, either, although he recognized he didn't have much of a say anymore. She didn't date much—Mike suspected the boys at her high school were intimidated by her—but she had gone out with a few musicians from Olcott, and now she was flirting with this opera singer, and Mike realized this was probably just the beginning. God help him.

She saw them and then bid the opera guy farewell with a kiss on the cheek. He beat a hasty retreat, so Mike assumed he wasn't supposed to know about this guy, although that was a conversation they'd be having later. She wasn't out of the house *yet*.

Then she ran over and let out a little squeal when she threw her arms around Mike.

"Congratulations, sweetie," said Mike. He hugged her tightly. "I'm so proud of you."

"Thanks, Dad." She took a step back and grinned. Then she hugged Gio. "Thank you too."

"You looked lovely up there, *cara*," Gio said.

Gio met Mike's gaze as Emma hugged Sandy and the boyfriend. Mike's heart was still pounding, but in a good way. Emma was an adult—almost—and was on the road to a successful singing career, and he could not have been prouder of his little girl. "You know, *amore mio*, this is an occasion for celebration, not for moping."

"I'm not moping."

Gio put an arm around Mike. "What do American parents usually threaten when their children move out? To convert their bedrooms into gyms?

Although, I suppose in your case, you intend to turn her room into the Emma McPhee Museum."

"I'm not that bad."

"Maybe in a few years we can sell tickets."

Mike laughed despite himself. "Or perhaps," Gio went on, "you can look at her impending independence as an opportunity to move on to the next phase of your life. Concentrate on being the king of renovations in New York. Or, alternately, you could just be my handsome husband."

"I thought I had that last one taken care of."

Gio smiled and gave Mike a brief peck on the lips. "You do. *Ti amo*."

"I love you too."

"Get a room," called Sandy.

Mike laughed. "Well, anyone who wants to come back to our place for a celebratory cocktail—virgin cocktails for you, Em—is welcome."

Emma stuck her tongue out at Mike.

"Let's go home," said Gio.

KATE MCMURRAY is a savvy New Yorker and voracious reader and writer. Her books have won several Rainbow Awards. She is currently serving as vice president of Rainbow Romance Writers, the LGBT romance chapter of Romance Writers of America. When she's not writing, Kate works as a nonfiction editor. She also reads a lot, plays the violin, knits and crochets, and drools over expensive handbags. She's maybe a tiny bit obsessed with baseball. She lives in Brooklyn, NY, with a pesky cat.

Website: http://www.katemcmurray.com
Twitter: http://www.twitter.com/katemcmwriter
Facebook: https://www.facebook.com/katemcmurraywriter

Also from KATE MCMURRAY

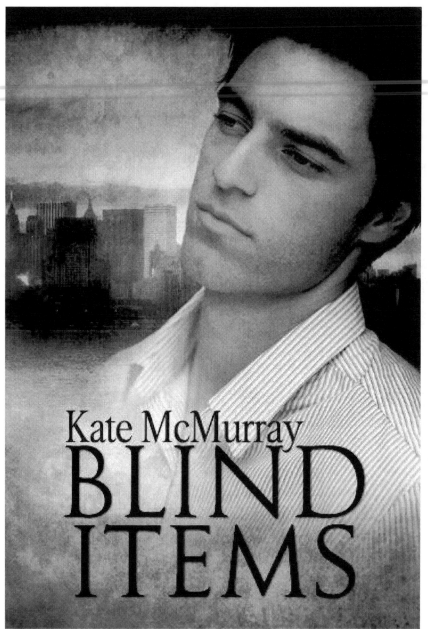

http://www.dreamspinnerpress.com

Also from KATE MCMURRAY

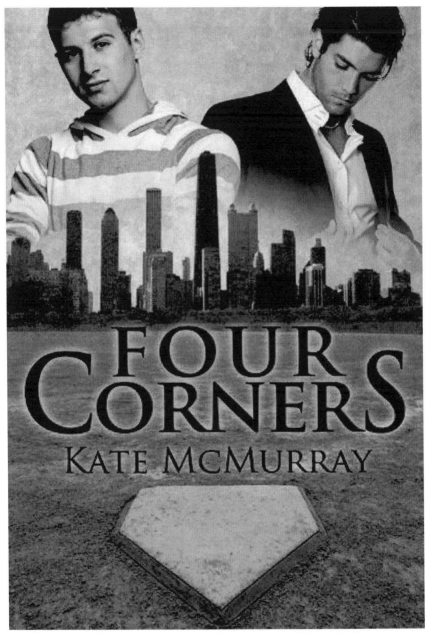

http://www.dreamspinnerpress.com

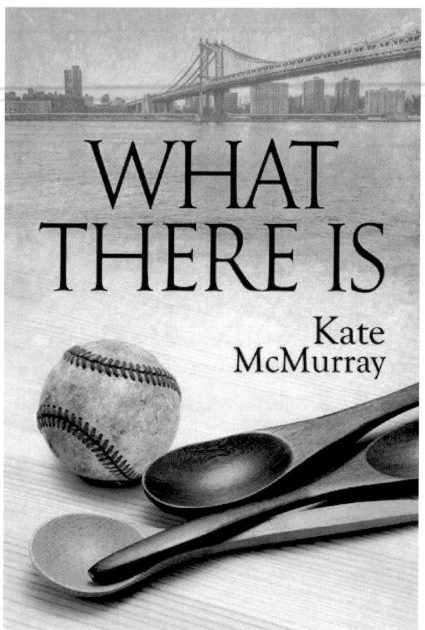

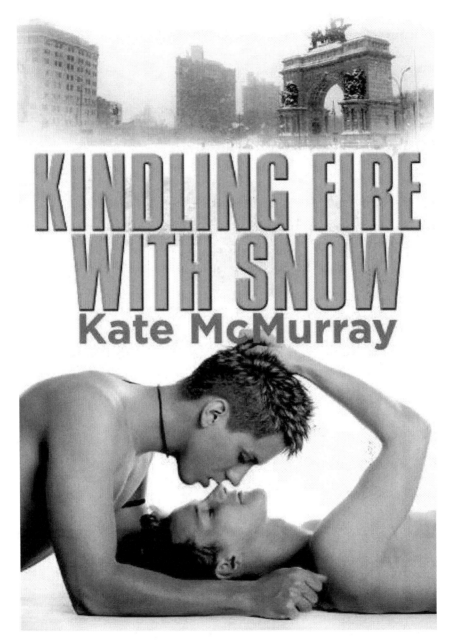

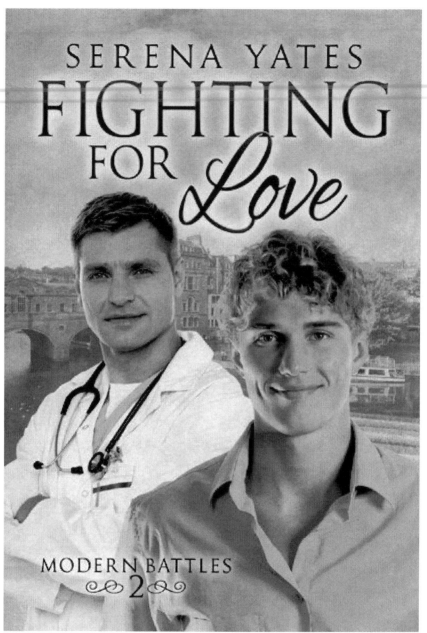

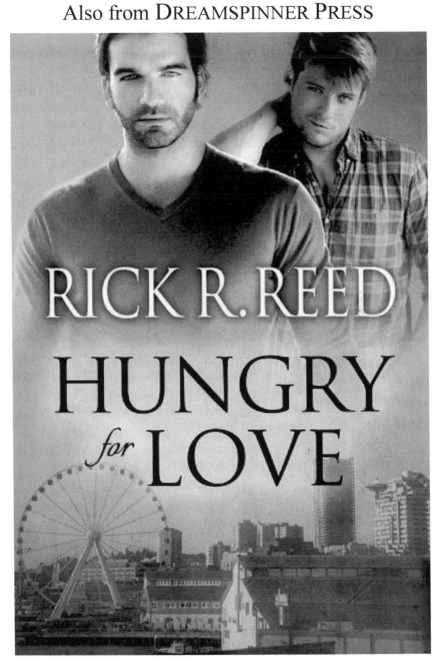

Also from DREAMSPINNER PRESS

Con Riley

salvage

http://www.dreamspinnerpress.com

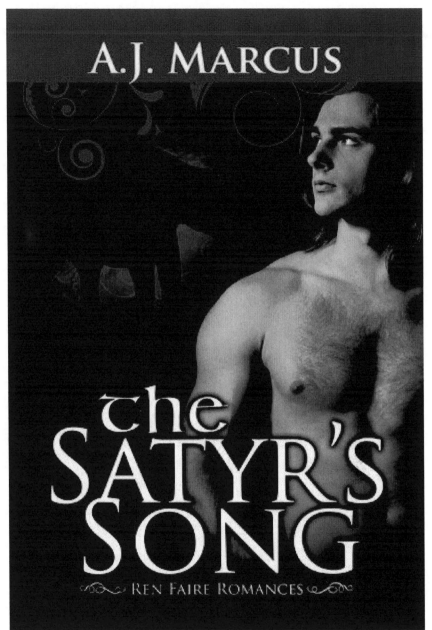